FIVE MOVES
OF DOOM

A NEWEST
MYSTERY

Praise for *Five Moves of Doom*

"A.J. Devlin does it again with *Five Moves of Doom*! It's fast and furious and fun, full of action, unexpected twists and turns, with a shocking ending that proves once again that Devlin is not only on his game, but in a league of his own. The best yet in the 'Hammerhead' Jed series."
— Dave Butler, Crime Writers of Canada Award-Winning author of *Full Curl*, *No Place for Wolverines*, and *In Rhino We Trust*

"I ripped through Devlin's latest. At times I felt I was in an MMA fight with dialogue as dry as a three olive Martini and descriptive prose peppering me with blows and throws. It may be a cliché, but this book's a knockout."
— M.N. Grenside, film/TV/music producer and author of *Fall Out*

"A.J. Devlin nails it with his explosive, hard-hitting fight scenes. A well-written and entertaining look into the most interesting sport in the world — Mixed Martial Arts — through the eyes of tough guy PI, 'Hammerhead' Jed!"
— Gerry Gionco, legendary Canadian fight promoter

"This time around, 'Hammerhead' Jed isn't the toughest guy on the block, and the adrenaline-pounding excitement when his investigation leads him to square off against a particularly ruthless and brutal MMA fighter brings to mind Rocky vs. Drago. Bigger, badder, and darker, Devlin's third installment reveals a deeper and more vulnerable side of our favourite wrestler-detective, adding gravitas to a case involving a world where second place often means death."
— J.T. Siemens, critically-acclaimed author of *To Those Who Killed Me*

"*Five Moves of Doom* is a fast-paced, rollicking rip through the vibrant and seedy neighbourhoods of Vancouver and surrounding area. With Devlin's usual cast of colourful, eclectic characters along with his equally colourful regular cast — including 'Hammerhead' Jed, cousin Declan, and VPD Detective Rya Shepard — this adventure took me back to many familiar haunts in Vancouver's skid row and some of the outlying regions around the city and the Lower Mainland. MMA, murder, mayhem and money make this a can't miss!"
— Joel Johnston, retired 28-year VPD Sergeant, Shotokan Karate and MMA Practitioner, Use of Force Subject Matter Expert, Writer and Technical Advisor

"It's a case of same place, different terrain as Vancouver's pro-wrestler PI grapples with new threats that force him to confront dark truths about his city and himself. In *Five Moves of Doom*, Devlin showcases a more vulnerable 'Hammerhead' Jed than we've seen before. While this installment features the signature comedy and charm of the first two books, it's the shadows, spilling from corners and pooling at feet, that give this latest mystery its true shape. A worthy cap to this trilogy."
— Niall Howell, Kobo Emerging Writer Prize-Nominated author of *Only Pretty Damned* and *There Are Wolves Here Too*

Praise for *Rolling Thunder*

"Professional wrestler-turned-PI 'Hammerhead' Jed is back, and not a moment too soon—trouble is brewing in the Greater Vancouver area on the roller derby circuit. *Rolling Thunder* is sheer fun. The dialogue is snappy, the action fast-paced. A.J. Devlin is the Canadian Carl Hiaasen. In fact, America will trade you Carl Hiaasen for him. I feel that strongly about this kid's future."
— Andrew Shaffer, *New York Times* bestselling author and humorist

"A.J. Devlin's latest crime novel packs a punch with nonstop action! His witty, entertaining style hooked me quicker than a figure-4 leglock and pinned me to the pages.

"*Rolling Thunder* is a must read for everyone who is a fan of sports, wrestling, suspense … or all three!"
— Jeanne "Hollywood" Basone, the first GLOW girl hired by creator David McLane

"*Rolling Thunder* has everything! Action, humour, mystery, and most importantly pro wrestling. I'm totally invested. Can't wait for the next one!"
— Cat Power, pro wrestler and former ECCW Women's Champion

"A.J. Devlin scores again as he sends 'Hammerhead' Jed on another no-holds-barred romp through the dark underbelly of Metro Vancouver. Brilliantly done."
— Bob Harris, writer, promoter, and archivist of pro wrestling vintage memorabilia

"Award-winning author A.J. Devlin hip-checks the reader from one captivating clue to the next in this gripping crime novel. *Rolling Thunder* is a laugh-out-loud mystery with unique and hilarious characters, and a realistic peek at the hard-hitting, counter-culture sport of women's roller derby."
— Jenna Hauck—AKA Hydro-Jenna Bomb—former Terminal City Rollergirls skater and multimedia journalist with the *Chilliwack Progress*

Praise for *Cobra Clutch*

"...masterfully blends humour, mystery, thrills, action, romance, and heart into a hell of a story featuring a lively wrestler-turned-PI hero. The action scenes are intense, the quiet times heartwarming and engaging, and the humour expertly interjected to accentuate characters and breathe realism into the story."
— John M. Murray, *Foreword Reviews*

"Set in Vancouver, BC, this intriguing debut offers a fast-paced, graphically violent mystery.... Fans of pro wrestling will appreciate 'Hammerhead' Jed."
— *Library Journal*

"...a very authentic-feeling world full of colourful characters, twists and turns and plenty of banana milkshakes."
— J.P Cupertino, *Gremlins Online*

"*Cobra Clutch* uses humour and gritty realism and includes a former tag-team partner, a kidnapped snake, sleazy promoters, and violence inside and outside the ring."
— *BC BookWorld*

Library and Archives Canada Cataloguing in Publication

Title: Five moves of doom / A.J. Devlin.
Names: Devlin, A. J., author.
Description: "A 'Hammerhead' Jed mystery."
Identifiers: Canadiana (print) 20210379553 | Canadiana (ebook) 20210379618 | ISBN 9781774390559 (softcover) | ISBN 9781774390566 (EPUB)
Classification: LCC PS8607.E94555 F58 2022 | DDC C813/.6—dc23

Board Editor: Merrill Distad
Cover and interior design: Michel Vrana
Cover images: iStockphoto
Author photo: Gina Spanos

NeWest Press acknowledges that the land on which we operate is Treaty 6 territory and a traditional meeting ground and home for many Indigenous Peoples, including Cree, Saulteaux, Niitsitapi (Blackfoot), Métis, and Nakota Sioux. NeWest Press acknowledges the Canada Council for the Arts, the Alberta Foundation for the Arts, and the Edmonton Arts Council for support of our publishing program. We acknowledge the financial support of the Government of Canada.

NeWest Press
#201, 8540-109 Street
Edmonton, Alberta T6G 1E6
www.newestpress.com

No bison were harmed in the making of this book.

Printed and bound in Canada

1 2 3 4   24 23 22

For Dianne and Susie

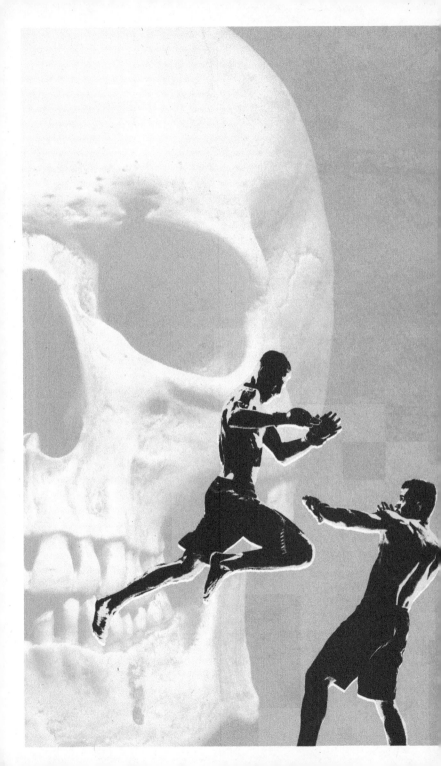

FIVE MOVES OF DOOM

A "HAMMERHEAD" JED MYSTERY

A.J. DEVLIN

NeWest Press

Five Moves of Doom:

\ ˈfiv \ \ ˈmüvs \ \ ˈəv, *before consonants also* ə; ˈəv , ˈäv \ \ ˈdüm \

1. A particular combination of moves that a wrestler tends to use in every match, often in the same sequence, usually ending with the finisher and a pinfall. This term is often used pejoratively. Popularized by pro wrestlers Bret Hart, The Rock, and John Cena.

PROLOGUE

You have a couple of options when you answer the door wearing nothing but a skin-tight pair of André the Giant boxer briefs before being arrested for murder.

ONE: *You accept what's happening and fully embrace your shame.*

TWO: *You man up and rock those undergarments with the same aplomb James Bond would while sipping vodka martinis (shaken, not stirred) at a no-limit baccarat table in the Casino de Monte-Carlo.*

I attempted to pull off the latter and tried to puff out my hairy chest, which was suddenly itchy as hell. I also quickly realized my torso was long overdue for a trim.

"Burt Reynolds on a bearskin rug ain't got nothing on you, Big Guy. And while I'm sure a bunch of tabloids will duke it out for the privilege of splashing this iconic pose all over the cover of a future issue, I'd hardly call that bulge the Eighth Wonder of the World."

Vancouver Police Department Homicide Detective Constable Rya Shepard, flanked by two uniformed officers, tugged on the lapels of her tan pantsuit blazer before nodding toward my junk and rolling her eyes.

"Hello, Rya. You seem chipper." I grabbed a T-shirt and pair of track pants on the banister beside me and slipped them on faster than it takes a piece of weakened two-by-four western red cedar to break in half over my forehead after winning a wrestling match.

"Detective Shepard?" asked one of the uniformed officers beside the woman I had long loved with feelings I had never shared.

Rya sighed audibly, looking downwards. "Cuff him."

One of the cops strutted forward, yanked my wrists behind my back, and handcuffed me while his partner pulled a laminated card from a pouch on his police duty belt and proceeded to read aloud my rights. "John Edward Ounstead, AKA "Hammerhead" Jed Ounstead. You are hereby under arrest for the murder of—"

I couldn't take it anymore. "What the hell, Rya?!?"

"Don't make this any harder than it has to be," she said, hanging her head.

I clenched my jaw as Officer Tweedledum snapped on the metal restraints.

"This isn't a heel turn, Detective. You know me. I'm not a murderer."

Rya crossed her arms and finally looked me in the eye. "I hope you're right, Jed."

"Hope? What happened to trust?"

She turned her back to me. "Take him away," she said softly to the officers.

SIX WEEKS EARLIER

"How many times have you been punched in the face?"

"Too many."

"Seriously, how many times?"

"You want an actual number?"

"Yes."

"Do glancing blows count?"

"What the hell are glancing blows?"

"In pro wrestling you throw a lot of big, dramatic haymakers, but you pull your punches. However, sometimes your fist gets away from you, and there is unintended but real contact. Got my nose broken twice that way."

"Kind of a pussy way to have your nose broken."

"Tell that to my deviated septum."

"Seriously, I want to know."

"If we're talking legit strikes to the face, then, I don't know. Two dozen times?"

"That's it?"

"Like I said, too many."

I felt an itch on the bridge of my nose and wanted to scratch it, but because it was likely psychosomatic due to all of the talk of face-punching, I managed to resist the urge. So I slipped my free hand into my pocket. My other hand held a large Dairy Queen banana milkshake. I took a big sip until the sensation on my schnoz had subsided.

Elijah Lennox smiled and ran a hand over his sleek, shaved head. "You and me both, Man." Even under his sweat-wicking Under Armour long-sleeved shirt and shorts overtop a pair of matching grey compression socks, I could tell he was at minimum an impressive five-foot-ten package of two-hundred pounds of tight, shredded muscle. Despite the countless strikes he had taken while competing in the UFC, he was still a very good-looking Black man who had a face more likely to star in Old Spice commercials than be on the receiving end of punches.

"We doin' this, Mr. Lennox? Or are ya gonna keep chattin' with Jon Snow on steroids over there?"

Both Lennox and I turned our heads to look at the lippy punk inside the MMA cage. He was a well-built Hispanic kid who looked to be in his late-teens or early twenties, and he had at least a couple of inches and a good ten to twenty pounds over my potential new client. The kid's sweat-drenched T-shirt was evidence of the effort he had been putting in during his one-on-one training session with Lennox.

"Keep your shorts on, Cisco," cautioned the man who had requested I visit him at his gym for an as yet unknown potential case.

"Yes, Sir," replied Cisco, in a much more respectful tone.

Lennox smirked and gave me a curt nod. "Give me a few minutes to finish this up."

I held up my favourite beverage as if I were giving a toast. "Have at it, Bub."

Elijah turned his back, touched gloves with his student, and the two resumed sparring. I tried to give them some space by occupying myself looking around the impressive gym.

Black-leather heavy bags hung from chains in one corner of the large, open space. Rows of kettlebells and cast-iron weights on racks lined a wall, while skipping ropes, headgear, padded gloves, and other MMA equipment dangled on another. A black-and-red Tatami mat lay by my feet, familiar from my grappling days when I competed in freestyle wrestling. The mat was two inches, thick and firm, but with just the right amount of give, making it excellent for striking and takedowns. However, the *piece de résistance* was without question the large, octagon-shaped combat ring in the centre of the mixed martial arts gym, with its chain-link fencing, padded posts and railings.

I turned my attention back to the combatants inside the octagon and caught the tail end of a flurry of punches by Cisco, all of which Lennox batted away with such ease as if his attacker had been moving in slow motion. Cisco grew frustrated and threw an aggressive yet sloppy side kick—which all but sealed his fate. Lennox blocked the strike with one of his feet before delivering two lightning quick crushing blows to his student's solar plexus, and the young fighter doubled over in pain and was hyperventilating in an instant. Lennox moved in for the kill but the kid tapped the mat repeatedly while he wheezed and tried not to puke.

"Never let emotion get the better of you, Cisco. Remember— calm mind, patience, and focus. That's the key."

Cisco nodded slightly as he continued to clutch his sternum.

"Go on, shower up," ordered Lennox.

Cisco slid out of the cage and hobbled toward the locker room while still suffering the effects of his teacher's painful punctuation on their sparring session. Lennox emerged from the octagon, grabbed a towel, and dabbed the sweat off his brow and body. "Sorry about that. Some of these kids are stubborn as hell and only learn the hard way."

"Roger that, Champ," I replied, while biting my tongue and purposely not mentioning the fact that I couldn't recall a time in my life I had ever seen a fighter instantly dismantle his opponent's offence with such ease.

Lennox slung the towel over his shoulder. "You look like you got something on your mind, Ounstead."

"Just that I feel like I'm at the MGM Grand right now. Except without tens of thousands of fans and a chilled, yard-long, lime-blended margarita in an oversized pink cup in my hands."

Lennox chuckled, hopping onto the ground. "You know, you look different than the photo on your private investigator website."

I smiled, scratched the short beard I had grown over the summer, and ran a hand through my hair, pushing back my bangs from my forehead. "I've started wrestling again, so I've let the hair go a bit. Longer locks help dramatize taking and making strikes and other in-ring moves. Trick of the trade."

Lennox seemed satisfied with my answer and nodded, waving a hand around his gym. "I've sunk a lot of my UFC money into this place. It was my dream after I retired. C'mon, let me show you the scene of the crime."

I had already checked out the thief's point of entry—the front door—and, as far as I could tell either a key was used or its lock had been masterfully picked. I followed Lennox over to a shattered trophy case to the left of the octagon. Shards of glass littered the floor, but fortunately I happened to be wearing a pair of aerated, thick-soled, Native Jefferson rubber shoes in addition to my usual black cargo shorts and matching T-shirt, one of my go-to outfits during the dog days of summer.

Greater Vancouver was suffering from a major August heat wave, so I was grateful that Lennox Kickboxing & Pankration had its own cooling system that kept the gym at a comfortable temperature. Glass crunched under my feet as Lennox reached into the broken trophy case, retrieved a framed photograph, and handed it to me. In the picture, he beamed while standing next to Dana White, who was handing him a custom-made, white-leather, diamond-encrusted, UFC Light Heavyweight Championship belt.

"Dana gave that to me when I retired as a thank-you gift for all I had done for the sport. It's worth over two-hundred-thousand dollars."

I almost choked on a sip of banana-flavoured goodness and had a small coughing fit as I fought to keep it from going down the wrong pipe.

"You all right?"

I cleared my throat and thumped a fist against my chest. "Yeah, sorry. I'm fine. But isn't Dana White known for being an SOB?"

"Maybe. But he also launched my career, so I owe him."

I took another sip of my shake and smiled.

"What's so funny?" asked Elijah.

"It's just that your missing belt makes the commemorative WWE Intercontinental Championship Title I have framed on my office wall look like a Mattel Toys replica for kids."

I handed Lennox the photo, and he lowered his head and shook it sadly. "I can't believe it's gone."

"Was the belt insured?"

"Up the wazoo."

"So, you'll be okay, regardless of how this plays out."

"That's not the point."

"How about the police? Did you file a theft report?"

Lennox nodded. "They were great, but let's face it, stolen merchandise ain't gonna light a fire under their asses. I want someone to make finding my belt top priority twenty-four seven. That's why I called you. You come highly recommended."

Although now fully licensed I was still only about a year into my tenure as a private investigator, and it had been a busy one. Since joining my father's detective agency, the recently renamed Ounstead & Son Investigations had seen a spike in paying clientele, mostly because I had been dragged into a couple of high-profile cases in the news, which were often recapped in the pages of the *Vancouver Sun*. My father was ecstatic. Personally,

I could have done without the attention. I had enough of that over the years.

"Look, Elijah, no offence, but why would you keep something so valuable here in the first place?"

"Well, the trophy case had double-paned glass and several locks. And I have a pretty good security system." He pointed to motion sensors mounted on the walls throughout the gym.

"Security cameras?"

"No. And I'm kicking myself for not springing for them."

"Still seems pretty risky to keep something worth two hundred grand in your gym."

Lennox placed the framed photo back on a shelf in the shattered trophy case and turned to face me. "You know why I do? The kids, Man. I do it for the kids."

"I suppose seeing that belt increases the number of them signing up for classes."

"It's more than that. I came from nothing. Grew up with a daddy I never met and a single mama who worked two jobs just to keep me fed and clothed. And for me to come from that kind of home, find this sport, learn discipline, develop toughness, build confidence, and then come into financial security?" Elijah paused before pointing a finger at the photo. "That's not just a belt, Man. That's a damn beacon for any kid out there who is struggling or has a challenging home life, so they can realize there is a light at the end of the tunnel if they're willing to put in the work."

I nodded, impressed with Lennox's conviction. "Listen, Elijah, that's very admirable. And I apologize in advance for this question, but I wouldn't be doing my job if I didn't ask—do you have any students who might have a criminal history or background?"

Elijah sighed and rubbed his shiny head again. "I train some at-risk youth who are either troubled or have even been recently released from juvie."

"Anybody you can think of off the top of your head who might be behind this?"

"These kids, for some of them I'm their last shot. And they come in here with huge chips on their shoulders because of the shitty hand they've been dealt, so they don't exactly open up overnight. It takes time to break down those barriers and attitudes and show them a path. Most don't last. But a few do, which makes it all worth it. This place gives them a purpose. Something they can hold on to. Not to mention that nothing's better for working out anger than punching the hell out of a heavy bag. I train everyone from beginners all the way to elites who have legit shots at MMA careers, but working with those kids, well, it's the best thing I do."

"Sounds like you're making a hell of a difference. But if I'm going to do my job, I'll need you to print out a list of the names of any kids or clients that recently quit as well as those of your at-risk students, in addition to anyone who has keys or private access to this gym. That will give me a place to start."

Lennox nodded. "Sure thing, I can do that. And I'll get your retainer fee too. Just sit tight." He walked past the octagon toward the back of the room to the door to his private office.

"Elijah?"

"Yeah?" he replied, stopping in his tracks and turning on a dime.

"How do these troubled kids manage to afford lessons at a top-of-line facility like this?"

Lennox smirked and responded without missing a beat. "Because I train them for free."

And with that he entered his office while I slurped back the remainder of my banana milkshake, wondering what kind of person would rob such a benevolent man of his most prized possession, one he used to inspire hope.

Twenty minutes later, I had a pretty good idea.

TWO

The windows were up and the air conditioning was on full blast as my Ford F-150 snaked down and around to the left of Moody Street. On the other side of the intersecting road, a large, electric, cursive sign bathed Parkside Brewery's patio in bright green light as dusk approached. Across the way, past Rocky Point, rays of sunshine fought valiantly to continue sparkling and dancing atop the dark blue water of the Pacific Ocean, but it was a losing battle.

I pulled into the parking lot and found a spot near a food truck. I stopped by the mobile eatery, ordered a slab of bacon pulled pork with onions on a ciabatta bun, then headed inside. Five minutes later I was at a picnic table eating my sandwich and nursing a pint of Parkside's Dusk Pale Ale while watching the sunset across the Burrard Inlet.

I finished my meal and nursed my pint, then pulled the folded envelope that Lennox had given me from my pocket. I left the retainer cheque to Ounstead & Son Investigations in the envelope, but retrieved the paper with the names I had requested.

The list wasn't long. Right off the bat, I dismissed those fourteen or under, as it's hard to believe that anyone that age would have the nerve to break in or the skill to pick the door lock without leaving so much as a scratch. That left five names of kids ranging between sixteen and twenty-one. I circled them. I'd get my old man to see what he could dig up on them on my return to the Emerald Shillelagh, our family pub, which was conveniently located beneath the second-floor office of our detective agency. I was about to refold the paper and return it to my pocket when a name at the bottom of the page caught my eye.

Wally Fitzgibbons.

I took a long sip of my beer. There was something about that name, but I couldn't quite place it. Fitzgibbons was listed as the lone janitor for Lennox Kickboxing & Pankration. According to the printout he had been employed there for several years. I took another swig of my brew and gave up trying to figure out why that particular name was causing an itch in the back of my brain. I pulled out my iPhone, but hesitated. Although my technology-challenged father had finally joined the rest of the civilized world by purchasing a smartphone, he still preferred an old-fashioned phone call rather than communicating via SMS or iMessage. I rolled the dice and decided to text my old man anyway, in the hopes that the pleasant summer evening I was enjoying would not be uprooted by an abrupt, gruff chinwag with an irascible senior son of a gun.

I fired off a text message to my father that, although the name *Wally Fitzgibbons* rang a bell, for the life of me I could not remember why. Three minutes later I had my response. My pop had quickly replied *"Robson Street."*

I was at a loss to know what he was trying to communicate, but I did appreciate the prompt reply, so I texted right back.

"What on Robson St?" Three dots flickered across my iPhone's screen as he took way too long to craft a response.

"Courthouse in the 90s," he replied. *"Dont u rmember?"*

I racked my brain for an answer, but drew a blank.

"Old case?" I messaged back.

Seconds later I received an iMessage response consisting of two eggplant emojis followed by an exclamation point. Not wanting to waste time, as I was sure my father had no idea what his newly discovered emojis actually meant, I responded with a curt *"What the hell does that mean?"*

"Two thumbs up," replied the Vancouver Police Department's living legend.

I shook my head as I informed my old man the meaning of what he had just texted.

"Pop, you just sent me two emojis of purple eggplants. They're used to symbolize penises."

I don't know if it was possible, but I swear the three dots were moving faster than usual across my screen as Frank fired off his retort.

"Jesus jumfed up Christ! Not dickz goddammit! Two big thumbs up is waht I meant!"

I threw in the towel and decided that any further attempt at text messaging tutorials on my end would only lead to trouble.

"Just tell me why you recognize the name Wally Fitzgibbons and if his age fits with any perp you're familiar with." Seconds later I had a response.

"It does. And I cant believe you dont remember. First time I ever brought you to see me testify in court was against Fitzgibbons."

I searched my mind for a memory, but still came up empty.

"Domestic abuse?" I guessed.

"Robbery," replied my father.

I killed the rest of my pale ale and scratched my head, still clueless about how the name Wally Fitzgibbons was connected to my past.

"Why can't I place him?" I asked.

"Dont know," came the reply. *"You would think youd remember the best jewel thief this city's ever seen."*

THREE

How could I have been so obtuse?

I felt like an idiot. But my chagrin was soon dispelled by more sips of the most delicious banana milkshake I had ever tasted.

After returning my empty Parkside Brewery pint glass to the bar I asked the hipster with a soul patch who had served me if he knew of the location of the nearest Dairy Queen. Soul Patch scrunched up his nose and winced. "Ugh, Dairy Queen? Really?"

I silenced him with a glare. "Watch yourself, Bub."

Soul Patch threw up his hands defensively. "Try Rocky Point Ice Cream across the street," he said nervously, pointing a shaky finger straight ahead. "Trust me."

I eyed him suspiciously and took my leave.

A few minutes later I was inside the Rocky Point Ice Cream Parlour, enjoying the vintage malt shop ambiance and sitting at a table beneath a signed framed headshot of Bryan Cranston while slurping back a dairy delight. I had never tried Walter White's style of pure meth, but was damn sure the high couldn't match the one I was getting from the liquid heaven between my lips. I returned to the pimply-faced, red-headed cashier with my empty cup.

"What was in this milkshake?"

"Excuse me, Sir?"

"The ingredients."

"Vanilla ice cream, whole milk, one-and-a-half bananas, and a specialty cane syrup."

"Show me this cane syrup you speak of."

The cashier scurried off, returning with a bottle of Torani Crème De Banana Syrup. I stared at the red, yellow, and blue label, and then snapped a picture of it with my iPhone before returning it.

"I need more," I said.

"Sir?"

"More milkshakes. Banana. Do you have to-go trays?"

"Yes, we do."

"How many shakes can you fit in them?"

"Um, four, but I suppose we could squeeze an extra one in the middle."

"Make it so," I said, snapping my fingers, then pointing my index at him.

He nodded and hurried off with my order. Minutes later, I was cruising down the Barnet Highway at ninety kilometres an hour while four banana milkshakes rested comfortably in a cardboard tray on my front passenger seat. The fifth one was in my lap between my thighs.

I called my old man on speakerphone between sips, and when he picked up I had a question ready to go.

"Jewel thief? Seriously?"

"That's the Wally Fitzgibbons I remember."

"You realize this is for the case in Port Moody we were just hired for, right?"

My old man grunted. "What was it again? We've been so busy lately I can't recall the details."

"A diamond-studded, UFC championship belt worth over two hundred grand was stolen, Pop. And your old jewel thief pal just happens to be working at Lennox Kickboxing & Pankration as a janitor."

"Are you sure?"

"I'm driving. You tell me."

I heard my old man's chair creak as he leaned forward and started to hunt-and-peck type with his sausage-sized index fingers on the new iMac I had insisted we purchase for our office. A few blunt keystrokes later I heard my father recline in his noisy chair.

"Sweet fancy Moses!" exclaimed my old man. "Tell me you picked up the retainer."

"I did. Why?"

"Because I just went to Lennox's website and Fitzgibbons's photo is on the Staff Page. It leaves out his criminal history, but I'll be damned if it ain't the same fella."

FOUR

It's not every day you witness a three-foot dwarf twerking beside a nearly four-hundred-pound Samoan man.

I came across this unique sight as I drove down Hastings Street and wondered why a gaggle of raggedy looking people were lined up around the block of Pigeon Park Savings, until I remembered that it was welfare day and many of the residents of Vancouver's Downtown Eastside were waiting to cash their cheques. A bare-chested man, who had turned his shirt into a makeshift bandana to beat the heat, pushed a rusty lawn-mower across the road as I waited for the light to turn green. I slurped back some more banana milkshake, and recalled that the nearest patch of grass was kilometres away from here. Nevertheless, the lawnmower man continued proudly pushing his mower along the sidewalk as if he were on an MLB field during spring training.

Once parked in front of the Emerald Shillelagh, I entered carrying the tray of Rocky Point Ice Cream banana milkshakes just as the dancing dwarf transitioned from aggressively jiggling his diminutive butt to popping-and-locking. Known in XCCW

AKA X-Treme Canadian Championship Wrestling as *"Pocket"*—one half of the sockless loafers and crisp white suit-wearing *Miami Vice* tribute tag-team *"Pocket and Tubbs"*—my diminutive pal was getting his groove on in the open floor space near the back of the room, while my cousin Declan was giving Queen and David Bowie a run for their money.

Although Declan St. James was a bartender best known in Vancouver for his talent of pouring a perfect pint of Guinness—and sometimes starting a scrap or two after imbibing one too many of his brilliant brews—I was stunned to see him belting out a tune, and a challenging one at that. I'll be damned if he wasn't delivering a killer rendition of "Under Pressure" on the Shillelagh's latest attraction, a state-of-the-art, Acesonic KOD-2800 Karaoke Machine, which came complete with a touchscreen, microphone, and stand.

My ex-pro wrestler turned roller-derby star girlfriend Stormy Daze was standing by the bar, looking as lovely as ever, bopping her head and waving her hands in the air as she rocked on. Pocket did a couple of twirls for her, bowed gracefully, offered her a tiny hand, and led her to the dance floor. Moments later both Stormy and Pocket danced fervently as my cousin reached the ballad's ending. Not one to be outdone, the other half of the current XCCW Tag-Team champions— the Polynesian mountain of a man *"Tubbs"*—lumbered onto the dance floor and broke into some kind of ceremonial Samoan dance complete with claps, thigh slaps, and plenty of stomps.

Never one to not make something his own, I quickly realized that while Declan's pitch and cadence were perfect, he had taken some significant creative liberties with the song's lyrics as he mimicked Freddie Mercury's climactic solo.

"Why can't we drink pints, drink pints, drink pints, drink pints, drink pints, drink pints, drink pints, drink pints, drink piiiiints?" crooned my cousin.

He then threw the wireless mic high up into the air, spun around, scooped up his full glass of Guinness with one hand,

and caught the microphone out of the air with his other. The nearly dozen grooving ladies in front of the small stage, a mishmash made up of mostly college coeds and cougars, all marvelled and swooned at my cousin's moves as they cheered him on. He lowered his vocal cords an octave or two and slipped into his best David Bowie impression in order to bring the song home.

"Cuz stout's such an old time-y brew, made with bar-ley, and wa-ter, and lots and lots and lots and lots of hops ..."

I shook my head and chuckled at my cousin who was having the time of his life. He held his Guinness high in the air and closed his eyes as the music reached its crescendo. Stormy, Pocket, and Tubbs threw themselves into the song's final verse.

I walked past the spellbound customers, who were giddily taking in the unusual sight of a former IRA operative turned bartender singing in front of a nearly six-foot Amazon woman whipping her red-and-blue tipped, shoulder-length, blonde hair around in circles while dancing between a spritely dwarf and a colossal Pacific Islander. I slipped behind the bar, put my banana milkshakes in the fridge, then started pouring myself some of Sir Arthur's nectar of the gods.

My cousin brought it home with style.

"Car-ing about beer, this is our best pint, this is our best pint, this is our best beer ..."

His voice grew softer as the song came to an end.

"Everyone drink up ... and be sure to tip me ... be sure to tip me ..."

The piano played its last notes and silence fell over the pub. All eyes were on Declan as he lowered his head. The room exploded into rapturous cheers and applause. Crammed around a table, a group of film students from the Vancouver Film School across the street stood up, held their pints aloft, and bellowed "CHEERS!" in unison. The rest of the patrons followed suit and the sound of clinking echoed across the pub as customers bolted to the great stretch of smooth Mahogany bar to toss toonies, loonies, and even some bills into the multiple glass gratuity jars.

Declan waved his hand graciously and gave a full and proper, post-performance, Broadway-style bow. He joined me at the bar while the karaoke machine switched off and much quieter house music kicked in. An instrumental, ambient music version of Coldplay's "Viva La Vida" started to play. My cousin pulled up a stool, knocked back the rest of his Guinness in a single gulp, and burped.

"Them Queen tunes tend to leave me a bit parched. Last time I sang 'Bohemian Rhapsody' I croaked like a bloody frog for days."

"You were really going for it up there."

I presented my cousin with a fresh pint and he took a thirsty sip of his stout. "Aye, an' I don' like to disappoint." He winked at a tableful of flustered middle-aged women who were fanning themselves and looked like they were having hot flashes.

"So I guess the investment is paying off then?" I asked, nodding at the karaoke machine.

Declan smiled and raised his glass toward the ladies, who all blushed and giggled before waving back. "Ya bet yer hairy arse it is, Boyo," he said proudly.

"Baby!" exclaimed Stormy Daze, charging over to me and grabbing a handful of my shirt, yanking me forward across the bar, and planting a forceful kiss on my lips. She was both statuesque and stunning, so far be it for me to resist her affection, but my girlfriend definitely packed a wallop. I braced myself against the bar as Stormy began to pepper my cheeks with kisses.

"Easy, Sweetie. It's nice to see you too," I replied.

Stormy released her hold, and blushed a little. "You remember these guys, don't you?" she asked. I smiled and turned to face Pocket and Tubbs. The little man was dabbing sweat from his brow and the neckline of the sky-blue shirt he wore underneath his ivory blazer with the matching handkerchief from his front chest pocket. Tubbs eased his large frame down onto a bar stool that creaked loudly, and for a moment we all held our breath. The solid oak seat withstood the weight and the big man took a sizeable swig of his mojito.

"You know I do. How's it going, Boys?" I asked.

"'Tis good, Braddah. Come, talk story wit me and dis Kolohe," said Tubbs, grabbing his little tag-team partner by the scruff of his blazer and picking him up and placing him onto the bar stool next to him with the ease that most people used lifting a pencil.

"Another time. Working a new case."

"Is that the one with the stolen belt you were telling me about?" asked Stormy.

"Yes. And I may have just cracked it."

"Jaysus, ya got a lead already?" said my cousin. "Enough with this wrestling shite. Frank is right, stick with the sleuthin'."

A low guttural growl slowly reverberated along the bar as Tubbs glared at Declan.

"Easy, Palāla," I said in Samoan Pidgin, which I had learned meant "brother." "I'm not going anywhere." Pocket soothingly patted one of Tubbs's massive biceps reassuringly.

"Maybe Declan's got a point," said Stormy softly.

"Don't listen to her, Bro!" snapped Pocket. "Just because she abandoned the ring doesn't mean that you should too!"

"Will you guys relax? Besides, how could I quit with our big six-man, tag-team match coming up on the next pay-per-view?"

"Can you believe the streaming platform Grasby snagged for that?" asked Pocket. "We're gonna make so much bank!" He drained the last of his extra-large Caesar, smacked his lips, then crunched into a stick of celery nearly the length of his forearm. "Damn, Bro, your cuz may be a dick, but he sure does make a killer cocktail."

"Aye, an' if this poxy pint-sized bollocks moved in a wrasslin' ring like he does on a dance floor he'd never lose a match," snapped Declan.

"If you like my dancing so much," snapped back Pocket, "then how about you hook up three sweet feet of sexy with another spicy Caesar?"

"The mouth on this wee bastard!" Declan and Pocket glared at each other for a moment, until mutual grins spread across their faces and they both started laughing. They appeared to call a truce with a fist bump.

Although their relationship had once been acrimonious, I was pleased to see that Declan and Pocket had developed a rapport, as dysfunctional as it may have been. My wrestling pals had been frequenting the Emerald Shillelagh quite a bit in the past few months, ever since the odd couple had moved into a nearby apartment complex.

"I'll catch up with you guys later to talk about our match. I have a hell of an idea for the finish."

"'Tis good to hear, Brah," said Tubbs.

"Now that's the 'Hammerhead' I know," chimed in Pocket.

I nodded at my cousin and gave Stormy a hug. She smiled and gently ran a hand alongside my cheek.

"I've got to get to Chi," she said, referring to the upscale spa where she was employed as a beautician.

"See you at my place later?" I asked.

"You better believe it, Bub," she replied, reaching over the bar again, but this time to smack me on my bottom before strutting out the door.

When I turned around, both Pocket and Tubbs were smiling and had their fists held out, so I reluctantly gave them the obligatory bumps they clearly wanted. Declan took my place behind the bar as I left my friends and coworkers and walked past the restrooms to the spiral staircase that led to the second-floor office of Ounstead & Son Investigations. I made my way upstairs to the familiar door bearing a big brass plaque engraved with the name of our agency, opened it, and stepped inside.

Frank Ounstead, all six-foot-five and two-hundred-and-sixty-plus pounds of him, was behind our shared desk and straining the hinges of the leather office chair. He was leaning forward and glaring at the Amazon Alexa unit we had recently purchased harder than he had the criminals he used to sweat for hours in VPD interview rooms back in the day.

"Alec, find me some Garth Brooks,"

After a ding Alexa responded. "Finding you some good books," she replied. "The nearest bookstore is Chapters-Indigo located at 1033 Robson Street, Vancouver, British Columbia."

"Goddamn it!" exclaimed my father, smashing a ham-sized fist down on the desktop with such force that Alexa jumped into the air like a kernel of bursting popcorn. The machine toppled onto its side and my old man sighed deeply. I took a seat in the client chair across from him, picked up Alexa, turned it off, and then placed the gadget right side up.

"Sorry, Son, I just can't seem to get this Alec fella to work right."

"Well, for starters, it's not a person, Pop. It's a virtual assistant. And secondly, it's a she and her name is *Alexa*, not *Alec*."

My father leaned back in the creaky chair and stroked his prominent salt-and-pepper moustache. "That might explain why it's been spotty when responding to my voice commands," he grumbled.

"Any luck on digging up a location for Fitzgibbons?"

My father smiled. "Dug up a number and gave it a call. Turns out he lives with his mama and the old gal was so grateful just to have someone to chat with she sang like a canary."

According to his elderly mother, Fitzgibbons spent most evenings at the Arms Pub in Port Coquitlam. My old man checked his watch then nodded.

"Fitzgibbons should be there until 9 or 10 PM. Apparently, it's Bingo Night."

I sighed and ran a hand through my hair. "Damn it, Pop, I was just out that way." After a moment I realized that to get to Port Coquitlam I would have to drive past the Rocky Point Ice Cream Parlour again, and just like that another forty-minute car trip suddenly didn't seem so bad.

FIVE

A beefy man wearing overalls and sipping liquor from a bottle in a brown paper bag gave me a nod and a wink.

"Evenin', Boss," he said, cheerfully. He was leaning against a red-brick wall outside of the Arms Pub. He wore no shirt underneath his denim shoulder straps, and with his long, curly locks and abundance of chest hair, was a dead ringer for WWE Hall of Famer Hillbilly Jim. I gave a curt nod and walked past him into the sketchy drinking hole.

The Arms Pub was located in a strip mall off of Coast Meridian Road in Port Coquitlam, which sat on the north bank of the Fraser and Pitt Rivers. The spacious pub, despite province-wide No Smoking laws, had a musty tobacco scent that lingered in the air. Bingo Night was underway, and a portly, bespectacled, balding man stood by a spherical, steel cage, and cranked a creaky lever to spin the numbered balls. He called out "B-15" with little enthusiasm. I recognized Wally Fitzgibbons sitting by himself at a table in the back of the pub. A gaunt man with a craggy face and stringy grey hair pulled back into a ponytail, he wore a tattered

Pink Floyd T-shirt so worn I half expected it to disintegrate at any moment. I made my way over to his table.

"Mind if I join you?" I asked.

Fitzgibbons gave me a quick glance before fiddling with a hearing aid. "Goddamn piece of no-good shit … say again?"

"May I join you?" I said, louder and clearer.

Fitzgibbons shrugged and used his green bingo dabber to mark one of the two cards in front of him. I took a seat and by the time I had settled in, a frumpy, blonde waitress chomping on a wad of gum appeared.

"Who's your friend?" she asked, giving me the once-over.

"Ain't my friend," replied Fitzgibbons.

"Can I get you a drink, Big Guy?"

"Water is fine, thank you."

Fitzgibbons placed his bingo dabber on the table right side up, leaned back in his chair, and glared at me. "I don't trust no man who waltzes into a pub and doesn't order a proper drink."

I sighed and conceded. "Do you have any IPA?"

The waitress blew a big pink bubble that popped loudly before resuming her chewing. "This is PoCo, Sugar. We got Molson or Pabst."

"Molson will do," I said. "But in a bottle, please."

"Sorry, Fancypants. Cans only."

The waitress trudged off toward the bar.

"She's just a ray of sunshine, isn't she?" I said. "Like Reese Witherspoon without the everything."

Fitzgibbons eyed me suspiciously. "What do you want?"

"I'm glad you asked me that, Wally."

If my knowing his name rattled him at all, he did a good job of hiding it. Fitzgibbons took a sip of his White Russian. "I seem to be at a disadvantage," he said, pushing the bingo cards away and checking out of the current game. "Who the hell are you?"

"Jed Ounstead. I'm a private investigator hired by Elijah Lennox."

"Stolen belt," he said, nodding and taking another sip of his cocktail.

"That's right."

"Wish I could help you. But that sucker's long gone."

"You seem awfully certain that two-hundred-thousand dollars' worth of diamonds can't be recovered."

Fitzgibbons leaned forward against the table and clued in. "You know about my past, eh?"

"I do."

He stroked his wispy goatee for a moment before leaning back in his chair, crossing his arms, and smirking. "*Ounstead*. Son of a bitch. You're Frank's boy, ain't ya?"

"I am."

"How is that crusty bastard? He must be well into his sixties now."

I nodded. "And running one of the top private investigator firms in Vancouver."

Fitzgibbons chuckled and took another sip of his drink. "Time catches up with us all. But good for him."

"You don't resent him for putting you away?"

He shook his head vigorously. "Your old man did me a favour. Probably saved my life. I was on a dark path, Son. While inside, I got myself sorted, picked up some skills, and when I got out, God bless Elijah because that man gave me a chance and believed in me when no one else would. I'd take a bullet for that guy."

For a potential suspect, Fitzgibbons was making a hell of a case to be crossed off of my list of possible culprits, and was doing so in a casual and non-defensive manner. He was either genuine or was one seriously smooth operator.

"Did Elijah know some people consider you to be one of the greatest jewel thieves the country has ever seen?"

Fitzgibbons stared me right in the eye. "Not 'one of,' Kid. *The greatest jewel thief in Canada*. Once upon a time. And you're goddamn right he did. I ain't never kept nothin' from Elijah."

"Yet he hired you anyway, despite knowing you'd be working every day right beside a trophy case that contained a once in a lifetime score. Isn't that like hiring a kleptomaniac to work at a Costco?"

Fitzgibbons scoffed at my question. "Elijah had faith in me. Why do you think I'm so loyal to him?"

The waitress reappeared and placed a lukewarm can of Molson Canadian in front of me. I thanked her, popped the top, and took a swig of what Declan referred to as "corporate swill." With its flat taste, I winced as I swallowed and immediately found myself agreeing with my cousin.

"The fact remains the belt is still missing and you're sitting here on a Wednesday night drinking and playing bingo rather than using your expertise to help Elijah track it down."

Fitzgibbons chuckled. "Expertise? Boy, back when I was makin' big scores you weren't even a twinkle in your daddy's eye. There are so many cameras and highfalutin security systems nowadays, I couldn't even swipe a chocolate bar from a 7-Eleven without getting caught."

I took another pull of my bland brew and considered his words. "All right, Wally. Let's say I take you at your word. You still work at Lennox Pankration five to six days a week. I would imagine that makes you the eyes and the ears of that place. And yet you have no idea who may have stolen Elijah's belt?"

Fitzgibbons sighed and killed what remained of his drink. "I … I don't know. I thought at first that maybe some of those punk kids we train might be behind it, but it wasn't a typical smash-and-grab job. I may not be up-to-date as a professional thief, but I'll be damned if I still can't tell if a burglary was done by a pro. Whoever took Elijah's belt definitely had some chops."

"Chops?" I asked.

"They managed to deactivate the security system for one. That's no small feat. And they left nothing behind. No prints, no DNA, no clues at all."

I pondered Fitzgibbons's response and appreciated his candour. He may have been a flawed man, but at this point I was certain he wasn't trying to hide anything.

"Is there anything you can do to assist me in helping Elijah?" I asked. "He hid it well, but I kind of got the feeling he was pretty broken up when I was at the gym earlier today."

Fitzgibbons popped an ice cube from his empty glass into his mouth and crunched it, sighing deeply. I could see that there was a battle raging in his head over what to say next, so I took another sip of my bland beer and bit my tongue. After a while, he spoke.

"There may be someone you might want to talk to."

"And who would that be?"

"*BINGO!*"

A young guy with greasy, shoulder-length hair and wearing a backwards Korn baseball cap a few tables over leapt out of his chair and thrust his pink-dotted bingo card into the air. There was tepid applause as the kid cackled riotously. "Suck it, Bitches!" he crowed, taunting the other players while doing D-Generation X crotch chops. The clapping stopped.

"I hate that asshole," muttered Fitzgibbons. "Second time he's won tonight."

"Wally?"

"Yeah?"

"You were about to tell me there was someone I should talk to?"

"Right. Look, I'm not sayin' he's the thief, but the guy gives me the creeps when he comes to the gym. And I've known some bad dudes in my time. There are also rumours that he used to run with the Hamlet Brothers."

"The gangsters? Aren't they in prison?"

Fitzgibbons shrugged. "I'm just tellin' you what I've heard."

I took another sip of my beer while more questions came to mind. "What's his name?"

"Jim Ratcliffe."

"If he's so shady, why does Elijah let him train at Lennox Pankration?"

"Guy brings in a lot of new clients. All of his juiced-up meathead buddies. Good for business."

"Where can I find this Ratcliffe?"

"If he ain't at Elijah's gym—which he won't be while it's shut down cuz of the robbery—then you'll find him down the street at Grimly's Gym. Word is he slings 'roids and dope out of the locker room."

"Last question. What's he look like?"

"A goddamn rooster."

"I beg your pardon?"

"He's got spiky, bright red hair on the top of his head and struts around on his chicken legs with his overdeveloped chest puffed out. I don't think the dumb shit has ever done a squat in his life. He's all vanity muscles and tattoos. You can't miss him."

I pulled a twenty-dollar bill from my wallet and placed it flat on the table.

"Thanks for your time, Wally. Enjoy another round on me."

"Ain't I the lucky one," he said sarcastically, getting a fresh bingo card ready.

I got up and started walking toward the exit.

"Hey, Li'l Ounstead." I stopped and turned around. "Tell your old man I said hi and wish him well." I nodded and noticed Wally's wrinkled face contorting as if he was trying to say more, so I stayed put for a few moments.

"Tread lightly with Ratcliffe," he continued. "I've seen him snap in the octagon before. Nasty temper. He might be a piece of shit, but he can throw down with the best of 'em."

I gave Fitzgibbons a courteous nod and wondered just what I had gotten myself into.

SIX

Hillbilly Jim was still outside the Arms Pub when I exited
through the front door, although he had finished his bottle of
brown-bagged liquor and had moved on to smoking a cigarillo.
He was still casually leaning against the rustic red-brick wall,
one hand holding his cheap smoke, the thumb of his other hand
tucked snugly underneath one of the straps of his overalls. It
didn't seem possible, but I could have sworn his thick, bushy
chest hair had grown during the short time I had been inside
the modest watering hole.

"Get lucky tonight, Boss?" he asked, as I passed him by.

"Verdict's still out, Bub," I replied.

Hillbilly Jim seemed to get a kick out of that answer and let
out a guttural chuckle.

Most of the cars in the parking lot in the strip mall had
cleared and it was fairly dark due to several street lamps that were
burnt out. I checked my watch to see that it was creeping up on
eleven o'clock. I slid behind the wheel of my Ford F-150, rolled
down my driver's side window in order to catch a light breeze

of the cool night air, and sat in silence for a few moments as I reflected upon my chat with Fitzgibbons.

Every which way I looked at it, it was hard to believe the guy wasn't telling the truth. His loyalty toward Elijah tracked and his kind words about my father, the cop who had busted him and put him behind bars for his jewel thievery, only made the veracity of what he had told me appear more rock solid.

The door to the Arms Pub swung open and Wally Fitzgibbons hobbled out past Hillbilly Jim, who was still dutifully puffing away on his smoke. They exchanged friendly nods. Fitzgibbons walked with a limp in his right leg, and after a few slow steps, he stopped on the asphalt ten feet away from the pub's entrance. He held up the twenty-dollar bill I had left for him to buy another round under the crackling, pink neon light from a large marijuana leaf sign from the next-door cannabis store and smiled.

I guess ol' Wally had better plans for the money than a few more White Russians.

I dug my phone out of my pocket and was about to do a web search for Grimly's Gym so I could determine their open hours before deciding upon a strategy of how and when to approach Jim Ratcliffe when I heard the sound. I knew before I even looked up what it was.

Screeching tires on asphalt pierced my ears and the racket was quickly followed by the pungent scent of burnt rubber. I looked left to see a beat-up purple Jeep fishtail as it rounded the corner from an adjoining gas station that was nearly a hundred metres away. I couldn't see inside the vehicle due to the limited lighting, but the driver shifted gears and gunned the engine—and it picked up speed as it made a straight shot for Wally, who had his back to the rapidly approaching Jeep. The old man hadn't moved a muscle and was still admiring his newly acquired cash.

"Hearing aid," I muttered to myself as it dawned on me Wally had likely not heard the screeching tires, and even if he did, with his limp there was no way he could get out of its path in time.

"Shit!" I exclaimed, before leaping out of my truck and making a mad dash toward him. I glanced over my shoulder and saw the Jeep was tearing up a strip, zeroing in on Fitzgibbons with each passing second.

I committed to my sprint, not risking another glance, but could tell by the rumbling of the Jeep's engine growing louder and closer that it was going to be tight.

"Wally!" I screamed at the top of my lungs, snapping him out of his trance. At that point I was only a few feet away. The old codger looked utterly confused at the sight of a six-foot-three, two-hundred-and-forty-plus-pound man barrelling toward him and a moment later I managed to shove him forward onto the sidewalk and out of harm's way.

The driver slammed on the brakes and squealed to a stop, but it was too late. The only choice I had left was to lessen the impact by trying to jump on top of the hood and roll. I did as much, but the vehicle still clipped me hard on my left side. One of my elbows smashed into the windshield, causing cracks to spiderweb across the glass. The next thing I knew I was rolling off the hood of the Jeep. I landed flat on the asphalt, the wind completely knocked out of me.

I was dazed for a few moments while my side and elbow throbbed, but I was able to assess that I hadn't been seriously injured. I focused on catching my breath.

I inhaled and exhaled, slowly but surely, while the ringing in my ears subsided. What I heard next while lying on the asphalt was almost as troubling as the vehicular assault itself.

"Wally, you sneaky old asshole! Where is it?"

I sat up in time to see the old man slowly push himself up off the sidewalk and use the red-brick wall to ease himself back up onto his feet.

Wally spat on the ground and sneered. "You stupid fucks! It wasn't me."

"Bullshit!" snarled a short, beefy twentysomething man with a high and tight military-style crewcut.

Beefy Crewcut was flanked by a guy around the same age who was a good six inches taller. He was all lean, sinewy muscle and sported an Everlast fitness wear tank top. Together, both men slowly started to circle poor Wally like hungry hyenas would an injured wildebeest, while it was all the elderly bugger could do to try not to wobble on his feet as he struggled to regain his balance.

BAM! BAM! BAM!

Beefy Crewcut and Everlast both looked back over their shoulders to see the Jeep's driver, a husky, melon-headed dude with multiple nose rings, hanging his giant noggin and left arm out of the vehicle's window. "Load him up and let's get the fuck outta here, Boys!" he commanded, banging the side of the driver's side door again.

I sat up and glanced around to see if a big dude like Hillbilly Jim might be willing to lend a hand. The overall-clad character had vanished and it was just me and Wally and his attackers alone in the parking lot. I sprang to my feet and approached the scene unfolding at a brisk pace.

"You know, the last time a person hit me with a car, it didn't end well for them."

Beefy Crewcut, Everlast, and Melon Head all stared at me.

"Fuck off, Samaritan. This is private business."

I stopped in front of the idling purple Jeep while the three thugs kept their eyes trained on me. "Yeah, well, it kind of stopped being private to me when you tried to run over a disabled old man and plowed into me with your piece of shit ride. What the hell do you even use a pile of crap like this for, anyway? In case the Joker wants to go on a safari?"

Wally liked that one and snickered, but his would be attackers didn't seem to care for the reference. Instead, they just stood around slack-jawed, looking back and forth at one another in a state of confusion.

Beefy Crewcut, who was seemingly the leader of this crack team of thugs with a collective IQ lower than my bowling average, had enough. "You gone an' fucked yourself now. T-Money, show this big bitch how we roll."

Everlast Tank Top, AKA T-Money, stepped forward, bouncing on the balls of his feet, flexing his lean yet ripped biceps and triceps. "Oooh, yeah. You like that, Baby?" he taunted. "Bet you've never seen striated guns like this before."

"I have not. But that's because those aren't guns. They're more like pipe cleaners."

T-Money let out a roar and came at me fast with a few short steps before throwing an overhand right with all of his weight behind it. I had to give him credit, his form was top-notch and the punch he threw looked good.

At least it did until I stopped it cold by catching his fist in my hand.

T-Money's eyes widened in surprise. He tried to pull his fist free but couldn't. I waited until I saw the fear creep across his face, then I squeezed my hand, snapped back his wrist to the point where I almost expected to hear bones crack, and pushed downwards. T-Money dropped to his knees faster than a fornicator with fibromyalgia in front of a faith healer.

"Oh, fuck, fuck, fuck!" he cried, bursting into tears. "Stop man! Fuck that hurts! You're going to break my wrist!"

I towered over T-Money, one rotation away from shattering his bony joint. "You want me to make the pain stop?"

"Yes, please! Please! Make it stop!"

I honoured his request by punching downwards with a fierce left hook, cracking T-Money flush on his cheekbone with my fist. I let go of his wrist and he was out cold before his lanky body collapsed to the asphalt.

Both Beefy Crewcut and Melon Head, who was still hanging outside of the purple Jeep's driver's side window, looked at one another in disbelief. I left T-Money behind me and walked closer to Beefy Crewcut. I caught a glimpse of Wally, who had steadied himself against the red-brick wall. He was smiling.

"You know what, Fellas? My bad. That Joker crack was way off. I mean look at the size of this moon-faced bastard's cranium," I said, motioning toward Melon Head. "Throw a striped shirt on him and a black mask on around his eyes and you got a dead ringer for the Hamburglar if he hot-wired the Grimace-mobile."

More blank stares from Beefy Crewcut and Melon Head. Hell, even Wally looked perplexed by that one. Either I was battling a generation gap on both ends of the spectrum or my pop culture wisecracking skills were waning.

"Alright, Josey Wales," snapped Beefy Crewcut. "You asked for it."

I threw my hands up in the air as the stout muscle-bound punk charged at me. "Seventies' Clint Eastwood cowboys you know, but not the McDonaldland Gang?" I asked in exasperation.

There was no time to elucidate the matter as Beefy was on me in a heartbeat. He fired off a series of strong jabs, all of which I dodged. He tried to snap off a front kick that I easily blocked with the sole of my shoe. He then followed up with a wicked haymaker. Although Beefy was too strong for me to catch his fists like I had his buddy's, I was able to stop the attack dead in its tracks with a block using my left forearm then hitting him in the sternum with an open palm, which sent him down and flat on his back.

"You pillow-biting shitheads!" crowed Wally. "That's a fuck-ing Ounstead you're messing with!"

I didn't have a chance to thank Wally for his politically incorrect cheerleading because Beefy quickly rolled onto his side, hacked up a lung, then climbed back to his feet. The kid was tough, I had to give him that. No barbs or threats this time. Beefy just pulled a switchblade from his back pocket, pressed a button, and six-inches of shiny razor-sharp steel sprung out of the handle.

While he may have had some skills as a combat fighter, it was clear from his wild stabs and swings that Beefy knew jack squat about how to wield a knife effectively. I baited him by leaning forward and slightly dipping my left shoulder toward him, and moments later he made a clumsy attack toward my upper chest.

That was all the opening that I needed.

I withdrew my exposed shoulder and took a lightning-quick, reverse quarter-spin backwards, then snaked out both my hands and grabbed his right forearm. I slammed it hard against the side of the still idling Jeep and the switchblade clattered to the ground. Beefy let out a cry as I palmed the back of his head and smashed his face down on the hood of the vehicle. He bounced back up like a kids' inflatable punching bop bag before falling backwards and landing on the ground with a thud.

Smoke filled the air as a panicked Melon Head slid back behind the wheel of the Jeep and gunned it, the vehicle spinning around as its off-road tires burnt rubber and spat up bits of black asphalt while he tried to make his escape.

Not on my watch.

I took two quick strides, leaping over the tailgate mounted spare tire and into the uncovered back of the all-terrain vehicle. I used the roll bar to pull myself up, but the second Melon Head saw me in his rear-view he started swerving back and forth so violently it was all I could do to hang on for dear life and hope not to be tossed from the Jeep as it started speeding away into the night.

He slammed on the brakes and cranked the wheel. The Jeep did a one-eighty, causing me to lose my grip and balance. Flailing while falling backwards, I was able to grab the roll bar at the last second with my right hand and pull myself back into the Jeep. Melon Head floored it again.

I had had enough. I used the roll bar to pull myself across to the driver's side of the Jeep, then leapt out of the speeding and swerving vehicle onto the running boards. My feet securely planted, I shuffled forward until I was face to face with Melon Head. He tried feebly punching me with his left hand while steering with his right, but it didn't make a difference. I was pissed and ready to get off this ride.

In a flash I snapped off a quick jab and hit Melon Head on the side of his bulbous dome, then grabbed the steering wheel and yanked it hard to the left. The Jeep teetered on two wheels for a moment as it jaggedly changed direction. As it levelled out and all four wheels were on the asphalt again I had jumped off of the running boards just seconds before the vehicle smashed into a concrete parking lot divider.

I heard the sound of the Jeep's front end crumple from the impact and braced myself before landing squarely on my feet. I tucked my head and allowed the momentum of leaping clear to carry me into a couple of commando rolls before coming to a stop. I dusted myself off and walked back toward the Jeep that had taken me on a less-than-pleasant joyride. Melon Head was moaning, clearly dazed, his enormous head bobbing up and down as it kept bouncing off of the white air bag that had deployed upon impact.

My truck was nearby so I jogged over to it and popped the glovebox. Retrieving the three items I needed, I trotted back to Melon Head and opened the driver's side door. He whimpered loudly as I helped him out of the Jeep.

Seeing the modest frame underneath his round, flushed face, I couldn't help but take a cheap shot at the punk. "Damn, your head looks like a cherry tomato on a toothpick." I pushed him up against the side of his ride. He yelped as I pulled his hands behind his back and zip-tied his wrists together. "Come on, the rest of the bonehead brigade are waiting for you."

I marched a stumbling Melon Head back toward Wally and the unconscious Beefy Crewcut and T-Money. Wally was still where I had left him, but was now surrounded by Hillbilly Jim and a handful of patrons I recognized from inside the pub. Wally's pals had brought their drinks outside, including a White Russian for the old-timer himself. The group all hung on Wally's every word as he recounted the attempted attack in between sips of his vodka cocktail. His face lit up when he saw me approaching with Melon Head in tow, and he pointed excitedly. "There he is! That's Li'l Jed Ounstead!"

Wally and his chums applauded my little escapade. I nodded politely, forced Melon Head down onto his butt, and finished zip-tying both Beefy and T-Money's wrists behind their backs. A moment later I heard the sound of sirens quickly approaching, so I took a several steps away from the thwarted assailants into the parking lot.

By the time two RCMP squad cars rolled up I had withdrawn my driver's licence and British Columbia private investigator's ID from my wallet and laid them flat on the asphalt in front of me. My hands were high in the air as cops sprung out of their cars with their weapons at the ready.

I lowered myself to my knees and interlaced my fingers behind my head.

SEVEN

The Arms Pub had closed for the night, but not a single patron had left. Instead, they were all huddled together around Hillbilly Jim at his red-brick wall perch while the denim-clad, one-piece garment aficionado gleefully recounted what had gone down in the parking lot half-an-hour earlier. Even the blonde bubble-gum-chewing waitress was lingering about and seemed perplexed that a customer of hers could have caused such a commotion in so short a time.

I finished giving my statement to a patrol cop, along with my phone number, and he returned my driver's and private investigator's licences, assuring me I had nothing to worry about since there were over a dozen witnesses in addition to Wally who all confirmed that I had saved the old codger's life and acted in self-defence.

Beefy Crewcut, T-Money, and Melon Head had all been tended to by paramedics and either loaded on gurneys or assisted into the back of an ambulance, which then left for a nearby emergency room with an RCMP escort.

Wally was sitting on the bumper of a second ambulance, his hand and elbow bandaged and wrapped in gauze from the scrapes he received when I shoved him out of the way of the Jeep and onto the sidewalk. I walked over and took a seat on the rescue vehicle's bumper next to him, just as he finished taking a hit of oxygen through a mask connected to a tank in the ambulance.

"Li'l Ounstead! My hero," he said, chuckling. "You want a hit of this? Paramedic left it on and I'm on my third whiff. This shit's like the fountain of youth. I feel twenty years younger and even had a little blood flow to my ding-a-ling. I'm pretty sure it moved."

"I'm good, Wally. And I'm happy for your … improved circulation."

Wally beamed and took another hit.

"You know why I came over here to talk to you?"

He nodded, wrapped up the dangling tube around the plastic face mask, and threw it back over his shoulder into the rear of the ambulance without looking. "You want to know who those punks were and why they had it out for me."

I nodded. "I got the impression from the way they fought that they're probably members of Lennox Pankration."

Wally scoffed. "Dipshit members."

"I heard their leader yell at you. He said, *Where is it?*"

"That charmer is Nicholls. Trent Nicholls."

I logged into my phone and typed the name into my Notes app. "And by it he meant—"

"Elijah's belt."

Just as I expected. "Any idea why they assumed you had it?"

Wally snorted and scratched the hair on his upper lip. "Yeah, I'd say I know exactly why they thought that. They figured I poached it."

"So they know about your history as a jewel thief."

"Yeah. I don't know how, but they managed to find out a few months back."

I kept pushing. "Okay, Wally. Fair enough. There's just one thing I don't quite understand."

"Shoot."

"They seemed awfully angry with you. Like you had screwed them over or something."

"That's because they're nothin' but a bunch of mouth-breathin' knuckle-draggin' goons."

"I don't disagree with your assessment. But I still feel like I'm missing something."

Wally sighed. "Frank taught you well, Kid."

I nodded but kept quiet, waiting for Wally to fill in the blanks.

"Once those bozos learned about my past, they followed me out here one night and sat their asses down at my table, just like you. And I'll give you one goddamn guess as to what they wanted me to do."

It immediately clicked in my head. "Steal the belt."

"Bingo," he said, with a smirk. "Hey, would you look at that? I got to say it tonight after all."

"So they figured you went ahead solo with their idea."

"Yeah. Except when they first came to me, they didn't want me to just nick Elijah's most prized possession for them. They wanted me to do it with them. To show them how."

"Why, so they could kick-start careers in thievery?"

Wally shrugged. "I figure it was something like that."

"What did Elijah say when you told him?"

"That's the rub. I never did."

That detail caught me off guard. For all his talk about loyalty to Lennox, it seemed odd Wally wouldn't warn his employer of clients conspiring to rip him off. "Why not?" I asked.

"Elijah had enough on his plate, especially with the new gyms he was about to open."

"He was expanding Lennox Pankration?"

"Three new locations across Greater Vancouver with a plan for more. He was applying for loans and leveraging himself quite a bit, so the last thing he needed was to be worried about a few chowderheads who couldn't even steal a rattle from a baby. Plus, I was keeping an eye on them. If I ever thought they were starting to pose a legitimate threat I would have gone to Elijah with what I knew."

I sat with what I had just learned while my grizzled new pal glanced around furtively, then reached back into the ambulance, grabbed the plastic mask, and took another stealthy hit of oxygen. While I was glad I was in the right place at the right time to save Wally from either a vehicular assault or a beatdown, I realized my investigation was in the same spot as when I exited the Arms Pub half an hour ago. Which left me with one direction and one direction only.

Red-haired Rooster Jim Ratcliffe.

I dug one of my business cards out of my wallet and handed it to Wally. "Those guys give you any more trouble you give me a shout. I'll be sure to leave Elijah out of it."

"Thanks, Kid. For everything."

I gave Wally a pat on the back, got up off the ambulance bumper, and started toward my car.

"Hey, Li'l Ounstead."

I turned around.

"You're a good egg. Tell Frank he did a hell of a job raising you right."

"Roger that, Old-timer."

I couldn't help but smile as I considered how quickly Wally had gone from a semi-hostile suspect to unexpected ally. I was satisfied that we were now on good terms. Unfortunately for me, my impending meeting with Ratcliffe would wind up being the opposite experience.

EIGHT

I was on my fifth and final set of deadlifts when Jim Ratcliffe walked into the gym. My form was tight and I was lifting over four hundred and fifty pounds, which seemed to catch Ratcliffe's attention, if only for a moment.

The sides of his head had been freshly shaved with a razor and I'd be damned if his pointy, ruby-red flat-top, overdeveloped upper body, and skinny legs did not in fact make him look like a 'roided up rooster, just as Wally Fitzgibbons had said.

My weight belt was cinched tight, supporting my lower back, and I remained focused on my strict form and breathing as I slowly cranked out reps until I hit my target of six. The silver Olympic barbell arced downwards while in my grip, the five forty-five-pound plates on each side weighing it down. Some gym members had huddled together across the gym by a long dumbbell rack, furtively stealing glances at me and whispering as I lifted the heavy iron. I was all but certain a few of them recognized me from my days when I was still in my prime and wrestling weekly on TV.

I had skipped leg day the week before while wrapping up a car accident fraud case I had been working, so I figured I should take the opportunity to punish my quads, hammies, calves, and glutes while working out at Grimly's Gym during my complimentary first session—despite the fact I had no intention of signing up for a membership. I finished my last rep and gently lowered the barbell to the floor. I grabbed my white sports towel, wiped the perspiration from my brow, tugged my sweaty xccw T-shirt foreward a few inches so it stopped sticking to my chest, then took a long and well-earned sip from my "Macho Man" Randy Savage stainless-steel water bottle. Having concluded my routine and display of lower body strength, the other gym patrons resumed their workouts. I watched in the reflection of the giant floor-to-ceiling mirror as Ratcliffe fist-bumped a couple of his pals before heading toward the men's locker room.

I took another sip of water and bided my time before slinging my towel over my shoulder and casually following him. In the change room Ratcliffe had already put on his gym gear. With his back to me, he popped in a pair of wireless earbuds and cranked the volume on his iPhone. Some kind of heavy metal started blasting so loudly I could hear the lyrics from where I was standing. I went to the sink and washed my hands until he walked into a bathroom stall and the latch clicked shut. I looked in the mirror past my reflection and noticed that Ratcliffe had left his gym bag on a bench outside of the toilet stall. Glancing around to ensure we were alone, I walked over and quietly unzipped the bag. I didn't have to root around for long before I found vials of anabolic steroids, Dianabol and Deca-Durabolin, as well as a prescription bottle of Oxycontin with the name "Julio Sanchez" typed on the label. I dropped the illegal drugs into my shorts pockets then retrieved my backpack from one of the lockers and slipped out of the change room like a cat burglar tiptoeing on eggshells.

Ninety minutes later, I was sitting at a table at the Grimly's Gym café and reading a deep-dive deconstruction on my iPhone's web browser about whether or not one of the greatest movies of all time—*Die Hard*—is, in fact, a Christmas movie (it is), when Ratcliffe lumbered out of the gym and ordered an American Body Building Blue Thunder, a lean mass-gainer drink. Ratcliffe turned his back on the barista, leaned against the counter, and surveyed the empty bistro before setting his sights on me. Once he paid for and was served his post-workout beverage, he made his way over to my two-seat table.

"Mind if I join you?"

"Does Hans Gruber like bearer bonds?"

"What?"

I clicked my phone off and sat up straight in my chair. "By all means," I replied. Ratcliffe took a seat and enjoyed a long slurp of his drink while I stirred the Rocky Point Ice Cream banana milkshake I had retrieved from a cooler in my truck while I was waiting.

"That was some sick weight you were deadlifting earlier," he said. I nodded and took another sip. "Whey protein?" he asked, motioning toward my beverage.

"Banana milkshake," I replied.

Ratcliffe winced, but kept up his inquiry. He was angling at something. "You're a big boy. Have I seen you around before?"

"You a pro-wrestling fan, Jimbo?"

Ratcliffe chuckled and nodded. "Hell, yeah. I grew up on that shit." His smile faded as he studied me. "Hold on ... that's where I know you from!" he exclaimed, snapping his fingers. "You're that wrestler guy, uh, 'Hammerman' Judd, aren't you?"

"'Hammerhead' Jed," I replied curtly.

"That's right," he continued. "So clearly you're keeping yourself in good shape." He leaned forward and spoke in a hushed voice. "You interested in taking your physique to the next level, *Brother*?"

I smiled. After a moment, his eyes widened. "Wait a minute. How did you know my name?"

"Well, I certainly didn't think it was Julio Sanchez."

That comment rattled him. "What the ... how ... why did you say that?"

"Because it's the name on the prescription bottle of Oxy I lifted from your gym bag."

Ratcliffe slammed both his palms down on the table. His drink toppled over and spilled onto the floor. Fortunately, I kept a tight grip on my banana shake and clutched it close to my chest in anticipation of such an outburst.

"You're going to want to calm down if you want it back. Not to mention the vials of Dianabol and Deca I snagged as well."

Ratcliffe jumped up from his seat, stomped around the table in a tight circle as he considered my words and ran his fingers through his ridiculous rooster-red hair. After a couple laps, he sat back down, angrily kicked his spilled drink across the floor, and gritted his teeth so hard I thought he might pop loose a filling.

"You are fucking with the wrong guy, Shithead."

"It's 'Hammerhead.' And maybe. Or perhaps you're underestimating the police contacts I have as both a private investigator and the son of a legendary VPD officer."

Ratcliffe sighed and scratched his head hard, nearly pulling out tufts of his scarlet flat-top. "What do you want?" he asked.

"Just a few answers. Then you can have your stash back."

Ratcliffe glared at me. Eventually, he nodded grudgingly. "All right," he said. "But you don't tell a soul about any of this, got it?"

I nodded agreement. "Fair enough."

"Ask your damn questions already."

"You train at Lennox Pankration, correct?"

"Yeah, so?"

"So, you might have heard that someone recently stole Elijah Lennox's diamond-studded championship belt."

Ratcliffe leaned back in his chair and crossed his arms so tightly the snaky blue veins on his biceps and forearms bulged out of his skin. "What of it?"

"I've heard you're a man with connections. And that if someone connected to the gym pulled this off, you might have an idea who it might be."

"Where'd you hear that?"

"Doesn't matter."

"It was that old geezer Wally, wasn't it? That fucking rat. I'm gonna break both his goddamn hips. He's always had it in for me."

"It wasn't him," I said, hoping to save Wally from a beating. "Come on, Bub. I know you used to run with the Hamlet Brothers. Tell me this heist doesn't smell a little funny to someone like you."

Ratcliffe uncrossed his arms and leaned forward. He glanced around to ensure we were alone before speaking in a hushed voice. "Look, I ain't sayin' this person did anything, okay? But I got word from a buddy of mine of something a little suspicious."

"Go on."

"There's this chick. Gabrielle something or other. I can't remember her last name but I know her a little. Trained her in kickboxing, even helped her set up a home MMA gym. Goes by 'Goddess Goldie.' She just became an IFBB pro. She worked out at Elijah's regularly until a few months back when she scored her ticket."

Having gone toe-to-toe in the squared circle over the years with some extremely jacked dudes, I knew that IFBB stood for International Federation of Bodybuilding and that getting one's card was no easy task. Whoever this Goddess Goldie was, she was legit.

"You think she stole the belt?"

Ratcliffe shrugged. "I don't know. But I wouldn't put it past her or her little bitch of a boyfriend."

"Boyfriend?"

"Yeah. He's like her manager and publicist or whatever. Books all her gigs. According to my friend, Goddess Goldie has been strutting around town flaunting a one-karat diamond engagement ring from that pussy she calls a fiancé."

As I absorbed his words a narrative began to form in my head. "One-karat diamonds are what Dana White used to adorn Elijah's championship belt," I said, piecing the puzzle together.

"And I could pop one loose in two seconds with a pocket knife," replied Ratcliffe.

I took a hit of my banana milkshake while I considered the big coincidence of Goddess Goldie snagging the same size diamond only days after Elijah's belt was stolen.

"Have you told this to anyone else?" I asked.

Ratcliffe shook his head. "Only you."

"Why did Goddess Goldie quit training at Lennox Pankration?"

"I think since her IFBB career has been ramping up she's focusing more on bodybuilding instead of MMA. But I don't know for sure. You'd have to ask her."

"You got a number or address that you can share?"

Ratcliffe sighed and dug out his phone from the gym bag I had raided earlier. "Yeah, right here."

I flipped over my business card and slid it across the table. Ratcliffe dug a pen out of his bag and scribbled down the contact info. Moments later I had the mobile number and home address for Goddess Goldie.

"One more question," I said. "Why didn't you tell Elijah about this yourself?"

Ratcliffe scoffed, "Man, to hell with that guy. He's always looked down his nose at me."

"If you dislike him so much then why train at his gym?"

"Uh, because it's the best and most badass MMA gym in the province. And if you think I move my product here, shit, it ain't nothin' compared to over there."

"Thanks, Jimbo. Let's keep this little chat just between us, okay?" I started to get up from the table when Ratcliffe cleared his throat. "Right," I said, sitting back down. I reached into my gym bag, retrieved the vials of steroids and bottle of Oxy, then covertly handed them back to Ratcliffe.

"You ever try something like this again and I'll fucking kill you. I don't care how famous you are."

"Nice hanging out with you too," I said. I stood up and slung my gym bag over my shoulder. "One more thing."

"What?"

"Cock-a-doodle-doo, *Brother*."

I had my back turned to him and was three steps away toward the exit when I heard him cuss loudly and angrily smack his palms down on the table for a second time.

NINE

"Guns out, buns out!"

That was the mantra I heard repeatedly shouted while I made my way backstage at the IFBB show Declan and I were crashing. "Goddess Goldie" AKA Gabrielle Jane Henderson, proved herself to be quite the challenging person to locate, but by the time I'd called in a few favours from some old bodybuilder buddies, I had a direct line on her whereabouts. I also learned that she was known to be a bit cagey, so it definitely made the most sense for me to try and pin her down for questioning in a public place.

The show theatre at the Hard Rock Casino Vancouver was nearly at its thousand-seat capacity, the audience buzzing as they awaited the opportunity to see some of the best physiques amateur and pro ranks had to offer step on stage. I flashed my father's old VPD badge at the box office, introduced myself as Detective Constable Frank Ounstead, and said I needed to speak to a competitor backstage. A mousy, young cashier gave Declan a funny look since he was wearing his usual, amber-tinted, aviator sunglasses and an Iggy Pop tank top that showed off his colourful arm-sleeve tattoos, camouflage cargo shorts, and flip-flops. Not exactly the kind of person one would expect to accompany a plainclothes cop. Before I could come up with a half-baked explanation, Declan leaned forward on the counter and put his face up to the glass.

"I know I'm a prize to look at, Lassie, but believe it or not, I ain't in the show."

"What are you doing here then?"

Declan flashed a smile and ran a hand through his hair. "Style consultant."

I shook my head while the cashier rang for someone to escort us backstage. We followed the usher down the main aisle and then to the left of the theatre beneath the stage, where he opened the door for us. I nodded as did Declan. A few moments later he and I suddenly had unfettered access to the dozens of sensational, sinewy spray-tanned ladies who were all oiling up, pumping weights, and practicing their poses, each waiting for their moment in the limelight.

"Janey Mack!" exclaimed Declan. "It's like an army o'sexy lady Rambos all givin' me a stiffener at once."

"I don't know why I continue to bring you to these kinds of things," I lamented. "I forget about your impulse control problems."

"Impulse control? Just cuz ya got yerself a steady gal doesn't mean ya need to ruin the fun for the rest o'us."

A moment later, I spotted Goddess Goldie in front of a mirror. I recognized her from a quick Google image search I had done earlier. She was wearing a sparkly pink bikini, the colours of which perfectly matched her lipstick and long braided hair. She was about five-foot-five, had an attractive and symmetrical face, and with her incredibly pouty lips and prominent and perfectly in place cleavage, it was hard not to assume that she had made some cosmetic enhancements. Striations in Goldie's bronzed muscles from her shoulders all the way down to her calves rippled as she switched from biceps curls to shoulder flys, her deltoids glistening as she cranked out rep after rep.

We started toward her, but I sensed at once that she was raising her guard as we approached.

"Who the hell are you?" she barked.

"Jed Ounstead. This is my cousin, Declan St. James. I'm a private investigator hired by Elijah Lennox to find his missing UFC championship belt."

Goddess Goldie let go of the handles of the resistance band she was standing on and it snapped to the floor. She picked up a gym towel from the bench beside her. "I didn't realize Elijah hired a PI," she said. "I heard about the theft, but haven't been by the gym in a while."

"Fair enough. And congratulations on your engagement, by the way," I said, nodding at the glittery diamond ring she was wearing. Goddess Goldie immediately covered the diamond with her other hand, before catching herself and trying to walk back the instinctive movement by adjusting the ring on her finger. "I didn't realize bodybuilders were allowed to wear jewelry during their pose downs," I continued.

"Fuck you," snarled Goddess Goldie, before looking directly over my shoulder.

Just then a diminutive man in a tan suit, polka-dot tie, and sporting a hot pink pocket square, which perfectly matched Goddess Goldie's skimpy outfit, strutted past me and up to her. He clutched a pen in one hand and a clipboard in another. He started chattering in a hyper manner, and as he yammered, he made notes, ticked boxes, and crossed things off the paper on his clipboard.

"First, the bad news. They ran out of Fiji bottled water."

Goldie huffed and put her hands on her hips. "You know that's the only kind I'll drink, Christopher!"

The little man threw up a well-manicured hand in defence. "Of course, Gigi, of course. I already have someone on it. What's exciting is that I pulled a few strings and your song is now approved for your pose down, despite the explicit language."

Declan and I looked at each other, taken aback by the little man's fastidiousness. "What are ya playin'?" asked my cousin. "'Botox Implosion' by Asphyx?"

Goldie instinctively touched her lips before scowling and moving to slap my cousin across the cheek. Little did she know whom she was dealing with, as one of Declan's hands snaked out lightning fast and caught her by the wrist before she could make impact.

Christopher did not like that at all. "Don't you touch her!" he snapped, and then threw his clipboard on the ground and shoved Declan's chest. His hands bounced off of my cousin's hardened pecs as if they were a trampoline. "Ouch!" Christopher cried, shaking his stinging palms in the air.

A huge grin broke out across my cousin's face. "That tickled," he said, amused.

"Enough," I said. Declan let go of her hand and he, Goldie, and Christopher all looked at me.

"Who are these uncouth brutes, Gigi?" Christopher asked, leaning in to give his goddess a peck on the cheek. If that was the little man's attempt at making an alpha move, he failed miserably.

"Just some punk-ass detectives," replied Goldie. "Apparently Elijah hired them to find his belt."

"Jaysus, you're a couple o'bloody charmers, ain't ya?" said Declan. "I'd rather scratch me arse with a cactus than have to watch the both o'yer lurid arses snog."

"You animal!" declared Christopher, taking a step back. "I think we're done here."

Christopher tried to leave, but I stepped to the left, blocked his path, and said, "Let's try this again. My name is Jed Ounstead. And I need your help, unfortunately, whoever the hell you think you are."

Christopher shared a brief look with Goddess Goldie as he smoothed out the creases on the blazer of what was either part of a made-to-measure suit or something off the rack for teenage boys. "Christopher Randall Alister Padmore," he announced, carefully adjusting the Windsor knot on his tie and regally holding his head high in the air, even though it didn't even come up to my shoulder. "I am Goldie's manager, valet, fiancé."

"Holy shite!" exclaimed Declan. "Yer initials are *CRAP*?"

Christopher's face turned beet red and Goldie hung her head in shame. "Why do you always feel the need to include *Alister*, you idiot?"

"You know that was my grandfather's name!" he replied defiantly.

"Look, I don't care if you go by Bubbles Splendiferous. Goldie here is sporting an engagement ring that features a one-karat, cushion-cut diamond, the same kind found on Elijah Lennox's stolen UFC belt. And I know she has a history with him."

"So what if there are similarities between my ring and his missing diamonds," sniped Goldie. "I told Christopher before he proposed that a cushion cut was the only kind I wanted. It's not a crime to have admired Elijah's belt for years while training in his gym."

I looked Goldie hard in the eye, but wasn't buying what she was selling. Too much of a coincidence, and I could tell she was holding something back.

"I think that's just about enough," said Christopher. "If you don't mind, we have a show to prepare for."

"Keep yer Alans on, CRAP," said Declan, holding up a hand. "No more foostering. Where's the bloody belt?"

Christopher's face scrunched up in confusion before picking up his clipboard and tucking it under one arm. He grabbed Goddess Goldie by the hand and escorted her away. We watched as they stormed off, quietly jabbering back and forth about our encounter as they made their way to another part of the backstage area.

I turned to my cousin and gave him a look. "Foostering?"

"Aye, ya know. Wastin' time."

"Next time just let me ask the questions, okay?"

"Ah, sod off. Yer just jealous cuz I almost cracked the case all by meself."

"Her diamond came from Elijah's belt," I said, bringing up a picture of Elijah Lennox's prized possession on my iPhone. I handed the device to my cousin so he could take a look.

Declan zoomed in on the gemstones. "Sure looks that way, Mate. So, what now?"

"Plan B."

"Well, good luck with all that. I'll find me own ride home."

"Where are you going?"

Declan smirked at me and winked. "Gotta keep crossin' things off o'me bucket list."

I sighed as I watched him approach a brunette bodybuilder he had ogled earlier. I couldn't hear what he said to her as he chatted her up, but within thirty seconds she was giggling while handing over a bottle of bronzer, and Declan began lubing up her many muscles.

I shook my head at my cousin's boldness as I left, and began formulating a plan to trick Goldie and CRAP into revealing the location of Elijah Lennox's diamond-studded belt.

TEN

A rat scurried across the weathered grey cobblestones in front of me, nearly running over my shoes. I walked past a row of dumpsters by a dilapidated concrete building as I neared the Salt Tasting Room, where I had recently taken Stormy for a date night. We shared a bottle of wine, enjoyed Vancouver's finest assortment of artisanal cheeses and small-batch cured meats, and stayed up until the wee hours of the morning talking about our favourite SummerSlam moments from years past. It had been a great night.

Despite being a hot and muggy evening, I decided to forgo the F-150's air conditioning, and to walk to my destination from the Emerald Shillelagh. I turned left off East Hastings down Abbott Street before cutting through Vancouver's historic Blood Alley. After a short jaunt down Carrall Street, I turned right on Powell, and then it was a straight shot to Van Lowe 'Vestigations, downtown Vancouver's second most popular PI agency after Ounstead & Son.

I wasn't surprised to find the office closed, even during business hours. And, since it was close to dinner time, I knew exactly where the proprietor would be. As I approached the square, orange building on the street corner, the bouncers working the door of the infamous strip club were pleased to see me. I had worked with both men back in the day before I became a private investigator, and we shot the breeze for a bit until they kindly granted me access without having to pay the cover charge.

A disco ball suspended from the ceiling lit up the room with a kaleidoscope of colours as the smattering of early-bird patrons sipped their drinks and watched an attractive, topless, raven-haired woman swathed in a feathered boa and pink light slowly gyrating while Fiona Apple's sultry voice crooned about being a bad, bad girl.

The last time I had been to the No. 5 Orange Showroom Pub was to request the assistance of disbarred criminal defence lawyer turned rival private investigator Melvin Van Lowe, so it seemed fitting that I was back again for the same reason. Although our initial relationship had been acrimonious, Melvin really came through for me at a time when I was at my lowest. Without his help, I would not have been able to save my father's life. For that, I would always owe him. While he could be quite sleazy, I believed that at his core he was a decent man.

I found my fellow private investigator in his usual spot in "gyno row"—AKA the front seating directly beneath the stage— where he was enjoying a steak dinner and admiring the current stripper's performance. I noticed his drink was nearly empty so I went to the bar and ordered his preferred beverage, Jack Daniel's and Coca-Cola, and a pint of draft lager for myself. I made my way over to Melvin, placed the cocktail in front of him, and took a seat. He slowly and reluctantly shifted his gaze away from the exotic dancer before grinning when he saw me.

"Ounstead, you overgrown son of a bitch. It's been a while."

"Good to see you too, Melvin."

We shook hands. Considering the last time I had greeted him by slamming his face down on the stage-side ledge, our relationship had come a long way. Despite the heat, Melvin was dressed in his standard garb of a light leather jacket over top of a white button-down shirt, complete with a skinny black tie and blue jeans.

"How's your old man?"

"Still going strong. He's currently fishing in the Rockies just outside of Cranbrook."

"Good ol' Frank," said Melvin, slurping the last of his Jack and Coke and then taking a sip from his fresh glass. "So, I take it you're not here for a lap dance?"

"I don't think that my girlfriend would be too pleased if I were."

"You got a girlfriend now? And you're a licensed PI? Look at you, wearing some big boy pants and being all respectable and shit. That's a far cry from getting all slathered up in baby oil and trying to hide a boner while bear hugging other muscly dudes in the ring, ain't it?"

I rolled my eyes as Melvin snickered. With his long, pointy nose, he looked like a mischievous weasel who just told a joke that only he found funny. I took the ribbing in stride and forced a smile, knowing all too well that Melvin couldn't resist taking potshots at my wrestling career.

"Tell me about this lady of yours. Another wrestler? Let me guess. Her name is 'Big Bertha'?"

Melvin snickered some more, but I had just about run out of patience.

"Actually, you know her. She was a previous client of yours."

That caught his attention. "Who?"

"Stormy Daze."

Melvin choked and spat up a little Jack and Coke before wiping his mouth with a napkin. "Holy shit! You hooked up with that smokeshow?" he asked, incredulously.

"She's a lovely lady, Melvin. And we reconnected when she hired me for my last big case." I briefed Melvin on how Stormy and I had become an item after she and her women's flat-track roller-derby team hired me to find their missing coach a few months back.

Melvin took a swig of his cocktail and shook his head. "I'm green with envy, Jed. She's a stunner and seems like a really cool chick."

"You're right. But let's get to what brought me here tonight."

"Lay it on me."

Melvin listened intently as I told him about Elijah Lennox, his stolen championship belt, and the trail of bread crumbs that I had been following. Of course, as both an active listener and a skilled multitasker, Melvin managed to tuck a couple of five-dollar bills into the stripper's G-string when she made her way by our side of the stage.

"Damn," said Melvin after I had brought him up to date on the case. "That's some solid detective work. But it sounds like you've hit a roadblock."

"And then some. Plus, I still haven't told you about CRAP."

"CRAP?"

"Christopher Randall Alister Padmore. Goddess Goldie's fiancé and manager."

Melvin killed the rest of his drink. "I'm anxious to hear all about him. But first tell me this—why come to me?"

I took a long sip of my lager and placed it back down on the side-stage ledge. "Well, I have a plan, but it involves a particular skill set of yours."

"Oh, hell no, Jed. Not a chance. The last time you had a 'plan' you nearly got me wasted by the baddest biker gang Vancouver had ever seen."

"It's not like that. This is strictly reconnaissance. But I need someone with your expertise to pull it off."

Melvin crossed his arms and smiled smugly. "I've only gotten better with my surveillance skills, you know," he said proudly. "The Spy Store has me registered as a gold star customer."

"I have no doubt they do, Bub. So, would you like to hear what I've got cooking or not?"

Melvin slapped a few bills down next to his nearly finished steak dinner and stood up. "Fill me in on the deets while we head next door," he said, leading the way out of the strip club and toward his one of a kind private investigator's office.

ELEVEN

ELEVEN

The lady orc's long braided hair was wrapped around her neck. She held the long handle of a battle axe between her cleavage and roared ferociously, showcasing her prominent lower jaw tusks, which pointed upward past her large nose ring. The sexy fantasy creature was just one of many well-endowed female figures painted on the glittery black walls, and she was right at home beside fanged lady vampires wielding broadswords and a bikini-clad babe hoisting a giant laser gun while standing triumphantly next to a crater on the moon.

Melvin had taken over his office space from a gothic-punk art gallery that had gone out of business, and not only had he not painted over the murals, he managed to turn them into a point of professional pride and effectively utilize them in the marketing of his private investigation business.

Melvin may have been a pervy little bastard, but I'll be damned if I didn't respect his hustle, especially since my pop and I had grabbed a stranglehold on the Vancouver PI market ever since I worked my first headline-making case. We had even floated Melvin some clients as a thank you for his assistance in rescuing my old man from a dire fate. He had built upon those contacts and extricated himself from his formerly exclusive, cheating-spouse surveillance service. Although he had a gift for catching philanderers in the act, the skeevy work left him feeling frustrated and unsatisfied.

"Place looks good. Is that lady orc a new mural?" I asked.

Melvin chuckled as he knelt in front of an open storage locker behind his desk, where he proceeded to load a duffle bag with binoculars, parabolic microphones, and recording equipment. "I had an artist for a client a while ago whose wife was screwing around on him with her personal trainer. Caught them bent over a treadmill getting it on after-hours at the gym even though the lights were out. Used a night-vision app on my phone to snap the pics while I was crouched behind a garbage can."

"Fortune favours the brave."

"Damn straight. Anyway, after the divorce, the guy tipped me by adding that badass blue bitch to my collection, free of charge."

"And they say there are no perks to a career as a private investigator."

Melvin slammed the storage locker shut, zipped up the duffle bag, and slung it over his shoulder. "You wanna hear about the time I caught a couple of retards jerking each other off on the top of a Ferris wheel?"

I sighed deeply. I'd forgotten that spending time with Melvin was like hanging out with a coked-up dirty uncle at a family reunion. "Let's save it for the stakeout," I replied.

We took separate vehicles to the home address Jim Ratcliffe had given me for Goddess Goldie. She lived in one half of a run-down duplex on a suburban road in the Greater Vancouver municipality of Surrey. Melvin parked his cherry-red Dodge Viper on the street a couple of houses away and I drove past him before doing a U-turn and parking across from Goddess Goldie's driveway. Melvin used a Bluetooth earpiece while I put my iPhone on speaker.

"Yo, Sasquatch, don't park so close or she'll spot you," he cautioned.

"I have a good view from here. And she's not a sniper, Melvin. I think I'll be okay."

"Your call, Big Guy. But in this shit part of town anything can happen."

"I appreciate your expertise on all things surveillance, but I need to be close enough to make my play. Just have my back, all right?"

"Roger that."

Twenty minutes later I watched as Goddess Goldie pulled into her driveway in a pink Volkswagen Beetle. What was it with this lady and the colour pink? I was out of my truck and darting across the road before she had even turned off the engine. As soon as the driver's side door opened, I said "Goddess Goldie. Nice to see you again."

Goldie got out of the car and glared at me. "You fucking stalker. I'm calling the police."

"Fine by me. My old man's retired VPD, so be sure to mention my surname Ounstead to the Mounties. It will expedite things for all of us."

Goddess Goldie slammed her car's door shut. "What the fuck do you think is going to happen here?"

"I was hoping for a quick chat."

Goddess Goldie scoffed at my remark. "Why? So you can try and get me to incriminate myself?"

"I have no interest in causing you or CRAP any trouble. Where is he anyway? Don't you guys live together?"

Goldie sighed. "Just because I showcase my muscular perfection in swimwear doesn't mean I'm not a classy and old-fashioned girl. We're not moving into his condo—which I'll have you know is in a better part of town—until I've made some money on the IFBB circuit and after the wedding, okay?"

Living on her own in this kind of neighbourhood seemed crazy to me if she had other options, but I let it go. "Well, I'm sure CRAP doesn't mind. Probably gives him extra time to organize his collection of colourful pocket squares."

"Stop calling him that," she snarled.

I threw my hands up in submission. "Look, I'm just a guy who has been hired to find a missing belt. If I can get it back—even if it's short a cushion-cut diamond—that's good enough for me."

"All you want is the belt?"

"Yes. So I can fulfill the promise I made to Elijah when he hired me."

Goddess Goldie dug a hand into one of the pockets of her Lululemon hoodie and pulled out a protein bar. She ripped the packaging off the top with her teeth, spat the plastic wrapping on the ground, then chomped into the snack as if it were a Snickers. I remembered regularly choking down such supplements back in my wrestling and bodybuilding days, and certainly didn't envy her for having to do so.

"You talk a good game, but there's no way I can trust you."

"Sure you can. You just need to get to know me better. Let's see ... I'm a Sagittarius, I love long walks along the seawall, and fancy myself a bit of a poet."

"You write poetry?"

"Hell-yeah I do."

"What kind?"

"Uh, well ... limericks, mostly."

Goddess Goldie took another bite of her protein bar and furrowed her brow. "Nice try. Look, it's nothing personal, all right? I'm just not saying shit. I have nothing to gain and everything to lose by talking to you or anyone else for that matter."

"Your call, Sister. I'm just trying to give you an out because I was told you and Elijah were friends. But make no mistake, I'm getting my hands on that belt one way or the other."

"I don't care what kind of pull you have with the cops. You come back here again and I'll call 911."

"Okay, Goldie. Have it your way."

"You're goddamn right I will. Now get the fuck off of my property."

I took a few slow steps backwards before I turned and crossed the road toward my truck. I hopped behind the wheel and drove off while Goldie watched me carefully. I was sure not to look back at her or at Melvin as I passed his car moments later. I drove a block before turning left and parking on the street. I locked up my truck, made my way down the sidewalk to the Dodge Viper's passenger side door, and squeezed myself into the car, scrunching my bulk inside the small vehicle as best I could. Melvin had his driver's side window open, was leaning to the left and aiming a clear plastic, parabolic microphone at Goddess Goldie, who had started pacing up and down her driveway. We blended in but also had a clear view from where we were. Melvin had found a great spot.

"What's she doing?" I asked.

"I think she's making a call."

I grabbed a pair of small binoculars from the dashboard and took a closer look. Goddess Goldie grimaced as she pressed her mobile phone to her ear.

"She hasn't even gone into her house yet," said Melvin. "I think you spooked her." A moment later Goldie stopped dead in her tracks and started talking frantically. Melvin passed me one of the two earbuds that were attached to the parabolic microphone. I slipped it into my ear and listened.

"I don't fucking know how he found me, but he's done it twice now. In one day! First at the IFBB show and now at my goddamn house. I didn't sign up for this!"

A muffled voice responded, but it was impossible to make out any words, let alone if the caller on the other end of the line were a man or a woman.

"No way to crank this up?" I asked.

"Who do you think I am, Tony Stark? I've already got it set at max volume."

I bit my tongue. A few seconds later Goldie continued ranting. "It's safe, I promise … No, I don't have it anymore … Are you kidding? With this kind of heat coming down on me?"

Melvin and I shared an excited glance. We were getting close to something.

"I had Christopher move it to a more secure location." There was a pregnant pause. "Don't you think it's better if you don't know? ... Yes, of course it's safe ... You do trust me, right? ... It's with a friend of mine ... Why do you need to know his name?"

Goldie listened to the person on the other end of the line before letting out a big sigh. "Sylvester Chang," she said eventually.

"Jackpot," I said.

"Why?" snapped Goldie into the phone. "Let's just say that Sly's got connections to some dangerous people. He's not someone you want to mess with."

Goddess Goldie ended the call, grabbed her gym bag from her car, then headed inside her house. Once the door was shut Melvin slammed his hand down on his steering wheel. "Holy shit! I can't believe that worked!" Ignoring Melvin, I replayed in my head a specific thing Goddess Goldie had said.

Connections to some dangerous people.

I had been mixed up with organized crime when working my first case, and I wasn't thrilled about dealing with those types again.

"Hello? Earth to Ounstead?" asked Melvin, snapping his fingers repeatedly in front of my face.

"Yeah?"

"Are we celebrating with some boobs and bubbly or what?"

"I appreciate the offer, Melvin, but I want to run with this lead while it's hot."

"Can't you just whip up a background check on the guy tomorrow and take the night off? Probably aren't a ton of dudes named Sylvester Chang out there."

"You're right. But I might have a faster way to both locate and find everything out about him."

"How the hell are you going to manage that?"

I smirked. "I know a guy."

TWELVE

The donkey wouldn't stop staring at me.

Its big black eyes tracked my every move as I made my way down the gravel path, past a coop of clucking poultry and a pigpen full of muddy, snorting swine. After about twenty seconds, I tired of being scrutinized, so I veered to the left and walked toward the donkey's enclosure. As I neared, the equine's tail started swinging wildly and her long ears flopped up and down. The donkey, named "Darla" according to a nameplate, approached the wooden corral and stuck her head over the top. I reached out and gently petted her on the snout. Her bristly fur made a soft rustling noise as it stirred back and forth. Although there was a "DO NOT FEED THE ANIMALS" sign attached to the enclosure, I made sure the coast was clear, reached into a pocket of my cargo shorts, retrieved a honey-almond sunflower seed bar, unwrapped it, and fed it to my new burro buddy, who gobbled it up.

I left Darla to enjoy her forbidden treat and continued on my way down the gravel path of Maplewood Farm on Vancouver's North Shore. Opening in 1975, it had become a well-loved tourist attraction. I had fond memories of my mother taking me there as a child. The best part, like many of the places we visited together, was that if I was well-behaved, we would stop at a Dairy Queen on the way home where I'd be rewarded with a banana milkshake.

Cows in metal milking sheds mooed loudly while automated machines relieved their swollen udders. Barks, gobbles, and quacks came from all directions as the path turned into a large patch of sunburnt yellowed grass surrounding a weathered blue barn.

The big doors to the farm building were wide open, and when I walked inside I saw stacks of hay lining the walls, a beat-up orange tractor with monster truck-style oversized wheels, and a horizontal rack in the middle of the barn that housed a copious number of shovels, rakes, and pitchforks—all things you would expect to find in such a place.

But what I saw next, well, let's just say I probably would have been more prepared to see llamas in top hats tap dancing and twirling canes.

The rear of the barn had been penned off into a rectangular space where twenty or more women and men transitioned from Downward Dog to Warrior One, while close to a dozen small goats bleated, bounced, jumped on people's backs, and ate from small piles of grain that lay in front of each yoga participant's mat. I stopped mid-stride when I took notice of this peculiar scene. I'm not sure how long I stood there gawking, before a familiar voice snapped me out of my trance.

"Mr. Ounstead, please, join me."

To my left, in a luxurious folding chair next to the goats and yoga participants, sat the stylish and urbane gentleman I met while working my last big case. His jet-black hair was perfectly styled and coiffed, and he was dressed in brown, sockless loafers, khaki pants, and a crisp, white polo shirt. Despite the shade inside the barn he wore his usual silver aviator sunglasses.

Familiar with the man's eccentric nature, I was only mildly surprised when I saw him holding a sleeping baby goat in his lap. I took a seat in the empty chair beside him.

"Hello, Sykes." He nodded toward the cupholder in my chair, which held an ice-cold bottle of Steamworks Pilsner.

"I am afraid I did not have the time to procure a banana milkshake," he replied.

"This'll work, thank you."

"Then it would be a shame for you not to drink it while still cold."

I took the hint, cracked open the bottle with the opener that was also in the cupholder, and enjoyed a sip. "Much obliged, Sir."

Sykes nodded courteously, taking a sip of a cocktail which was dark and orange and looked to be a Mai Tai. His glass also sported a lime garnish and a tiny umbrella on a plastic toothpick that had speared three bright red maraschino cherries.

We sat in silence for what felt like an eternity before I couldn't take any more of Sykes's cagey mind games.

"Are you really going to make me ask?"

"First, a toast," he said. I held up my beer. "To Brutus."

"Who's Brutus?"

"We will get to that."

We clinked our drinks together. Sykes wet his whistle, then placed his cocktail back in his cupholder. He stroked the white baby goat in his lap with his other hand. "I am assuming you are a bit perplexed by the presence of my goats?"

"No, Sykes, I want to know if that old tractor over there is for sale. Of course I'm confused by the damn goats. And why the hell are these people doing yoga with them?"

"Goat yoga is the future of the spiritual and ascetic discipline, Mr. Ounstead."

"Goat yoga?"

"Correct."

"What the hell is goat yoga?"

Sykes slid his sunglasses down the bridge of his nose and looked at me with his icy blue eyes. "I would say it is fairly self-explanatory, would you not?"

I took a sip of my beer and licked my lips. "I just meant—why goats? What's the point? And where is Napoleon?" I asked, referring to Sykes's prized racing dachshund. The dog and I had forged an unexpected kinship. The last time I had seen the speedy pup was when he was crowned champion at the annual Vancouver Wiener Dog Race at Hastings Racecourse. The little rascal even made my cousin and me some money when we bet on him to win.

"Napoleon is on a well-deserved vacation at an exclusive canine spa and retreat for dogs of his pedigree," explained Sykes. "And, if I am so fortunate, he is also currently siring a new generation of champion dachshunds."

"Hard to argue that he hasn't earned that," I said.

"With regards to the goat yoga, I am afraid you are missing the essence of the exercise."

"How so?"

"Some people who seek out this activity suffer from PTSD or other challenging mental health issues. Goat yoga has been proven to be a very effective and relaxing form of animal therapy, in addition to offering the traditional breath control, meditation, building of flexibility, and strengthening of joints that many find so soothing and alluring."

I glanced through the wood-fenced pen and saw a goat standing on a man's back produce half a dozen marble-size turds, before an attendant scurried over to clean up the mess with a pooper scooper.

"That's a pretty ripe type of allure," I quipped.

"Trust me when I say I do not take my business ventures lightly." The baby goat in Sykes's lap awoke and started fussing. "Mr. Ounstead, this is Brutus. If I could trouble you to hold him for a moment?"

Sykes lifted the baby goat into my arms and handed me a bottle of milk. Before I even knew what was happening, the little thing was nipping at the bottle and I was petting it while it nursed.

"Well done. You are a natural. Brutus can be fastidious and often is reticent when meeting new people."

"Like owner, like goat, I suppose."

That elicited a deep chuckle from Sykes, which was amazing, because I had never heard the man laugh out loud.

"Very good, Mr. Ounstead," he said. "Very good."

I looked at Sykes while the kid loudly suckled at the plastic nipple of the bottle of milk. "Perhaps it's time we discussed the matter I brought up over the phone?"

"Yes, of course," said Sykes. "But first, this is owed to you after our last business endeavour together."

Sykes handed me an envelope. I opened it with one hand and was surprised to find a cheque for twenty-five-thousand dollars made out to the Spinal Cord Injury Foundation of British Columbia, an organization near and dear to me, signed by none other than professional wrestling legend Bret "The Hitman" Hart.

"It appears your exhibition match with Mr. Hart was an even bigger success than any of us could have anticipated," said Sykes. "He said that he very much enjoyed working with you and to consider this an additional donation to be made on his behalf. He insisted I give it to you personally."

I stared at the cheque while I tried to process it. I had already lived out my dream by wrestling my childhood hero for charity, earned his respect, and even had a few backstage beers with him after our match where we bonded and traded war stories. But to learn that he also made such a generous donation to a cause that I cared so much about? It was almost too much.

"Mr. Ounstead? I assume you are satisfied?"

I composed myself, tucked the cheque and envelope into my pocket, and returned my attention to the hungry kid on my lap.

"Yes. Thank you, Sykes. This means a great deal to me."

"I assumed as much," said Sykes confidently. "So, now that our previous business has been concluded, I imagine that you would like to discuss Sylvester Chang?"

I scratched Brutus behind his ears while the little fella smacked its lips and drained the bottle of its remaining milk. "Yes. And I'm not surprised to learn that he's on your radar. It's why I thought to give you a call."

"I know many, many people, Mr. Ounstead. It is, after all, my business. Mr. Chang and his compatriots often make substantial wagers with me."

"Fair enough," I replied. "But there's a particular reason I'm interested in him."

I told Sykes about working for Elijah Lennox and the events that followed as I pursued his missing UFC commemorative championship belt around all of Greater Vancouver.

If Sykes, ever the cool cucumber, were at all surprised by my tale, he certainly didn't show it. Instead, he lifted the tiny animal off my lap and patted its back.

"Come, Brutus," he said. "Burp for Papa."

As if on command, Brutus the baby goat let out an epic belch.

"I must say, it does appear that your profession as a private investigator tends to bring you into the peripheral orbit of some unique individuals."

"Sykes, I just bottle fed a baby yoga goat some milk before you patted its back until it belched so loud frat boys at a kegger would have been impressed. How is that any different?"

"Touché, Mr. Ounstead."

The yoga teacher in the pen instructed her students to switch from Side Plank to Half Moon pose while the bevy of goats continued to bounce around and bleat. I waited for Sykes to continue.

"Have you considered that Sylvester Chang might be a more dangerous individual than you are accustomed to? Given my growing fondness for you and vested interest in your well-being, I must strongly suggest that you avoid him completely."

"Aw, shucks. You're going to make me blush."

I saw a smirk appear and then vanish from Sykes's face as he got up out of his chair, then lifted Brutus over the wooden fence, and placed him in the pen. The diminutive kid immediately made a beeline for a pile of kibble in front of a fuller-figured woman who was using a balancing block in order to perform Triangle pose. Sykes sat back down in his chair and enjoyed another sip of his cocktail.

"I appreciate your concern, Sykes. I really do. But I need to speak with this man."

Sykes sighed. "As you wish, Mr. Ounstead. But please do mind my warning. Mr. Chang and his associates—and believe me when I say he will be with his associates—are not people with whom one should trifle. Chang is the head of an organized crime syndicate that call themselves the *Red Guard Boys*. His restaurant is a front for much of his illegal business, and he has a reputation for being a particularly ruthless individual. He might not take kindly to you walking into his establishment and accusing him of receiving stolen goods."

"Duly noted."

Sykes slid his sunglasses down the bridge of his nose again and gave me a more solemn than usual look. "I hope for your sake you will come up with a reasonable strategy before attempting to engage him with your line of questioning."

I nodded. "Thank you, Sykes."

"I will text message you the address of the location where you can find Mr. Chang. But I implore you to remember my words as I would hate for our burgeoning relationship to come to a premature end."

I took a big sip of my beer then placed the empty bottle back in the cupholder as I stood up. "As would I," I said, extending my hand.

Sykes glanced at my palm as if he had just been offered cheap caviar on a two-hundred-foot yacht, but after a moment, he shook it. "I wish you well, Mr. Ounstead."

I left Sykes with his clients and yoga goats and exited the barn, only stopping on the way back to my truck to feed Darla the donkey a handful of kibble I had swiped from the top of a fence post.

THIRTEEN

Moo Shu Chinese restaurant was located in a small building at the bottom of the hill off Boundary Road in Burnaby—the city immediately east of Vancouver—and was just down the street from a now defunct neighbourhood sports bar that my cousin Declan loathed since tasting his first pint of Guinness in Canada there. Declan was aghast at the local version of Éire's famous stout. He denounced it as an "abomination," and made one hell of a scene before storming out of the place. He was thrilled when it closed up shop.

Sylvester Chang's Moo Shu restaurant was also only minutes away from my girlfriend's condo, so Declan and I took two cars. Stormy and I had made plans to order in dinner, watch a movie, and have a sleepover after I had confronted the notoriously violent gangster.

I pulled my F-150 into a small parking lot and waited. I took a sip of my large DQ banana milkshake and watched cars zip up and down the long road while I waited for my cousin.

Finally, I heard the familiar roar of Declan's 1974 Pontiac GTO as it tore down Hastings Street, wheels screeching when he took a right turn, before pulling up beside me. Declan slid out of the rolled down window of his muscle car and landed on his feet. He was wearing another rock 'n' roll tank top, jean shorts, and the ugliest pair of orange Crocs I had ever seen.

"Door jammed?" I asked, as Declan flicked a cigarette upwards, caught the filter between his lips, and lit the tobacco end with his lighter, all in one smooth motion.

My cousin took a long drag, exhaling a cloud of smoke and shaking his head. "*Dukes O'Hazzard* marathon on the telly."

"Is that why your shoes match the General Lee?"

Declan liked that one and chuckled. I caught him up on things since I had left him lathering up the muscular brunette who caught his fancy backstage at the IFBB show. He listened intently as I recounted recent events and was motionless save for moving his right hand back and forth to inhale puffs of smoke.

"Who do ya think the Goddess was talkin' to when that shite-sniffer Marvin had the mic on her?"

"His name is Melvin. And I don't know. But whoever it was, it's clear they're the one calling the shots regarding Elijah's stolen belt."

"I still don't understand why Lennox would keep somethin' so valuable in his gym. Has the bloke never heard o'a safety deposit box?"

"That belt means a lot more to him than just its price tag. He sees it as a symbol. A beacon of hope. Something that the at-risk youth he works with can look at and believe that if Elijah came from nothing and made it, then so could they."

"Aye, fair enough. But why would the Goddess o'all people be the one holdin' on to it? If it were me, I'd be selling that thing on the black market or poppin' the diamonds off one by one and lookin' for some greasy tosser to fence 'em *tits sweet*."

I ignored my cousin's mangling of the French expression for *right away* and responded. "All I know is that I'm close, D. But we need to tread lightly. Especially with this Chang character. He comes with a pretty big warning label. I can't have you going off half-cocked in there."

Declan flicked his cigarette to the concrete and stomped out the butt. "Aye, roger that, Boyo. I'll follow yer lead."

I gave my cousin a grateful pat on the shoulder. We walked toward the front of the building, past some wilted shrubs lining the entrance, yet more vegetation victims of Greater Vancouver's brutal August heat wave. A humming, yellow *OPEN* sign flickered in the window of the modest stucco structure and chimes above our heads jingled as we entered the restaurant. The lights were dim and the sun was setting outside, so it took a moment for my eyes to adjust. I enjoyed the final sip of my shake with a loud slurping sound. This caught the attention of the stocky Asian man in a too-tight Affliction T-shirt who sat behind the bar. The man folded the Chinese newspaper he had been reading and leaned forward on his stool.

"No outside food or drink," he growled.

"All finished," I said, shaking the empty cup as proof. "I don't suppose you have a garbage can back there, do you, Bub?"

He stared at me blankly for a moment before waving me over. I walked across the tacky, Chinese New Year red-and-gold carpet and did my best not to step on a monkey, pig, or horse as I passed an empty hostess's podium. Declan followed me. When I was halfway to Affliction Shirt, he whistled. By the time I reached the bar, three heavies, all wearing tank tops showcasing their beefy, tattooed muscles and sporting scowls on their faces, exited the kitchen and began to encircle me, like a pack of wolves zeroing in on their prey. Declan stepped forward next to me in an instant.

Affliction Shirt flicked a switch on the countertop and I heard a crackle and zap behind me. I glanced back over my shoulder to see the yellow *OPEN* sign go out only to be replaced by a humming, red *CLOSED* sign.

"What the hell is a 'Bub'?" Affliction Shirt asked.

"You know. 'Bub.' Like when you call someone 'Guy,' 'Fella,' or 'Friend.'"

"I ain't your friend. And you got about twenty seconds before I show you what the opposite of that is."

"Let's just all take it easy now, yeah?" said Declan. "Ya see, we're just a couple o'grand ol' boyos. Ain't never meanin' no harm. We're just makin' our way through this banjaxed world by poundin' some pints the only way we know how."

Affliction Shirt and his cronies were speechless and gawked at us in between stealing glances at one other in a state of utter confusion. I shot my cousin a look, but the son of a gun just smirked. Affliction Shirt was not impressed. He slid off his stool and kicked it hard, sending it flying until it slammed loudly against a wall.

"Enough games!" he bellowed.

"Easy, now," I said. "I'm just here to have a quick chat with Sylvester."

Affliction Shirt really didn't care for that comment. "And who the fuck are you?"

"Jed Ounstead. I'm a private investigator."

That triggered all four men as they immediately and collectively began rolling their shoulders forward, flexing their arms, and cracking their necks by snapping their heads side-to-side. They were moments away from attacking us. I had to talk fast.

"I just have a couple of questions and then we'll be on our way," I said, slowly placing my empty milkshake cup on the counter in front of me before submissively half-raising my hands into the air.

"How did you know to come here?"

"I'm a detective, remember?" I said, not willing to rat out Sykes.

"Get the fuck out of here," growled Affliction Shirt.

"Nope."

"Excuse me?"

"Come on, Sly. I just want a quick word."

Affliction Shirt's eyes widened in surprise. "How do you know who I am?" snapped Chang.

"Four tough guys, all ready to lay into two—and each one of your crew keeps eyeballing you for direction? It wasn't hard to figure out."

"You have no idea what I'm capable of."

I nodded. "Actually, I do. And make no mistake, you have my respect. I have no interest in causing any trouble."

Chang eyeballed me for an eternity while his loyal enforcers stayed silent. After a while, he reached beneath the bar, retrieved a green bottle of Tsingtao beer, popped off the lid, and took a big swig.

I glanced at Declan, whose gaze kept shifting back and forth between Chang and his three goons who still surrounded us. He caught my eye and gave me an encouraging nod.

"Fine," said Chang, relenting. "Two questions. Then you and the Mick are gone."

I tried to remain calm despite the ethnic slur toward my cousin. "Thank you," I said, politely. "Now the first thing I have to ask—because I'm afraid I just can't help myself—were your folks huge *Rocky* fans by any chance?"

Chang shot daggers at me with his dark eyes and took another pull of his beer.

My old man had drilled into me that the key to interrogating or questioning suspects or witnesses, especially if they were hostile, was to try and keep them off balance. I excelled at this. Perhaps a bit too much.

"*Rambo?*" I asked. "*Cobra?* Please tell me it wasn't *Stop! Or My Mom Will Shoot.*"

"Enough from this fool!" Chang bellowed, and the enforcer on my left cocked a fist and stepped toward me.

Bad call.

Like a flash of lightning, Declan spun around behind me, our shoulder blades touching for a split second, before he snapped off a side kick with such force it hit the approaching goon square in the sternum and sent him flying off his feet onto his back.

What happened next was a combination of a flurry of motion and a cacophony of grunts, shouts, and clacking metal. The remaining two goons still on their feet drew pistols and tried to aim them at Declan and me, but they were too slow, as my cousin moved so fast it was like two guns magically appeared in his hands.

By the time Chang's goons levelled their weapons at us, Declan's arms were spread wide, his trusty Browning 9mm pointed at one henchman while a Glock 19 Gen4 was lined up directly with the face of the other.

"Would ya bloody well look at this," said Declan. "A Mexican standoff with an Irishman and a couple o'Asians! Are we multi-cultural or what?"

Chang reached under the counter and retrieved a sawed-off shotgun. He laid a box of cartridges down on the countertop and slowly and methodically began loading the weapon. I glanced at Declan. He was in control. The goons he had in his line of fire looked nervous and both had beads of sweat forming on their brows that began to trickle down their faces. It was now or never.

I took a slow step forward toward Chang. "Easy, now. Let's all keep our cool."

Chang looked up from loading his shotgun and pumped the sliding handguard on the gun's forestock. "You have one question left, Asshole," cautioned Chang. "I suggest you make it count."

I heeded his advice. "Where are you keeping Elijah Lennox's championship belt?"

That caught Chang's attention. After a few moments, he spoke. "I don't know what you're talking about."

"I think you do," I replied. "And if things here escalate, you're going to have half a dozen police cars outside your restaurant in minutes."

"Bullshit," snarled Chang.

"I'm afraid not. You see, I left out the part about how I'm something of a celebrity since I'm also a former WWE professional wrestler. At least ten people know exactly where we are at this very moment. If they don't hear from me soon, well, there would be trouble."

Chang eyed me cautiously. "So what? No bodies, no evidence. My boys know how to hold fast."

"Maybe so. But even you and your organization couldn't withstand the wrath of the entire Vancouver Police Department."

I could feel Chang's confidence falter. "What the fuck is that supposed to mean?"

"It means I saved the best for last, Sly. My father, retired Detective Frank Ounstead, is a damn VPD icon. And if his PI son and favourite nephew didn't return from their visit to a known gangster's headquarters while following up a lead, it's safe to say you'd immediately find yourself in the crosshairs of the Gang Crime Unit."

Chang slammed a fist down on the countertop and gritted his teeth. He might not have been pleased, but it was clear my words had made an impact. Declan tensed and his index fingers were all but touching the triggers of his pistols.

"Easy, Cuz …"

Chang clutched the shotgun across his chest and glared at me. I stared right back at him, unflinching.

"Ounstead," he said. "I know that name. Isn't that the old cop who took down the Steel Gods?"

Chang wasn't wrong, but I didn't feel the need to go into detail about how I was actually the Ounstead who was responsible for the biker gang pushing up daisies.

"One and the same."

Chang eyed me cautiously, slowly putting the shotgun back under the counter. He barked something in Chinese and moments later his goons lowered their weapons. My cousin kept his pistols trained on both men, and Chang waited to see what I would do next.

"Stand down, D."

Declan muttered to himself in Gaelic before following my command. However, he did not holster his pistols, instead holding them flat against his thighs and pointed toward the floor.

Chang cautiously looked me up and down, as if seeing me with a newfound respect. "Say I do know something," he said. "Why are you looking for this belt?"

"Because its owner Elijah Lennox hired me to find and retrieve it."

Chang stared at me for several moments, his expression betraying nothing. I couldn't read him even if my life depended on it. Eventually, he turned around and walked slowly through the swinging doors and into the kitchen. Thirty seconds later, Chang returned carrying Elijah Lennox's belt. The dim lighting was still bright enough for the many diamonds on the former UFC champion's prized possession to glitter and sparkle. Chang handed me the item I had been hired to find.

"Get out of here. Now."

I nodded courteously. Declan did the same, flicking on the safety switches on his guns with his thumbs and tucking the weapons back into his waistband. He then gave a thousand-watt smile to Chang and his goons, including the one he kicked so hard he was still flat on his back, moaning and squirming on the floor.

I had questions. Many questions. How and why did Sylvester Chang get involved in this caper? What was his connection to Goddess Goldie? Did he know who was ultimately responsible for the theft itself? Given Goldie's phone call in which she unwittingly gave up Chang's name, the person responsible for the robbery was still unknown and at large. But I knew better than to push my luck. I had done my job and successfully recovered Lennox's belt. That was all that mattered.

My cousin nudged me and nodded toward the door behind us. "C'mon Flash, let's get yer arse outta here."

"Ten-four, Rosco." My cousin smirked at the mention of the Duke boys' slow-witted Sheriff nemesis. As we backed up toward the exit I maintained eye contact with Chang and his crew, before nodding slightly and disappearing out the door.

FOURTEEN

There are a lot of different ways to carry the strap.

Back when I was one half of the WWE Tag-Team Champions, I wore it the traditional way, around my midsection, same as my partner "Killer" Colt Cruickshank. But when I struck out on my own in singles matches, and eventually won the Intercontinental Championship for the first time at WrestleMania, I carried the gold by slinging it over my shoulder and did so during my entire run as IC champ.

Some guys like The Rock carried the strap almost disrespectfully by lugging it around by their side as if it were a burden, but I'll be damned if ol' Dwayne didn't look like a million bucks when he climbed a turnbuckle in the ring, snapped the strap upwards, and hoisted the gold into the air. "Stone Cold" Steve Austin used to carry the belt over-the-shoulder akin to the way I did, while Triple H was a traditionalist and wore it cinched around his waist. Although I didn't watch the product much anymore, on occasion I would catch a clip of a pro wrestler sporting a strap and had noticed a new technique for showcasing the belt—the champs would wear it buttoned-up and around their necks. I thought it looked stupid, but then again, my WWE pro-wrestling days were long behind me, so what the hell did I know?

I was, however, certain that Stormy Daze was happy to see me when she clapped her hands and jumped up and down in the doorway of her condo while I strode triumphantly down the second-floor hallway with Elijah Lennox's championship belt slung over my right shoulder. Stormy leapt into my arms, and I stumbled backwards as the nearly six-foot-tall Amazon beauty peppered me with loving kisses. I managed to pry her muscular body off me and followed her into her condo, and with its dark red furniture and walnut brown coloured chairs, end tables, and ottoman, it was no wonder Stormy referred to her stylishly decorated domicile as her "chocolate-covered cherry." Half a dozen flickering candles were strategically placed throughout the dimly lit kitchen and living room. There were two glasses of Gray Monk Pinot Gris waiting for us on the countertop in her kitchen. I laid the belt flat on the granite and joined Stormy in a toast before enjoying a sip of chilled wine on a hot summer night.

"Look at those diamonds!" she exclaimed.

"One karat, cushion-cut," I replied.

"It would be a real shame if one of them popped loose," she said, winking at me.

"Let's not go there," I replied, pointing out the missing jewel on the belt and thinking of the headache Goddess Goldie and her engagement ring had already put me through.

"So another case closed," she said. "You know, I must say, you're getting pretty good at this detective thing."

I shrugged my shoulders. "I just followed the bread crumbs."

"Oh, come on. You got creative and you know it."

"Perhaps a little," I replied, taking another sip of wine. I told Stormy about the encounter with Sylvester Chang and his goons at his restaurant.

"Jesus, Jed. That could have backfired on you big time."

"Why do you think I brought Declan along?"

"I definitely feel better when he's with you," she confessed. "I guess I just don't like it when you put yourself in dangerous situations."

"Part of the job, I'm afraid."

Stormy took another sip of wine, then placed her glass down and nuzzled up to me. "I still don't have to like it. I mean, what would I do without you around?" she asked coyly.

"I don't know. Find a less handsome meathead who also appreciates cheesy movies and gives good foot rubs?"

Stormy snickered and flopped onto the couch. "Show me what I have to lose then, Hotshot."

I sat down and slipped my lap underneath Stormy's feet while taking two generous pumps from the container of moisturizing cream she had on the end table. I started rubbing her toes and she purred with satisfaction.

"I don't think there are many meatheads who can massage feet this well," she cooed, before turning on the TV and tuning in to *SportsCentre*. "Just promise me you'll stay safe, you big galoot."

"As you wish," I replied.

Stormy smiled. "*The Princess Bride*."

I started working on a tight knot in her right foot. "Touché, Darlin'. There ain't no flies on you."

Stormy closed her eyes, and began dozing off while I continued to knead her tense soles and caught the highlights of that evening's Blue Jays game.

"I love you, Jed," she said quietly, and I stopped massaging for a moment. Neither of us had ever used the "*L-word*" before in our relationship, but hearing it from her felt good.

I may not have been ready to reciprocate, but I did continue to rub my girl's feet and had her snoring softly within minutes.

FIFTEEN

The Barnet Highway was a fickle mistress.

I always enjoyed the curvy route nestled between an abundance of foliage and how the road offered a drive that was both high-speed and serene. I cruised by the entrance to Barnet Marine Park and saw a dozen men in tank tops and board shorts carrying a dragon boat on their shoulders as they marched their way toward the Pacific Ocean. Despite the blistering heat, the stretch of evergreen trees lining both sides of the highway was as vibrant and emerald as the grass in the Irish countryside. I turned off my air conditioning and rolled down the F-150's windows, letting the summer air breeze pass through the vehicle. As I entered the city of Port Moody, I took my first left off the Barnet, then followed the road down toward Rocky Point.

I snagged a parking spot right out front of the Rocky Point Ice Cream Parlour. The same pimply-faced, ginger-haired kid rolled his eyes when he saw me stride into the shop, before immediately plucking a bottle of Torani Crème De Banana Syrup off the shelf and going to work making a banana milkshake.

I received a few odd looks while I waited for my shake, but chalked it up to the fact I had a two-hundred-thousand dollar, diamond-encrusted UFC commemorative championship belt slung over my shoulder. After all of the hoops I had jumped through to recover the stolen item, I wasn't about to leave it sitting unattended in my truck. Regardless, Elijah's prized possession certainly made for a peculiar sight in a malt shoppe, which is why I took my Torani Crème-infused banana shake to go the moment it was ready.

I zipped up the corkscrew roadway until I reached Clarke Street, then it was a straight shot to my destination. I parked across from Lennox Pankration and made my way toward the entrance, which still featured a boarded-up front door sporting a hand-scrawled *TEMPORARILY CLOSED* sign.

The lights in the gym were off, but the door was unlocked, so I let myself in. I had left a voicemail message for Lennox to let him know I would be coming by with an update on the case. I patted the diamond-studded strap on my shoulder as I entered and hollered excitedly.

"Elijah! I got something here I think you'd like to see."

I blinked a few times as my eyes adjusted to the darkness before fumbling a hand around on the wall to my right while searching for a light switch. Finding one, I flicked it on. I rubbed my eyes as a florescent glare lit up the gym. The place was silent save for the slow creaking of metal on metal.

That's when I saw Elijah Lennox, with a thick, silver, weight-lifting chain wrapped around his neck, face swollen and purple, his corpse slowly swaying back and forth as it hung lifelessly from the chin-up bar of a squat rack.

SIXTEEN

The Port Moody Police swarmed the gym.

While suicide had been decriminalized in Canada, the response to my 911 call was prompt, and a handful of uniformed cops and a pair of detectives were all over the scene like fire ants swarming carrion in the desert.

I sat alone on a leather flat bench in the corner of the gym, clutching Elijah's precious strap in my arms. I was in shock. I couldn't for the life of me figure out why Lennox would have killed himself. The evidence on hand was mounting and appeared to indicate that the former UFC champion was responsible for taking his own life. There was only one problem.

I didn't buy it for a minute.

Elijah Lennox had hired me to find his missing commemorative championship belt, something I had accomplished pretty efficiently. I had not called ahead to tell him I had retrieved it from Sylvester Chang, but elected instead to surprise him in person when I walked through the front doors of his gym. Turns out I was the one who was caught off guard when I came across his hanging corpse.

I tried to play devil's advocate. Let's say Lennox did off himself. What would have been his motive? I hadn't made any inquiry regarding his mental health before accepting the case—there was no reason to, and tracking down a stolen belt seemed like a pretty straightforward job. As far as I could tell, Lennox was a solid guy looking to take the next step to recover his stolen property. He seemed sincere when he hired me, and I truly believed that his championship belt meant more to him than just eye candy from his fighting days.

Dusk was approaching. I looked out the window, caught a glimpse of the sinking sun, and thought of its rays dancing across the dark blue water of the Burrard Inlet. The PMPD officers and detectives had clustered together and were going over their notes and engaged in conversation while waiting for the Medical Examiner to arrive. In the meantime, all the cops present seemed oblivious to Elijah's corpse, still hanging from the chin-up bar with chains wrapped around his neck.

I laid the belt down on the bench and walked over to the body. I slipped my phone out of my pocket and surreptitiously took some pictures of Elijah from different angles. I dropped into a squat and examined his feet and legs then slowly stood up until we were face to face. My former client's lifeless eyes had begun to cloud over and I peered into them as if hoping to find some answers. There weren't any.

I noticed that Elijah had fresh contusions on his cheekbones, in addition to a fat lip. I looked back at the wall-mounted hooks, from which hung gloves, elbow pads, and headgear, among other equipment. I turned back to face Elijah and snapped a few close-up shots of the bruises and lacerations on his face. I knew from experience it was usually mandatory in training facilities such as Lennox's gym that headgear be worn during all sparring matches. So how did Elijah wind up with injuries to his face in spots that the headgear would have protected? Something didn't add up. I bent over to look at his hands and wasn't surprised to find his knuckles bruised with numerous small cuts around which blood had coagulated.

"Hey, get away from there!" hollered a uniformed officer sporting a shiny, high pompadour hairstyle. The cop and his partner charged toward me and inserted themselves between Elijah's body and me. They puffed out their chests and glared.

"What do you think you're doing?"

"I was just having a look at the body."

"Listen, Private Dick," Officer Pompadour declared. "We have your statement. You can hit the bricks now."

"No, you listen, Bub. I'm the one who found him like this while you were still brushing in your Brylcreem for the day. Lennox was my client. I'd at least like to stay until the ME arrives and does his initial exam."

"I don't think so," snapped the puffy-haired cop.

I decided to throw my weight around. "Do you know who you're talking to?"

"Yeah, yeah. You're Frank Ounstead's boy, the big shot wrestler-detective. I could give a shit. In case you haven't noticed, this is Port Moody, not Vancouver."

"My old man is tight with the top police brass from Hamilton Street to Hope. You sure you want to kick me out of here, Elvis?"

Pompadour furrowed his brow and gritted his teeth. He opened his mouth to tear a strip off me, but before he could say anything, he was interrupted by a familiar voice.

"Officer, may I have a word?" her melodious tone simultaneously conveying authority and allure. Once I caught a whiff of citrus-scented Burberry perfume, I knew the woman who had long held a special place in my heart had arrived on the scene.

VPD Detective Constable Rya Shepard was dressed casually in a short-sleeve, white pillowy blouse, a pair of light-blue jeans, and sandals. Her wavy brown hair was pulled back in a scrunchie, but despite her dressed-down appearance she looked as beautiful as I had ever seen her. Her green eyes sparkled as she strode over to me and the two PMPD cops.

"Detective Shepard," said Pompadour. "What are you doing here?"

"I just spoke with your Captain. Mr. Ounstead has been given permission to remain on site under my supervision as a professional courtesy."

Dumbfounded, Officer Pompadour looked back and forth between Rya and me.

"Yes, Ma'am," he said obediently. He shot me a dirty look and brushed my shoulder with his as he walked away.

Having won our pissing contest, I was inclined to let things go. But after the bastard bumped into me intentionally, I couldn't muster the restraint.

"Remember, Officer, that sale on mousse at Shopper's Drug Mart ends at midnight. Just don't forget to use the discount code VOLUME in order to get thirty percent off."

Pompadour grumbled to his partner as they retreated toward the other cops huddled near the octagon. Rya turned to face me shaking her head.

"You really can't help yourself, can you?"

"Hey, that sale is legit. And with a high maintenance bouffant like that, well, let's just say he needs all the help he can get. You have no idea how much money I used to spend on hair-care products back in my WWE days when I rocked a lion's mane."

Rya looked me straight in the eyes. "You're an idiot."

"And you look as lovely as ever, Detective."

"We have really got to stop meeting like this, Jed."

I nodded softly and feigned a smile. "Agreed. But it's always great to see you, Rya. Why are you here, anyway? Port Moody isn't in the VPD's jurisdiction."

"I was just down the street. My boyfriend took me out for an anniversary date-night dinner at Rosa's Cucina Italiana. Darren swears it's the best Italian food in all of Greater Vancouver."

"Anniversary?" I inquired, meekly.

"Yes. Six months."

I did my best to stifle my jealousy. "So the Rocket's here?" I finally asked.

"Please don't call him that. His name is Darren."

Rya jabbed a thumb over her shoulder and I saw her companion Darren "The Rocket" Stein through the gym's window. The handsome and fit son of a gun waved and gave me me a thumbs up, which I reciprocated.

"I love that guy," I said, despite the fact his dating Rya stirred up mixed emotions within me.

"Jed?"

"Yeah?"

"There's a dead man hanging from chains wrapped around his neck who was your client. Can we stay on point?"

"Roger that. How'd you even get wind of this?"

"I have friends in the Port Moody Police Department. And they are aware of our ... atypical friendship. One of them reached out to me once she learned you of all people had called in a suicide."

"Alleged suicide," I corrected.

Rya sighed and put her hands on her hips. "Okay, lay it on me, Big Fella."

I told Rya about being hired by Elijah Lennox to find his missing championship belt and the steps I had taken to do so. I also explained how I didn't buy for a second that Lennox had killed himself and shared my discovery of the curious bruises and lacerations on the body. Rya listened carefully as I told the story, scribbled in her notepad, didn't interrupt my recounting of events, and betrayed no emotion one way or the other.

"So, you had no idea Lennox was dead when you entered the building?"

"None. I was hoping to surprise him with good news. Now I'm beating myself up for not calling ahead. Perhaps if I had, he might be alive."

"You don't know that."

I shrugged. "I still feel like shit."

"I hear you," she said. "But the best thing you can do for yourself right now is go to the Shillelagh for a pint. You did your job. Let these boys do theirs. I promise I'll keep tabs on this case and ensure you're in the loop."

"I don't know if I can do that, Rya,"

"Christ, not this again," she grumbled. "Listen to me. You're done. You're no longer part of the equation."

"But—"

"Go, Jed. I'll be in touch."

I nodded, my eyes cast down at the floor. Rya stood up on her toes and leaned forward. My heart skipped a beat. A moment later, she ran her fingertips alongside my newly grown facial hair. "I like the beard," she said softly.

We shared a smile before I left without another word.

SEVENTEEN

I tried to keep myself busy in the time after Elijah Lennox's death, which was officially ruled a suicide by the Coroner and the Port Moody Police Department. They had simply written off Lennox's fresh contusions due to him being a retired MMA fighter and gym owner. Despite my protests, the PoMo Police didn't give it another thought. Cops like things neat and tidy, which allows them to close the book on a case and move on to another. I, on the other hand, didn't mind a bit of messiness. Something didn't add up, and although my job was complete, I didn't like how things were left with the Lennox case. Not one bit.

Rya had kept her word and ensured I remained in the loop with text messages regarding Lennox's death. I had a feeling she leaned hard on her Port Moody Police Department and VPD colleagues in order to keep up with developments in the case. I also noticed she had gone out of her way to avoid speaking to me by phone. Like an insecure teenager, I wondered if her relationship with "The Rocket" played a role in that. Regardless, Lennox's death was quickly swept under the rug. The belt I had worked so hard to retrieve was left to Elijah's mother, as was Lennox

Kickboxing & Pankration and his other remaining assets. Never having married or had children, Lennox's last will and testament bequeathed his entire estate to the woman who had raised him all on her own.

I kept myself busy since finding Elijah's body with a few gigs that Ounstead & Son Investigations had been hired for, including a detailed background check on a client's new lover and a recent skip tracing job. Both were pretty straightforward assignments and I quickly resolved them.

I had started to move on from Lennox's death when something unexpected occurred eleven days later, while I was wrestling at the Commodore Ballroom for xccw's Ballroom Brawl Beatdown IX, the indy pro-wrestling promotion's latest pay-per-view extravaganza.

The six-man tag-team match between Pocket, Tubbs, and myself versus The Tombstone Trio—three cowboy-themed "brothers" named Billy, Bobby, and Bart "The Fart" Bonanza (with Bart naturally the trio's overweight comic relief, who utilized a bum-to-the-face finishing move called "The Stinkface," made popular by WWE legend Rikishi). Our six-man showdown in the squared circle went off without a hitch. The match even co-headlined as a main event for the evening because the show had sold out and significant interest and momentum had built up on social media. I had only wrestled singles matches since my limited return to xccw and the fans seemed eager to witness my dynamic with Pocket and Tubbs and their popular *Miami Vice* gimmick.

I switched up my gear for the special occasion by wearing a teal-blue T-shirt underneath a crisp white linen blazer over top of my usual spandex pants and boots, and my altered appearance was a hit with the fans. When we arrived ringside, Tubbs kicked things off with some thunderous right hands and fierce Samoan clotheslines before getting winded. Naturally Pocket saved his partner by tagging in and leaping into the squared circle with some dexterous flips, rolls, and crotch punches (it was a no disqualification match after all). However, the tiny terror soon found himself in big trouble and on the cusp of a chokeslam at the hands of Bart "The Fart."

That was my cue, and I waited for Pocket to deliver yet another cheap shot to the groin before the little man dove across the ring with his undersized hand extended for a hot tag. Once I was the legal man in the match, I went to town. I grabbed Pocket by his wrists and started twirling him around the ring like the blades of a chopper and the diminutive dude's small feet, in sockless loafers, successively cracked each member of the Tombstone Trio in the jaw.

"Hell yeah!" bellowed Pocket mid-spin. "Eat my size fours, Bitches!"

After half a dozen rotations, and seemingly having knocked all of our opponents out cold, I dropped my dwarf compatriot onto the canvas and pinned Bart "The Fart" Bonanza. I rolled up the sweaty, blubbery, big man for a one-two-three count then basked in the cheering and applause alongside Pocket and Tubbs. The crowd went wild. It was great to see such hard-working mid-card wrestlers like Pocket and Tubbs so happy to finally be stealing some of the spotlight.

Forty-five minutes later I was backstage enjoying a cold beer with my tag-team partners and unpacking our match when XCCW owner and promoter Bert Grasby interrupted us with some excellent and surprising news.

"Great job tonight, Guys. Top-notch shit. Online polling already has you as the Match of the Night."

"Hell yeah, Bro!" crowed Pocket. "We killed it out there! Did you see that helicopter finish and how fast Jed whipped me around? I thought I was going to fly away!"

Grasby smirked and used the lapel of his white velour leopard embroidered tracksuit to dab the sweat from his brow. His apparent nervousness, combined with the unusually generous compliment, made it clear something was up with my part-time boss.

"You're right, Pocket. That shit was aces," said Grasby.

"We do good tonight, Brahs," said Tubbs, patting both Pocket and me on the shoulders with his giant hands.

"Everything okay, Grasby?" I asked, taking a pull of my bottle of Red Truck Lager.

His mouth formed a thin line and he looked at the ground. "First, let's take care of business. Here's your cut for tonight." Grasby handed me a thick envelope of cash. On the front, he had already written *Spinal Cord Research BC*. I did a double take at Grasby, who shrugged. "Thought I'd save you the trouble."

I nodded. "Thank you."

The portly man leaned forward and gave me an awkward pat on the shoulder. "My pleasure, Big Guy."

"Yo, you legit donate all your earnings from xccw to that charity cuz of that thing that went down with Mad Max?"

"*Anonymously*," I said with an edge. Pocket took the hint.

My little friend lowered his head before speaking. "Yeah, of course, our lips are sealed. That's amazing, Bro. Seriously. Good on you."

"There's one other thing, Ounstead," said Grasby.

"What's that?"

"Some old lady is waiting out there and asking for you. The grunts are already packing up the ring, but she refuses to leave until she gets a word."

"Did she say what she wants?"

Grasby shook his head emphatically, his jowls jiggling side to side.

Pocket and Tubbs watched me walk toward the hallway before stepping through the curtain and coming out of the side backstage entrance into the Commodore Ballroom. A waifish, elderly, Black woman dressed in a purple skirt, matching jacket, and small hat sat at a table near the bar. She was nervously wringing the strap of her purse with her leather-gloved hands.

"Ma'am?" I said, as I approached her like one would a fawn in the forest. She forced a soft smile and slowly stood up before offering a hand to shake.

"Hello, Mr. Ounstead. My name is Alma. Alma Lennox."

I shook her purple-gloved hand gently and took a seat. She sat back down, looked at the floor, and resumed wringing her purse strap. Because of her cowhide gloves, every time she did so it made a squeaky leather-on-leather sound.

"Mrs. Lennox, I assume you are related to Elijah?"

"He was my son," she said proudly, meeting my eyes as her own welled up with tears.

"He seemed like a good man."

"He was, Mr. Ounstead," she said. "And I can't make sense of why he would have killed himself."

"I'm inclined to agree with you, Ma'am."

Alma Lennox dabbed one of her eyes with a handkerchief. "That boy was strong as steel. And if he needed help, he would have come to me. We were very close. I would have known."

I nodded and waited for her to continue. "Elijah spoke very highly of you, Mr. Ounstead. Which brings me to the invoice your company sent him."

"Invoice?"

"That's right."

My father. I had been logging hours in the Ounstead & Son office, but attempting to solicit the outstanding balance after Elijah turned up dead had completely slipped my mind.

Mrs. Lennox produced an envelope and slid it to me across the table. "This is what's owing along with a generous tip for services rendered."

"Mrs. Lennox—"

"Don't hurt an old woman's feelings, young man."

I nodded and took the envelope.

"There is one more matter," she said.

"Which is?"

"I want to hire you."

"I'm sorry, Mrs. Lennox, I don't quite follow. Hire me for what?"

"To find out if Elijah really did kill himself. And, if so, why a sweet Catholic boy would ever do such a thing."

I sighed and leaned back in my chair. But it was already settled. By the time I looked her in the eye again I knew I couldn't turn Alma Lennox down.

"I liked him. And he was a hell of an athlete, even in his retirement. Plus all that work he did with at-risk youth spoke volumes about his character."

"He was special, Mr. Ounstead," she said. "But it's torturing me. I just can't make sense of why he would have taken his own life."

"I apologize for asking, but were you aware of him having any mental health issues? Depression or anything of the sort?"

"No. Not my Elijah. Not without me knowing."

I nodded solemnly.

"So, you'll take the case?"

I took a deep breath. After a moment, I responded. "I'd be lying if I said I wasn't already tempted to look into it."

"Thank you, Mr. Ounstead," she said, pulling another envelope from her purse. "Here is your customary retainer."

I took the other envelope without protesting.

"So, what now?" she asked.

"Now, I go to work."

EIGHTEEN

I escorted Alma Lennox back to the Granville Street SkyTrain
station because she stubbornly refused a ride home, despite my
repeated offers. She lived on her own nearby, apparently, and
hugged me tightly before she boarded a train heading east. She
patted my cheek lightly with one of her gloved hands.

"You're a good man, Mr. Ounstead. I know you'll do right
by my boy."

I squeezed her hand softly. "Thank you, Ma'am. I'll be in
touch soon."

She nodded before stroking my cheek again and boarding the
train. Once the engine whined and the train sped off, I exhaled a
breath I didn't realize I had been holding and ran a hand through
my hair.

What the hell had I just done? Although I had my doubts,
according to the experts, Elijah Lennox had taken his own life
for some reason, and now I had agreed to take a suffering old
woman's money in exchange for trying to give her the peace of
mind she would likely never have. After a while I stopped beating
myself up, because Alma Lennox was clearly hurting and if I have

a soft spot for anything in this life it's for a mother's love for her son. I had lost my own beloved mom to cancer as a teenager, and although time helps with acceptance, the gaping hole in my heart had never really healed. The late Linda Annalise Ounstead was the closest thing I had ever known to a saint. She believed in me my entire life and was right there in my corner when I felt the need to pull away from becoming a cop for the lure of professional wrestling. Even though it had driven a wedge between my father and me, my mother always had my back and encouraged me to chase my dreams. Regardless, I had no doubt that if she were still alive and I had suddenly died under circumstances similar to Elijah Lennox, my mother would have ripped the universe a new black hole through sheer force of will if it meant getting answers.

As I walked back down Granville Street toward the parking lot where I'd left my truck, I sidestepped groups of twenty-somethings stumbling drunkenly down the street as they chowed down on fast food between swigs of alcohol and bellowing out punchlines to crass jokes.

I made myself a promise. I couldn't guarantee that I would be able to provide the most comforting news, but I was sure as hell going to do my best to find out the truth about what happened to Alma Lennox's son.

NINETEEN

Declan wasn't having any of it.

"So ya promised an' old, grievin', wee li'l lady that ya'd find out why her boy up an' *tiomanta féinmharú*?

"*Tiomanta féinmharú*?"

"Aye. 'Tis Gaelic. For, ya know …" Declan held up an index finger to his throat and made a slicing motion.

I took a sip of my Guinness and nodded solemnly. "I still think the suicide is dubious at best. But even if I'm right I don't know how to prove it."

"Who the shite do ya think ya are, David Caruso?"

"Well, I'm sorry. I didn't have the heart to tell her I wouldn't even try to help."

Declan squinted and pursed his lips like he had just sucked back on a slice of lemon. He plucked his trademark pair of amber-tinted aviator sunglasses out of his pocket, flicked them open, and slid them slowly onto his face. He followed that up by putting his hands on his hips and using his best dramatic monotone voice.

"So maybe this suicide … ain't a suicide after all."

I shook my head at the sight of my cousin's over-the-top Horatio Cane *CSI: Miami* impression when he took things to the next level.

"YEEEEEEEEAAAAAAAAAAAHHHHHHHH!" he screamed, leaping over the bar top, darting to the karaoke machine, and punching in a song. The next thing I knew Declan was belting out the lyrics to "Won't Get Fooled Again" by The Who.

I slid off of my bar stool, caught my cousin's eye, and gave him a salute. He nodded in return, grinning and raising his eyebrows repeatedly as the ladies in the pub got up from their tables and booths and made their way over toward him, surrounding the makeshift stage and swaying back and forth to the music.

Nearly an hour later I found myself at a sketchy residence I never thought I would return to. It was close to midnight and I was not expecting a positive response after ringing the doorbell. My instincts were spot on. The front door swung open and there was Goddess Goldie, her voluptuous bust all but bursting through her pink mesh halter top.

"You!" she bellowed, clearly not pleased to see me again. "How dare you show your face here after all the shit you caused!"

"Elijah is dead," I said.

"I know that, Asshole."

"The police claim it's a suicide."

Goddess Goldie crossed her arms defiantly and glared. "So?"

"You knew him. Do you really believe he would do that?"

Goldie's eyes began to well up with tears. I didn't trust her. She had proven herself to be secretive and shady, but my gut told me that her emotions in that moment were genuine.

"Look, Goldie, Elijah's mother hired me to find out if there was any possibility of foul play and, if not, why he would take his own life. I promised her I would try. So, it's hard for me to not keep circling back to the diamond engagement ring that you're wearing—not to mention your association with Sylvester Chang. In case you don't know, it took some convincing, but I was able to get Chang to hand over Elijah's belt. I'm not sure how exactly, but it's clear to me that you were involved in the heist."

Goddess Goldie raised a hand to her forehead and shook slightly as she choked back tears.

"There was no heist."

"What?"

"I didn't steal the diamond," she said, holding up her ring. "Elijah said I could take one off of the belt for helping him out."

I looked at her curiously. "That doesn't make sense."

"Actually, it does. That was my reward for holding on to it for him."

"Are you telling me that Elijah stole his own belt?"

"Yes."

I furrowed my brow as I tried to process this unexpected revelation. Was Goldie lying? If so, to what end? With Elijah dead she had no reason to fabricate such a wild story.

"Why?" I asked.

"I'm not exactly sure. He said something about needing to cash in on the insurance money or something and owing a debt."

"He had a good career in the UFC. He didn't have any savings?" I asked.

"Not with the new gyms he was opening. He sank most of his capital into them. Look, I don't know much else. I helped a friend and got a free engagement ring out of the deal. That's it."

"But why did you hand off the belt to Chang? And how do you even know a guy like him?"

"Because you were sniffing around like a goddamn bloodhound! And Sylvester and I go way back. We dated pretty seriously in high school and stayed close friends. Nowadays he thinks of me as a little sister. Plus, I figured that given his current occupation, the belt couldn't have been in safer hands. How you got him to give it up is beyond me."

I shook my head in disbelief. "Okay, if that's the case then—"

"Of course it is! Why would I lie now that Elijah is dead?"

If what she said was true, then stashing the belt with Chang made sense. His restaurant was probably the last place anyone would expect to find a diamond-studded belt worth over two-hundred-thousand dollars. I cleared my throat to continue my questioning when a lime-green Mitsubishi Eclipse, with a spoiler so big and wide you could eat Thanksgiving dinner off of it, raced down the street behind me at a speed that must have been close to one hundred kilometres an hour. The engine noise was deafening and I waited until it faded in the distance. By the time I spoke again, the wind had caught a plume of exhaust and it washed over both of us like steam in a sauna.

I coughed a few times and fanned the smoke away from my face. I could tell Goddess Goldie was mortified that she lived in such a crummy neighbourhood and I didn't want to make her feel any more self-conscious than she already did.

"Why did Elijah hire me if he wanted the belt to appear stolen?" I asked.

"To make it look legit. He wanted everyone to know you were on the case, especially after all the press you and your agency have gotten over the last year. Unfortunately, it appears as if he underestimated your abilities."

I stroked my beard for a moment as I considered what I had learned. There was clearly a lot more at play than a simple robbery.

"I'm telling you the truth," continued Goldie. "This whole thing was Elijah's idea. How it wound up with him killing himself, I have no idea. That's everything I know, okay?"

Goddess Goldie sniffled and wiped her eyes. I don't know how long I stood on her front stoop trying to process what she had shared. Eventually, Goldie said, "I'm going inside now." She retreated behind the door and I heard a flurry of locks and deadbolts being turned. I walked slowly back to my truck. I didn't know how to move forward. The entire course of my investigation had now changed.

TWENTY

"So ya solved couple o'cases that got yer big arse in the news.
I don' see ya getting' a key to the city."

"It's not that, D. It's the fact that if Elijah had done a simple
Google search and picked a run of the mill private investigator,
the guy probably would have just logged his hours and come up
empty. Which would have allowed Elijah to pull off his insurance
scam. Instead, because of our publicity, he called unaware just
how deep Frank and his VPD connections run, not to mention
that I had connected guys like Sykes in my corner. Elijah didn't
realize I had a real shot at finding out the truth—even though
that was the last thing he wanted."

"Ya left out the part about ya bein' a thick bollocks who
doesn't bloody quit. Ever."

I shrugged while my cousin slung a towel over his shoulder
and topped off our pints of Guinness, etching shamrocks into
their creamy heads.

We clinked our glasses and I took a long sip, desperate to
change the topic. "So you're really leaning into this karaoke
thing, eh?"

"Are you kiddin'? The Shillelagh has almost doubled its biz since we snagged that glorious contraption," he said, nodding at the karaoke machine. "And aye, I'll admit it, I get a wee kick out'o singin' a tune from time-to-time. It certainly comes with its perks."

Declan nodded at a group of middle-aged ladies who were all squeezed into a booth together, making googly eyes at my cousin. A few of them were fanning themselves with menus as if trying to keep hot flashes at bay.

"Fair enough. I just didn't realize that *performing* regularly would ever become part of your job description."

"Ya know how I feel about me milfs, Boyo."

I chuckled despite myself. "I'm just pleased to see you so happy, D. But you can't fault me for taking the piss a little."

"Aye, roger that."

"Where's the old man?"

Declan took a large, contented gulp of his pint, licking the foam off of his stubbly upper lip. "Catching up on some book-keeping in the office."

Declan slipped me another pint of Guinness I didn't even realize he had poured. "For Frank."

I picked up the drinks and took them with me as I headed up the spiral staircase leading to the second-floor office of Ounstead & Son Investigations. I let myself in without knocking and took a seat across from my father who was seated at the executive desk we shared as partners. I found a couple of coasters on the desktop and placed our stouts down in front us. My father grumbled to himself while pushing up his eyeglasses, which kept sliding down the bridge of his nose as he read over a binder full of case reports and invoices. I knew better than to disturb him and quietly nursed my Guinness until he yanked off his spectacles, tossed them onto the desk, rubbed his tired eyes, grabbed his pint, and held it up in the air.

"Cheers, Son."

We clinked our glasses. "Cheers, Pop."

My old man took a big sip and a deep breath. "So? What's the scuttlebutt? You said you had an update on the Lennox case."

I brought my father up to speed regarding Elijah Lennox, my doubts about how he died, his mother hiring our agency to discover the motive for his apparent suicide, and Goddess Goldie's revelation about Elijah faking the theft of his championship belt. My father nodded and I could tell, despite his usual gruffness, he felt sympathy for Alma Lennox and her suffering.

After a few moments of silence, he spoke. "You did a good thing, Boy. I'm proud of you."

"Thanks. I assume you can take care of this?" I asked, tossing the two envelopes onto the desk. "Lennox's outstanding balance and the retainer his mother gave me."

My father smiled. "Well done," he said, opening the envelopes. His bushy eyebrows jumped up his forehead like they were on fishhooks and he whistled. "Hell of a generous tip."

"Which also made it tough to say no to the new job. The problem is I don't know what to do or where to go next. I want to help Mrs. Lennox, Pop. More than anything. But I feel like I'm at a dead end."

Frank leaned back in his chair and it creaked from the sheer weight of his six-foot-five, linebacker-like bulk. He crossed his arms across his chest and rocked back and forth a few times before leaning forward and thumping his elbows on the desktop.

"Do you believe this Goldie person?"

"I do."

"Then that's a good place to start. Lennox was up to something. We don't know what. But he clearly had some kind of plan that went off the rails. How long has he been dead?"

"Coming up on two weeks," I replied.

"So, his place is likely still intact."

I hesitated before answering. "You're saying I should go there and snoop around?"

My father waved the gorilla mitts he called hands back and forth. "I'm saying maybe he left his front door unlocked, and you just happen to enter as part of the new investigation you are conducting on behalf of his mother."

"There's a good chance Mrs. Lennox has a house key," I replied.

My old man stroked his salt-and-pepper moustache and gave me a stern look. "And do you think this is something that poor woman needs to be burdened with right now? Especially considering you have the skills to deal with such a situation on your own?"

I nodded. "Ten-four."

"All right, then. I'm around if you need me. Otherwise, I would advise you to get after it."

I thanked him for his guidance, finished my Guinness, returned the glass to the bar top, fist-bumped my cousin, retrieved my last remaining Rocky Point banana milkshake from the beer fridge, and headed off to see what secrets Elijah Lennox's residence might contain.

TWENTY-ONE

Elijah Lennox was a neat freak.

Everything in his home was clean, folded, organized, labelled, and perfectly arranged. Even the brass knocker on his front door was freshly polished.

I walked around the Port Moody Klahanie Townhouses and Condos a couple of times after finding a guest parking spot. The complex was nestled amidst an abundance of beautiful foliage, directly across the street from a trail that led to Rocky Point Park—which doubled as the home of my new favourite ice cream parlour.

Once I reached Lennox's front door with my trusty lock-picking kit and was certain that no nosy neighbours were eye-balling me, I picked the deadbolt and slipped inside.

I did a quick scan to get the lay of the land. Everything looked copacetic. I made my way up two flights of stairs before finding Lennox's office and started snooping. His place had either been given a quick and simple once-over by the Port Moody Police, or they hadn't even bothered as part of their investigation into his apparent suicide, because nothing appeared disturbed.

There were framed photos of Lennox with other fighters on the walls, many featuring him duking it out with fellow combatants in the octagon. Among the prized pictures was a snapshot of Elijah and Dana White posing and smiling side-by-side from his UFC days, as well as posters of previous pay-per-views he had headlined. Interspersed among them were carefully mounted pairs of striking gloves that had clearly been worn in the ring. I sat in my former client's office chair, clicked his computer's mouse, and was surprised to find that the PC wasn't password protected. I searched through his files and sought something—anything— that could be of help.

I had almost given up hope when I came across a folder labelled *Jerry Cripps* and clicked on it. Once opened, I selected some files and icons which brought up a flurry of photos. I worked my way through the grainy black-and-white images of fighters on what appeared to be several different rooftops, engaged in one-on-one bare-handed fisticuffs, while their fellow scrappers watched. I leaned back in the chair wondering what exactly I was seeing.

I took a few screenshots of the photos with my phone, closed the files, and put the computer to sleep. I had no idea how, or if, someone named Jerry Cripps figured into Lennox's death, or what it may have had to do with rooftop bouts.

But at least now I had a place to start.

TWENTY-TWO

My mind wandered, trying to make sense of the Lennox / Cripps connection as I drove by the Stadium-Chinatown SkyTrain station. The brakes of the automated rolling stock whined as they slowed, replaced by the whirring of the rapid transit cars on the adjacent track zipping off in the other direction. I sped past the enormous Vancouver Canucks NHL team banners that hung outside the Rogers Arena as questions popped up inside my head faster than the subterranean varmints in a game of Whack-A-Mole.

Who was Jerry Cripps? Apparently a member of some kind of rooftop fight club. But why was Lennox interested enough to have photos of him on his computer? Were they friends? Did he hire someone to photograph the rooftop fights, or did he snap the pics himself? It was a lot to process and I clearly had my work cut out for me. I called my old man and he agreed to do a rundown on Jerry Cripps in an effort to try and find out how he might be connected to Elijah Lennox.

We made plans to meet at the Dairy Queen on Robson Street in an hour. That gave me just enough time to hit a few European delis and dessert shops on my way back to Vancouver so I could procure the specialty item I desired. I found a metered spot on the street to park and used an app on my phone to buy myself an hour to avoid being towed.

Robson Street was bustling with shoppers, and the side-walk was so packed I brushed shoulders several times with folks toting either Lululemon bags stuffed to the brim with yoga wear, or colourful packages from Lush cosmetics shop, which were emitting whiffs of citrus and blackcurrant. When I arrived at the DQ Grill & Chill I found my old man inside in a corner booth, with a manila envelope and pineapple sundae in front of him, as well as a large banana milkshake waiting for me on my side of the table.

I slid into the booth and placed the brown paper bag down in front of me. My father chastised me as I pulled the bottle from the bag.

"What the—you're going to get us kicked out of here, Boy. And this is also a sign that you might have a problem."

I placed the brightly coloured bottle of Torani Crème De Banana Syrup on the table, opened it, popped off the lid of my milkshake, poured a shot into the cup, and then stirred vigorously with the straw.

"Take a closer look," I replied, forcing back a smirk.

My old man leaned forward and his eyes squinted behind his half-moon reading glasses. "Crème De … what in the blue hell?"

"High-end, European, banana-flavoured cane syrup, Pop. It's the evolution of milkshakes as we know it. We're talking next level stuff here."

My father folded the copy of the *Vancouver Sun* he had been reading, slid off his eyeglasses, and massaged the bridge of his nose.

"I don't know what it is with you and bananas," he said, sighing.

"Yes, you do," I replied.

My father looked me in the eye and we both smiled softly. We needed not speak of her, but we both thought of my mom and how banana milkshakes were the treat she had spoiled me with as a child. We basked in her memory and enjoyed our frozen desserts for a little while in silence.

Then, my old man cleared his throat and got down to business. "Well, Son, I'll give you this. You sure know how to pick them."

"Cripps?" I asked, taking another big sip of my now altered—and much improved—milkshake. My father nodded his head, opened the manila folder, and passed me a photo of Jerry Cripps lying on a rooftop. His face was badly bruised with copious amounts of blood pooling beneath his skull, one arm broken and dangling beside his limp body at a sickening angle, while two masked and gloved EMTs tended to him.

"Holy crap," I muttered, staring at the shattered body. "Wait a second." I pulled out my phone and brought up the snaps I had taken off of Lennox's computer. It took me a minute because of how battered Cripps's face was in the photo, but eventually I placed it. In two of the photos, he was standing in the circle of fighters cheering on the combatants, but in the third he was competing himself, caught mid-motion throwing an overhand right toward the jaw of his roughed-up opponent. Something told me Cripps knew how to handle himself, which made his savage beatdown all the more perplexing.

"Who took this photo?" I asked my old man, tapping on Cripps's prone image.

"One of the EMTs. Not exactly protocol, but he thought it might help the cops after he saw the state of the guy. Even took the time to make a follow-up inquiry and give a statement that in the twenty-plus years he's been riding the meat wagon he'd never seen anything like that. EMTs wasted no time getting him to the hospital. Poor bastard nearly died on the way."

"And they found Cripps alone on the rooftop?"

"Yep."

"Which one?"

"The Astoria."

The Astoria Hotel in the Downtown Eastside was a dingy dive that served crappy beer, offered rooms with roaches as roommates, and featured a regular showcase for punk and metal bands in its dilapidated lounge. It was also only a ten-minute walk from the Emerald Shillelagh and the Ounstead & Son Investigations office.

"Let me guess. Anonymous tip called it in?"

"See what happens when you use your noggin for something other than a punching bag?"

"How'd you get all this?" I finally asked.

My father grinned. "Why my PI magic, of course."

"If by *magic* you mean locking yourself out of the office computer, regularly deleting emails, and buggering up the private investigator software so badly because you visited a sketchy Asian porn site, then yeah, Pop, you're a regular David Copperfield."

"That was your cousin, goddamn it," he growled. "And it wasn't porn! It was ThaiCupid.com, a respectable place to find beautiful local Thai women on the interwebs."

"*Internet*, you troglodyte. Look, if you want a date, let me hook you up, okay? I'll find you a nice, respectable, non-gold-digging woman in your age bracket. Hell, I can only imagine what you and Declan get up to when I'm not around."

My father grumbled to himself and crossed his arms defiantly.

"Keep going," I said, motioning to the folder. Not appreciating the ribbing, my old man gave me the stink eye before finally relenting and letting out a sigh.

"I had my old pal Tuck from the VPD send it to me, all right, Smart Guy? He's no longer in Criminal Records and Fingerprinting, but he's well-connected. Anyway, there's one critical piece of info that's not in this little portfolio."

"Which is?"

"Cripps has been in a coma for over a month. May not ever come out of it. And even if he does, the docs think he could have permanent brain damage. Case remains open."

"It's all connected somehow, Pop. Elijah having photos of Cripps fighting. This clandestine brawling on different rooftops around the city. The only thing I can't figure is how Lennox's insurance scam with his belt and *apparent* suicide figure in. There has to be something I'm missing."

"Keep grinding, Son. You'll get there." My father scooped some more pineapple topping and ice cream up from his sundae, popped it in his mouth, smacked his lips, and used a napkin to remove the residue from his bristly moustache. "So, what's next, Wonder Boy?" he asked.

I spun the folder around and skimmed the summary on Cripps's bio. "Says here Cripps has a wife and two young boys. Maybe I can start there."

"Good thinking. But tread lightly. His wife is probably pretty distraught."

"I'm on it, Old Man. But honest to Pete, pineapple on a sundae? I can understand a Hawaiian pizza, but this is sacrilege."

My father stifled a burp and leaned forward. "You know I like to work my way around the DQ menu."

"Yes, but come on. A line has to be drawn somewhere. This is essentially blasphemy to the Ice Cream Gods."

"Oh, Moses, smell the roses! I'll be circling back to Peanut Buster Parfaits soon enough. There's only so much dairy-themed adventure a man can take, you know."

"There's the crotchety bastard I know and love," I said, in a tone of relief.

He smiled, then slid the manila envelope across the table toward me. "Get to the bottom of this Cripps thing. If you do, I think it could open up doors that might help you get Mrs. Lennox some of the answers she hired us to find. Don't forget, she's our client now. Not her son. We're square with him."

"That's a little cold," I said.

"We're running a business here. And we're not the cops."

I nodded obediently, took another sip of my custom-flavoured shake, put the bottle of Torani Crème De Banana Syrup back into the brown paper bag, and stood up to leave.

"Message received, you geriatric, ice cream-gobbling, pineapple-topping-popping son of a gun."

My father was still laughing as I exited the Dairy Queen.

TWENTY-THREE

From my home office, I made a quick call to Wally Fitzgibbons,
the ex-jewel thief turned janitor who was the eyes and ears of
Lennox Pankration. After saving him from a beating, I seemed
to be the old codger's new best friend.

"Hey! Li'l Ounstead! We were just talking about you."

"We?"

"Yeah, me and Otis."

"Otis?"

"You know, the big feller in the overalls."

Damn it, I thought to myself. I wasn't far off with the
"Hillbilly Jim" nickname after all. I tried not to let the disappointment get the better of me.

"Right, Otis," I said.

Wally continued. "We was hopin' to get you to come out to
the Arms again later this week and join us for two-dollar beer
night. Our treat."

My beer snobbery in full effect, I winced at the mere thought
of having to choke down more canned, room-temperature Molson
Canadian or PBR. "That's very nice of you, Wally. I'll take a look

at my schedule and get back to you. In the meantime, I have a quick question."

"Shoot."

"Does the name Jerry Cripps ring a bell?"

I heard the sound of Wally scratching his wispy goatee over the phone. "Cripps … Cripps … nah, I don't know nobody named Cripps."

"You sure he never worked out at Lennox Pankration? Even for a brief period of time?"

"I'm sure."

"Are there any logs you could check?"

He chuckled. "Hey, I know ol' Wally might look a little worse for wear, but my mind is a steel trap, Kid. The most accurate logs are all in my head. And I can tell you without a shadow of a doubt, there ain't never been no guy named Cripps around the gym."

I was disappointed by the dead end, but trusted his word. "Fair enough. Thanks anyways, Wally."

"Wait, Li'l Ounstead?"

"Yeah?"

"Did you tell Frank I sent my regards?"

"I did. He appreciated it and sends his own in return, along with a message."

"What message?"

"He said next time he sees you he won't bring the latex gloves."

Wally burst out into laughter. Considering the grizzled bugger's track record as a jewel thief, I stopped my imagination cold in its tracks, not wanting to even contemplate what my old man's words may have meant.

"Take care, Wally."

I hung up the phone and returned to the papers from the Lennox file that were spread across my desktop. I was missing something. I scribbled "no contact with gym" on a notepad that listed the facts I had ascertained about Jerry Cripps. But his lack of involvement with Lennox Pankration only made his connection with my former client more puzzling.

Why would Elijah care so much about a fighter who had never even trained at his facility to the point of having JPEGs of him on his computer? Something didn't add up. I called Cripps's residence and left a message, but over the next couple of days, it went unreturned. I started calling Cripps's other family and friends, including his wife Lynette's employer, and learned something interesting—no one had seen or heard from her or the children in almost two weeks. Lynette Cripps and her two sons were off the grid, or if they were staying with family, they were covering for her. I confirmed this when I reached one of Cripps's attending nurses in the ICU at St. Paul's Hospital. She told me that after visiting her comatose husband daily for extended periods of time, Lynette had stopped coming in altogether. Growing frustrated in my inability to trace Lynette Cripps's whereabouts, and because she might not even be aware of her husband's dangerous nocturnal hobby of fighting on rooftops, I put a pin in that line of investigation. I decided to play the only other card I had left that might help me sniff out this shadowy combat league—an organization to which both Cripps and my former client were directly connected.

The Vancouver Seawall is a great stone barrier constructed around the perimeter of Stanley Park to prevent erosion. I always found the park stunningly beautiful, densely filled with lush shrubs and evergreen trees. The seawall is popular with runners and cyclists alike, with each having a designated lane. The view from this concrete route snaking around the park is gorgeous, and in the late summer the Pacific Ocean shimmered with a beautiful dark blue as speedboats, yachts, and commercial freighters passed back and forth in the distance on the Burrard Inlet.

With a large DQ milkshake in one hand, I approached Sykes as he sat on a bench with his legs crossed. He was dressed in tan leather sandals, khaki pants, and an aquamarine Casablanca shirt. Sykes's silver sunglasses reflected the sun's rays. Taking a seat next to him, I recognized the white baby goat I had recently fed a bottle of milk. Brutus wore a black harness around his chest which connected to a matching leash, and his fluffy tail wagged excitedly behind him.

"You know, Mr. Ounstead, if we keep meeting like this, some people might make the assumption that we are friends."

I smiled as my upscale bookmaker associate kept his gaze on the ocean and scratched Brutus behind the ears. "Works for me. I'd be lying if I said I haven't come to enjoy your company."

I dug a silver flask from my cargo shorts, popped the lid, and topped up my banana milkshake. Sykes's eyebrows rose with a mixture of surprise and disdain.

"A bit early in the day, would you not agree?" he asked.

I sealed the flask, put it back in my shorts, and stirred my shake. "Not for Italian banana crème cane syrup, it isn't."

Sykes winced ever-so-slightly. "Your metabolism and exercise regimen are quite impressive given your penchant for those caloric monstrosities. Come," he said, rising to his feet. "It is time for Brutus to have his walk."

I accompanied Sykes as Brutus began trotting along the seawall, his tiny, cloven hooves clip-clopping on the concrete pathway. We strode along in silence for a minute or two. I had spent enough time with Sykes to know that patience was a virtue he valued highly. When he was ready, he would speak. Luckily, I didn't have to wait too long.

"I was relieved to hear of your successful interaction with Mr. Chang," he said, finally.

I nodded politely, not even bothering to wonder how Sykes had gotten wind of the result of that confrontation.

"However," he continued, "I was equally disappointed to learn of the passing of your client, despite you successfully fulfilling the task for which you were hired."

"Thank you, Sykes. And before we get to why I wanted to meet today, may I ask you a question?"

"But of course," he replied.

"Why are you walking a baby goat around the Stanley Park Seawall?"

"This is a crucial time for Brutus and his development, and I need him to be at his best both physically and cerebrally."

"You're concerned about a tiny goat's mental health?"

"Indeed. You see, I am expanding my new venture to another location, and Brutus will be spearheading my second team of talent. Despite being diminutive, this little one has an astounding vertical leap and has been known to even jump directly from the back of one yoga participant to another. It is quite remarkable and will truly set my goat yoga venture apart from others."

"There's more than one goat yoga business in Vancouver?"

"Oh, Mr. Ounstead. Your naiveté is almost charming."

I nodded, and at that moment, a flurry of poop pellets tumbled from Brutus's backside. Sykes made no effort to stop and pick them up, and seconds later a sweaty, shirtless, young jogger passed us and stepped in the pile of excrement.

"What the hell?!?" he snapped. "Clean up your fucking goat's shit, Asshole!"

The jogger started aggressively toward us, until I turned around, took a step forward, rolled my shoulders, and flexed my arms. The jogger stopped dead in his tracks, muttered to himself as he scraped the sole of his shoe on a concrete ledge, then continued his run in the opposite direction.

I returned to Sykes's side. "Thank you for that," he said dryly. "Two visits over a matter of weeks. To what do I owe the pleasure?"

"This one is a bigger ask, I'm afraid. And I'll owe you yet again if you're able to help. But I figured if anyone would know how I could connect with this particular group, or be able to point me in the right direction, it would be you."

Sykes nodded. "All in due time, Mr. Ounstead. Rest assured I will reach out when there is a matter with which I could utilize your unique skills."

"Fair enough," I said. I told him how Alma Lennox hired me to find out if Elijah had really taken his own life and shared my own skepticism. I also told him about the photos I found on his home computer and how they were the one definitive link that connected Lennox and Cripps to what appeared to be an under-the-radar fight club.

Sykes took in the information, and true to his nature, didn't react at all. We continued to work our way around the seawall. A man on a Sea-Doo zoomed by in the water way too close to shore, leaving waves and a trail of white foam behind him. The roaring of the Sea-Doo's engine startled Brutus, who let out a couple of nervous bleats.

Sykes petted the young goat soothingly and fed him a handful of kibble from a small Ziplock bag he retrieved from his pants pocket. Brutus gobbled it up and resumed his trot. After a minute or so, Sykes finally said, "I believe, Mr. Ounstead, that I can be of assistance."

My heart skipped a beat. Now I was getting somewhere. "Thank you, Sykes. I must admit, up until now I've been struggling to keep my investigation moving forward."

"Quite understandable." Sykes stopped and took in a long breath of the fresh ocean air then exhaled slowly. Brutus obediently waited for his owner to proceed with their walk and twitched his fluffy tail again.

Sykes continued. "About six months ago, I heard rumblings from a client of such a discreet organization having been formed. I did not pay it much mind at the time until I received more of the same chatter. It was clear something unusual was occurring, and, as a result, I soon began covering wagers placed on 'main event' bouts."

"Have you seen it first-hand?" I asked.

"No. And the bets being placed were occasional and scattershot, but have slowly picked up steam of late. I recently sent trusted employees to attend and conduct business on my behalf. They say this particular fight club is most unusual and can be quite … brutal."

"Did you hear of any association between this club and Elijah Lennox?"

"I am afraid not. But I can reach out to my associates and ask if they have. I will do the same with regards to this Cripps gentleman. Allow me to follow up on this matter so the next time we speak I can provide a more thorough and detailed report."

Brutus suddenly bleated again and jumped up in the air a few times for no apparent reason. "Easy, Brutus," said Sykes, giving him another handful of kibble. "Save it for your training session this afternoon." Brutus shook his head and his ears flapped back and forth before he settled down.

"Well, Mr. Ounstead. As always it has been a pleasure, but I believe this is where we go our separate ways. Brutus and I must make haste if we are to attend our next appointment on time."

I offered a hand to the man and he shook it with a firm grip. "I really appreciate this, Sykes." Sykes nodded courteously, if ever-so-slightly. I headed back along the seawall in the other direction, making sure to step around Brutus's surprisingly large number of poop pellets.

TWENTY-FOUR

I was one DQ-and-Torani-syrup milkshake and a pint of Guinness deep when Detective Constable Rya Shepard sidled up next to me at the Emerald Shillelagh's mahogany bar. Sykes had called earlier with a wealth of information he had gathered since we walked Brutus the day before. I had written up half a dozen pages to add to my case notes. I closed my notebook and hoped Rya hadn't glimpsed any of its contents. Odds were in my favour because my penmanship was so awful it could easily be mistaken for the mad scribblings found in the Unabomber's manifesto.

"Drago," she said, by way of greeting.

"Ripley," I replied, a bit surprised to hear my more obscure nickname.

Rya smiled as we referred to each other as Dolph Lundgren's and Sigourney Weaver's most iconic film roles. It had been a running gag we had engaged in for years, but not for a long time. Such playfulness had ended when tragedy struck my life and forced me to walk away from my white-hot and lucrative professional wrestling career. However, since I began working as a private investigator, that old familiarity between us had slowly returned. I knew Rya had feelings for me, though maybe not the kind I wanted her to have, and to this day she could still make my heart flutter like no other woman I had ever known. It was nice to resume our lighthearted banter from back when Rya had begun working as Frank Ounstead's newly minted partner and protégé during his twilight years in the VPD Homicide Unit.

The special dynamic they had was probably also the reason why Rya and I never really progressed past the friend zone. My old man had a father's love for Rya, and despite the fact that spending time with her pulled my heartstrings, courtship was simply too big a risk with too much at stake should nothing come of it. Besides, I was out of town so much during my time in the WWE, travelling from city to city. Unfortunately, timing just never seemed to be on our side.

Declan scurried about behind the bar serving drinks to the many customers who had jam-packed the Emerald Shillelagh during happy hour. When he noticed Rya sitting next to me, he immediately stopped everything he was doing and, in a flash, whipped up an ice-cold Grey Goose martini, with three green olives speared on a toothpick. He knew Rya's preferred drink and, more importantly, what she meant to my father and me.

"Thank you, Declan."

"Anything for you, Love."

I spun around on the rotating bar stool to face Rya and slipped an elbow onto the bar top. "So, Detective, what brings you to these parts?"

"Just checking in," she said matter-of-factly, before taking a sip of her cocktail.

"How's the Rocket?" I asked.

Rya grimaced slightly. "I really wish you would call him Darren."

I chuckled. "I would under different circumstances, but I get the feeling he likes his nickname. Hell, I love it when people call me 'Hammerhead.'"

Rya shook her head in disapproval. "You boys never grow up, do you?"

"Not when you stumble across an awesome moniker that sticks, you don't."

"I have an update for you about Lennox."

I nursed my malty pint of Guinness. "I'm listening."

"I called in a few favours with the Port Moody PD. There's something odd that keeps coming up."

"What's that?"

"Word of mouth is that Lennox may have been involved in some kind of local fight club. I don't know if that relates at all to his death, but I find it interesting a well-off, former UFC champion would get caught up in such a thing."

I nodded slowly, choosing my next words carefully. I hated to withhold anything from Rya, but after being hired by Alma Lennox, learning of Cripps, and receiving the info Sykes had just relayed, I was way ahead of her and the Port Moody Police.

"I think there was a lot more going on with Elijah than anyone realized," I replied.

"I'm assuming you've moved on?" she asked.

I hesitated before answering, but decided to share at least one kernel of truth. "Actually, his mother, a kind woman who is still in mourning, hired me to find out if he actually took his own life or if there might be a chance of foul play."

Rya almost choked on her martini and quickly grabbed a napkin to dab her mouth. "What? How could you take advantage of an old woman like that?"

"I didn't. She's hurting, Rya. Knowing I'm out there looking into the incident has brought her a bit of peace."

Before Rya could respond, my old man lumbered down the spiral staircase from the second-floor office and bellowed so loudly everyone in the pub heard his question. "Is that my little *Doll-Faced Dynamo* at my bar?"

Rya looked at me and rolled her eyes.

"Now that's a solid nickname. The crusty old bastard has never called me 'Hammerhead.'"

Rya slid off of her stool as my father lumbered toward her, and a moment later she was enveloped so fully into an enormous Frank Ounstead bear hug she all but disappeared. He lifted her off her feet and swung her gently side to side like a rag doll then placed her back on the ground. I also now had a pretty good idea of what it must have looked like when gorillas hugged Dian Fossey in the jungle.

Rya chuckled, stood on her tippy-toes as my old man ducked down, and planted a kiss on his cheek.

"Good to see you, Big Bear," she said. "It's been too long."

He cupped the side of her face and beamed. "Far too long, Sweetheart. We need to resume our weekly brunches at the Red Wagon."

Rya nodded. "Definitely. I've just been so swamped with—"

My old man shushed her. "You don't have to explain. I get it. More than most."

Rya smiled. "I know you do."

She sat back down while Frank Ounstead pulled up a stool at the bar. It was lovely to see them reconnect, but I realized that there was a potentially embarrassing gap between what my Pop and I knew about Lennox and what I had been withholding from Rya.

"Rya was just telling me how Lennox may have been involved in some kind of fight club," I said, catching my father's eye and raising one eyebrow ever so slightly, a signal my father picked up on at once.

"No shop talk," he commanded. "Let's all just have a drink and catch up."

Over the next hour, we did just that, and it was wonderful. We told old stories, laughed a lot, and Declan was even able to spring himself to join us for a bit after happy hour had come and gone. I had forgotten the chemistry we all had together, and in many ways, it felt like a family reunion—except I considered Rya more the woman I had always wanted to be with and less the surrogate sister my father imagined her to be. I felt a surge of guilt for having such feelings for Rya, and reminded myself that she was with a good man and I was in a committed relationship with Stormy Daze, a woman I had strong feelings for and who was the sweetest, kindest, and most thoughtful girlfriend ever.

I bottled up my swirling emotions just as my father excused himself to go home, most likely to listen to some vinyl Hank Williams Jr. recordings and read a bit of crime fiction before calling it a night. He kissed Rya on the top of her head, fist-bumped Declan, and slammed a mammoth hand down on the right side of my trapezius—which stung like hell—before leaving the Emerald Shillelagh for the evening. All in all, it was a great and long overdue visit. Rya attempted to square her bill by paying for an appy of deep-fried pickles and two vodka martinis, but Declan wouldn't hear of it.

"Ya know yer money is no good here, Detective," he said. "As far as I'm concerned, ya already overpaid by putting up with these bloody Ounstead orangutans for far too long—this overgrown bollocks in particular," he said, jabbing a thumb in my direction.

Rya chuckled despite herself. Declan shot me a furtive wink as he trotted off down the bar. Just like that, Rya and I were alone again.

"Coming from Declan, that's high praise," I said.

"It certainly is. Damn, Jed. I miss being around you guys."

"So come by more," I blurted out, perhaps too quickly.

There was an awkward pause before I tried to walk back my knee-jerk response.

"Of course, I know you've got your hands full," I stammered. "And you're with the Rocket—I mean, Darren—now."

"And you're with Stephanie Danielson."

"Yeah," I said slowly. We both nursed our drinks and an uncomfortable silence hung over us until the metaphorical light bulb above my head flicked on and I changed the topic. "I've got some stuff coming down the pipeline with this Lennox investigation," I said, in a transparent effort to segue. "If you're okay with it, I might need to reach out to you soon."

Rya finished what was left of her second Grey Goose martini and fought back a smile. She placed the glass on the bar top, stood up, and straightened her blouse before leaning forward and speaking softly into my ear.

"Anytime, you Big Lug. Just stay safe, smart, and—most importantly—calm out there."

And with that she kissed me gently on the cheek for what felt like an eternity. My pulse started racing, and in that moment I felt as if Aphrodite herself was bestowing me with a small but potent gift of love. Rya pulled back from the kiss, wiped lipstick off my cheek with her thumb, and left without another word.

As she exited the pub I found myself short of breath with goosebumps popping up like wildfire all over my skin. I checked my watch and realized my infatuation with Rya had caused me to run late in rendezvousing with my current girlfriend.

TWENTY-FIVE

I left the Shillelagh and made haste to meet Stormy back at my Coal Harbour townhouse. If she was miffed, she didn't show it. She had a key to the place and her own drawer in my bedroom dresser, so when I arrived home she was already wrapped in a towel, freshly showered, and blow-drying her long blonde hair. A light-blue sleeveless blouse, white summer shorts, and a pair of Birkenstocks were laid out on the duvet covering the bed.

I tossed aside the notebook with the details of Sykes's fight club intel before sweeping Stormy into my arms and kissing her. She was caught off guard, but returned my affection. After I don't know how long we ended our passionate lip lock.

"Wow, what has gotten into you, tonight, Mister?"

Only at that moment did it occur to me that I may have been fired up because of Rya's goodbye smooch. I was immediately overwhelmed with guilt.

"Sorry," I mumbled. "Emotional day."

"Don't apologize. I like this side of you."

Stormy ran her hands through my hair and gave me another soft kiss. It was lovely. Eventually, I pulled back. "Where are you going?" I asked, nodding toward her clothes laid out on my bed.

Stormy chuckled and began applying ruby-red lipstick to her heart-shaped lips. "It's date night, remember?"

"Right," I said, without conviction and only then remembered our plans.

"Don't tell me you want to bail, Babe."

"No, not at all. But do you think we could just visit the lounge at Cardero's?" I asked, referring to the harbour-side Live Bait and Marine Pub across the street. "I'm not really up for much else."

"You got it, Bub," replied Stormy with a smirk.

I grabbed a beer from the fridge and swapped out my cargo shorts and Chris Jericho *"Ayatollah of Rock and Rolla"* pro-wrestling T-shirt for some blue jeans and a white polo shirt so crisp that it made me feel as if I should be posing with a tennis racket for a country club-themed magazine photoshoot. While Stormy finished dressing, I capitalized on the bonus time by grabbing the notebook and slipping into my office to review what I had jotted down of my conversation with Sykes. He had not minced words when he contacted me earlier, and it had been all I could do to keep up with the detailed information that he'd shared. Apparently, this rooftop fight club that both Lennox and Cripps were involved with had blown up over the past several months. Little was known about it other than that fights mostly took place on weekends on a different rooftop, making them difficult to track. It was all but impossible to pin down a location without an invitation or prior knowledge from the host or hosts of these combat sessions.

When not working as a freelance personal trainer, Cripps had a reputation as an aspiring professional MMA fighter, and there were rumours that people in the rooftop club had some serious connections to that sport. So it made sense that Cripps would be involved. Why a fighter of Lennox's calibre would want to compete in such a shady organization, however, was beyond me. The man was a decorated, light-heavyweight legend and had literally done it all in the UFC. He had nothing to prove, and according to Sykes, this rooftop fight club consisted primarily of upstarts and wannabes. While apparently technically legal, the fight club was not sanctioned by anyone and remained steeped in mystery.

There were no referees. The fighters were not insured. There were no real rules in place. And, possibly the most troubling, there was no provision whatsoever for any medical personnel to be present. The use of ever-changing rooftop venues was the hallmark of this nameless club. But that's where someone as connected as Sykes came in. Through sources I dared not ask about, my bookmaker friend managed to ascertain not only the location of the next fight club meeting, but also arranged for me to attend as a guest combatant.

According to Sykes, the application process was simple and straightforward. It was strictly invitation only, but a client named McIntyre, who had been a member of the club since its inception, agreed to vouch for me as a favour to Sykes. As a result, I was to have a tryout fight in a couple of days at two AM on the rooftop of the old city jail at Main and Cordova in the Downtown Eastside, a few blocks down the same stretch of East Hastings Street from the Astoria, where Cripps had been found beaten into a coma. The jail was also directly across a double alleyway from the historic Empress Hotel, part of my old man's beat as a VPD patrol officer. "The Emp," as it was more commonly known, was a hotbed of activity, especially its notorious pub, where cops and ne'er-do-wells were known to drink. Not to mention the fact that the building was said to be haunted. So, all in all, the location for the event seemed like the perfect venue for some middle of the night, no-holds-barred, rooftop fisticuffs. I was not at all surprised that Sykes was able to arrange this so quickly. Despite the magic I'd seen the guy make happen in the past, I remained impressed by—and grateful for—the dachshund racing, goat yoga marketing bookmaker's endless connections.

I took a sip of my Widowmaker IPA from Backcountry Brewing, leaned back in my chair, and tried to envision my initiation into this rooftop fight club. I was so focused on trying to figure out what may have brought Lennox to the point of suicide that I hadn't stopped to acknowledge that I was placing myself in potential danger by infiltrating this exclusive and shadowy club. I took another sip of the IPA and purged any self-doubt by reminding myself of my extensive combat training. Although professional wrestling was part acting, part improv, and part stunt show, it still required an incredible amount of athleticism. I had also spent years training in Judo, Olympic and Greco-Roman wrestling, Brazilian Jiu-Jitsu, and a little Krav Maga. Reflecting upon my training brought me peace of mind before my upcoming bout. I had nothing to prove and no intention of trying to rise amongst the ranks of this club. I just needed one fight under my belt to earn respect and trust from its members. Then I might obtain answers to the questions I had about Elijah Lennox and Jerry Cripps's association with this underground—or should I say very much above ground—combat organization.

I thought of Declan, who was in many ways a much better candidate to infiltrate a fight club. But I also had to acknowledge that, while deadly and nearly undefeatable, my cousin had the subtlety of a carbon steel sledgehammer. Eliciting the answers I needed was going to require finesse, so despite my initial impulse to bring Declan along as backup, I concluded it wasn't worth the risk. I loved him as much as anyone in my life, but my cousin was known at times to be a hotheaded pisstank, and the awful potential scenarios were rattling around in my head like bingo balls bouncing inside a spinning metal barrel.

For better or worse, I was going to play this one close to my chest.

"Baby!" shouted Stormy from my doorway. She looked stunning in her outfit, but bore a concerned look.

"Yeah?"

"I had to call your name three times."

"Sorry, Stormy." I closed the notebook, left my chair, walked over to her, and hugged her tight. "You look absolutely beautiful."

Stormy smiled and grabbed my hand. "Let's go."

We left my townhouse and walked to Cardero's. After sitting at the bar underneath a clothesline with dozens of colourful international flags that were used instead of clunky plastic pagers to let customers know when their tables were ready, eventually a peppy waitress announced that a patio table had become available and led us outside. We grabbed our drinks and followed her as she led us to our seats at the end of the patio. We were greeted by a spectacular view of both the adjacent harbour and the Pacific Ocean. Moonlight danced off of the dark blue water while the dozens of shiny yachts in the harbour swayed ever so slowly.

I closed my eyes for a moment and inhaled the salty air. Stormy reached across the table, taking my hand in hers and squeezing it.

"Are you okay?" she asked.

I smiled and squeezed her hand back. "Yes. Just have a lot on my mind. Work stuff."

"Do you want to talk about it?"

"Honestly, not tonight."

"Good. I think we've done enough talking for one evening," she said, smiling deviously and sliding her foot up and down my leg under the table.

I realized what she had in mind. "Yeah?" I asked.

"Hell, yeah," she replied.

We finished our drinks and our appetizers of naan with pesto and feta hummus and blue shell mussels in coconut curry sauce. I paid our bill and we walked hand-in-hand back to my townhouse. We fell into each other's arms, and for the first time in a while my mind became tranquil and quiet. As our passion intensified, everything else melted away and my world felt wonderful and safe.

Had I known what was coming, I would have wished for that moment to last forever.

TWENTY-SIX

The empty beer bottle grazed my ear as it whipped past my head and shattered on the red-brick wall behind me. A couple of shards of glass needled the back of my neck, but after a quick check with my hand, I was relieved to discover they hadn't broken skin. The homeless woman who had thrown it cackled loudly while clapping in some kind of drug-addled celebration. I let it go and began my ascent up the rusty fire escape that led to the rooftop of the old city jail in the Downtown Eastside, just as I had been instructed.

It took me a minute to climb up the side of the derelict building. The ancient fire escape creaked more than a haunted house on Halloween. Cheap red, yellow, and blue neon signs from nearby businesses buzzed loudly, their light bouncing off of the numerous puddles on the pavement. Earlier that afternoon Vancouver had been hit by a brief—but much needed—rainfall that had cooled down the city and lessened the severity of the August heatwave.

It was a quarter to two AM. As Sykes had suggested, I arrived a bit early to acquaint myself with the set-up before my scheduled bout. I made it to the top of the building and dusted off my plain black T-shirt and athletic shorts, then bent a knee and cinched up my professional wrestling boots. The reinforced footwear was similar to the kind of boots worn by pro-wrestling greats like Brock Lesnar and Randy Orton, and the shiny synthetic black leather provided excellent ankle support.

My hands and wrists were taped up, while my bare fingertips stuck out of a pair of lean, padded, MMA gloves. By the time I stood up at least two dozen fighters and fans were staring at me. I had come prepared, clearly ready to rumble, and they knew it. I cracked my neck by rotating it from side-to-side a few times while jumping up and down on the balls of my feet, warming up my body. I turned my back on those eyeing me and did a bit of shadow boxing, exhaling hard with each phantom strike, before a stout and solid five-foot-six man approached me cautiously.

"Ounstead?" he asked.

I stopped warming up and looked down at the muscular little man in his blue tank top and boxing shorts. "You must be McIntyre."

"Didn't recognize you at first with the beard." The diminutive fighter stuck out a hand. I hesitated a moment before shaking it. "And call me Reggie."

I nodded.

"You know, you're bigger than you look on TV."

"You a wrestling fan?"

"Once upon a time. I can't believe you're here. Sykes said something about you having some questions?"

"Yeah, something like that. I want to know about Elijah Lennox and Jerry Cripps's association with this club." Reggie's face drained of colour and his Adam's apple moved up and down as he swallowed.

"Look, I, uh, I can't get into that right now. And don't breathe a word of it to anyone else. Famous or not, you're a newbie, which means you're gonna need to prove yourself before anyone even thinks about giving you or your questions the time of day. Just get a win and we can go from there."

"Okay. I appreciate you doing this, Reggie."

He chuckled. "Are you kidding? For Sykes, it's the least I can do."

"I can relate."

Reggie gave me a pat on my shoulder. "Good luck."

"Thanks."

Reggie returned to the flock of fighters and fans who were spread out across the rooftop. I could feel their eyes on me but tuned them out and focused on preparing for my upcoming fight. I had a few butterflies in my stomach, the way I often did before pro-wrestling matches, but it was a feeling I was used to and one that always seemed to bring out the best in me. I took a break from shadow boxing and stretched out my groin, calves, quads, hammies, triceps and biceps, then returned to my fight stance and fired off a few more strikes and practice kicks.

I sized up the other fighters while I continued to loosen up. Some looked seasoned and pretty tough, while others appeared to be rank amateurs. But I knew from experience not to judge a book by its cover. I had gone toe-to-toe with guys in the past who may not have looked like much, but could brawl with the best of them. Not to mention the fact that people willing to engage in combat on a rooftop in the middle of the night clearly had some issues they were working through.

A heavy, metal fire exit door that led from the top of a stairwell swung open. Out stepped a beast of a man, whose shaved head was so glossy, all of the light around it bounced off of his dome like it would off a candy apple. He wore desert-pattern camouflage pants tucked into a pair of black tactical boots and a dark green, skin-tight, tank top. His massive shoulders were covered in numerous military tattoos, including a Canadian Special Operations Forces Command one I had seen before on the arm of one of my old man's VPD buddies. Another large tat on one of the hulking man's football-sized deltoids featured a knife driven through the top of a skull. Finally—and most curiously—the behemoth wore a silver chain from which hung more than a dozen military dog tags, instead of the customary two.

The crowd grew quiet until the only sounds came from the nightlife three storeys below. The door slowly creaked shut behind the massive figure. To his left, a group of more than a dozen guys dressed in nice suits, who looked like they belonged more in the Financial District than a sketchy rooftop, gazed upon the monstrous military man in awe. The fighters had instinctively huddled together, silent and still. I remained alone in the corner of the rooftop where I had been warming up, but followed suit and turned my attention to the big boy. I clocked him as at least six-foot-seven and three-hundred-plus pounds of titanic muscle. He surveyed his surroundings, his eyes lingering on me briefly. His expression betrayed nothing and he turned to face everyone else present.

"Welcome," his deep voice boomed. "If you are here tonight, it is because you have been invited, which means you must be a person of some significance. It also goes without saying that extreme steps will be taken to ensure that whether you are a spectator or a participant, what goes down tonight remains confidential."

A slender man from the spectator's group in glasses and a charcoal suit raised a hand. The Man-Beast nodded permission for him to speak.

"Do ... do you mean, like, an NDA?"

Man-Beast smirked. "If that helps you," he said, crossing his arms, which were the size of two slabs of beef, across his broad chest. "But without all of that tedious paperwork." The behemoth raised an eyebrow and everyone caught on pretty fast. Slender Spectacles nodded quickly and folded himself back into the collective safety of his pod of spectators.

The giant man continued. "You may call me Mr. C. This is my associate, Mr. F."

As if out of nowhere, a six-foot man hobbled forward until he was by Mr. C's side. He had a solid build and a crewcut, held a clipboard, and was dressed in drab military T-shirt and cargo shorts. However, I imagine most people barely made note of his outfit, but stared instead at Mr. F's artificial right leg.

"Mr. F will be taking your wagers this evening. Our first fight commences now. Walker. McIntyre. You're up."

The spectators in suits swarmed Mr. F in order to place their bets. I held my ground as the fighters fanned out into a circle. Inside the makeshift ring my new fight club pal and Sykes's contact Reggie McIntyre popped in a black mouthguard and started dancing on the balls of his feet so smoothly Fred Astaire would have been impressed. Reggie stole a glance at me, and I gave him a supportive nod.

The other fighter, Walker, was about five-foot-eight so he had a couple inches on Reggie, but was much leaner. Neither man was wearing any gloves or protective padding and they circled each other like hyenas preparing to pounce on their prey. After a minute Mr. C whistled and Mr. F turned his back on the group of fight fans who had been eagerly placing their bets. Mr. F nodded back to his boss, and Mr. C's voice reverberated across the rooftop.

"*Jangaidal!*"

The spectators burst out into excited cheers. Before I even had a moment to wonder what "*Jangaidal!*" meant, Walker was throwing deep jabs from far away. His reach was deceptively long, and although Reggie dodged all of his blows, the unexpected punches had already impeded his footwork, which had been so impressive only moments ago. Walker took advantage of Reggie's off-balance stance and landed a solid left-hand jab to his jaw. Reggie rolled with the punch, only to catch two more quick shots to the side of his head. Reggie spat and gritted his teeth. He got his feet back underneath him, and the next time Walker fired off a long jab, he was ready. Reggie blocked the swing only to find Walker following up with a rushed overhand right.

That was Walker's mistake. Reggie batted away the right hand and grabbed the wrist, dropping to the ground, splitting his legs, and taking down his string-bean opponent hard with a scissor foot sweep. Walker lost his balance and fell forward, barely getting his left hand up in time to cushion his fall, but it was too late. With his legs still scissor-pinching the lanky man, Reggie rolled and chopped Walker hard on the back of the neck, forcing his head to smash onto the roof's concrete. There was a sickening crunch as Walker's nose broke, and as he gasped, he threw back his head and spewed a cloud of red mist up into the air.

The gamblers loved the bloodshed and bellowed enthusiastically in between high-fives and fist bumps. Reggie released the scissor hold, scrambled behind Walker, and put him in a rear naked choke. Walker struggled to breathe, making horrible gagging and gurgling sounds like a cat hacking up a hairball. Within moments Walker tapped out, and as quickly as it had started, the fight was over. Reggie released his grip and started to climb to his feet when Mr. C let loose a thunderous bellow.

"*Tarsara-kawal!*"

Reggie hesitated. He made eye contact with Mr. C, whose pupils were on fire. Reluctantly, Reggie dropped down and slipped Walker back into a rear naked choke, compressed his carotid artery, and within seconds the man passed out. Mr. C began applauding and everyone present, fighters and spectators, quickly followed suit. Mr. C whispered something to Mr. F, who then snapped at a few of the combatants. In response, they scrambled over to Walker, dragged his limp body into a corner of the rooftop, and applied smelling salts from a first aid kit. Mr. F headed over to the group of spectators and paid out the winning wagers. Just as Mr. F was concluding his business, Mr. C stepped forward.

"It looks as if we are off to a great start tonight. Next up, Santana and Ounstead."

There were some hushed rumblings among both fighters and spectators, which led me to assume some of them were aware of my fame as a pro wrestler. I caught Reggie's eye as I stepped into the combat circle and he gave me a solid *you got this* nod. I was joined by Santana, a six-foot-two, two-hundred-and-thirty-pound Hispanic bruiser. He pulled off his white T-shirt to reveal his shredded upper body, then jumped up and down and threw a few dangerous looking punches into the air. The fans chatted excitedly among themselves before bursting into a flurry of activity and rushing to place their bets. I bounced back and forth on the balls of my feet until all wagers had been placed.

"We don't wear those here," said Mr. C, pointing at my padded MMA gloves. I slipped them off and tossed them aside, my hands and knuckles bare save for the veteran tape job I had applied underneath.

"*Jangaidal!*" commanded Mr. C.

Santana came at me guns blazing. He unloaded a flurry of strikes, but I covered up effectively and blocked them all. While I matched Santana's impressive speed with my own, I had yet to throw a punch. My opponent grew frustrated by not being able to land a blow and, as a result, threw an impetuous and wild right. It was a bad call.

I pounced on the opportunity, dodged the punch, and grabbed his right wrist with both my hands. In a flash I rotated his arm over my head, ducked underneath, turned my back to his chest, and implemented a modified *Seoi nage*—commonly known as a one-armed shoulder throw. Santana flipped over my back and hit the ground hard. Before he could move, I delivered a whopping anvil of a right-hand square to his face. The impact was so hard, the back of his skull made a cringeworthy sound as it impacted the concrete.

Santana was dazed, but rather than jump on top of him in a ground-and-pound position and start whaling on the guy, I simply stood up and backed away. Reggie was not pleased with my decision to exercise sportsmanship. "What the hell are you doing?!?" he screamed. "Finish him!"

I ignored his plea. Santana took a few moments to collect himself before climbing to his feet. He touched the back of his head, then looked at the ruby-red blood on his fingertips. What happened next I did not see coming. Santana licked the blood off his fingers and started laughing maniacally. I glanced at the other fighters and fans who had formed a circle around us, and all of them looked shocked—except for Mr. C, whose face was contorted in anger. Santana came at me again like a man possessed. I struggled to keep his blows at bay before he launched into a series of side kicks, one of which caught me off guard and delivered a crushing blow to my ribs. I clutched my side and stumbled backwards, but Santana showed no mercy. He continued attacking my weak spot with more kicks and strikes, and before I knew it, I was hunched over favouring the left side of my torso. Santana pounded my injured ribs with a vengeance, while I desperately tried to counter with some feeble punches of my own. Santana dodged them easily, spinning around and delivering a devastating elbow to my damaged side. I fell onto my ass and dragged myself away from my attacker until my back was against the ledge at the roof's edge.

"It's over!" yelled Reggie. "He's had enough!"

Santana disagreed and, despite my helplessness, rained down haymakers so brutal on my face and cheekbones that they likely rattled my Irish ancestors.

"Cassian!" screamed Reggie to Mr. C, running to me and placing himself in between me and my opponent. Santana took the hint and took a few steps back, but paced back and forth like a jungle cat waiting to finish off its prey.

"Hang on, Man," said Reggie, before helping me up and onto the building's ledge.

I leaned forward, clutching my surely broken ribs while my face throbbed.

Mr. C, AKA Cassian, slowly approached me. Reggie instinctively backed away from the big man, who towered above us both. The other fighters and gamblers were silent and motionless. Every other person on the rooftop held their collective breath as they waited to see what Cassian would do.

"You had him, Ounstead. What was that? Mercy?"

"I call it not being an asshole," I muttered.

Cassian squatted down until we were eye to eye, the dog tags around his neck clinking against each other. Pain spiderwebbed through my ribs with each deep breath I took. "In this club, we fight until someone is unconscious or incapacitated."

I wiped the blood trickling down from my nose on the back of my taped hand and cleared my throat. "I prefer whisky, myself. Provides similar effects, but without all the mess and mayhem."

"Is that so?"

"Yeah. And by the way, since I have you here, would you mind if I shared an observation about your little combat clique?"

Cassian seemed bemused. "By all means."

"From what I know of the guy, I find it hard to believe that a good man and great fighter like Elijah Lennox would take part in something this sketchy and barbaric."

Cassian stood back up and glared while towering over me. "Seems to me that 'sketchy' and 'barbaric' just whupped your ass."

"Bullshit. I beat him clean and you know it. He got lucky with that first blow to my ribs."

Cassian gave a slight nod, reluctantly agreeing with my assessment. "So Elijah was your friend, eh?"

I stared down Cassian before responding. "Client."

Cassian nodded. "Tell him I say hello."

With that, he spun around faster than a tornado and round-house kicked me directly on the temple. I toppled over the ledge and fell three storeys, bounced off the rusty fire escape twice, then a dumpster, finally landing in the alleyway behind the Empress Hotel.

In a final fleeting moment, I had but one thought. That my life had come to an end.

TWENTY-SEVEN

(Declan)

WHAT. THE. SHITE?

When admitted to the hospital, me cousin seemed as good as dead. Gettin' kicked off o'a building will do that to a fella. I was so bullin' over him actin' the maggot that I may o'been a bit out o'me mind. If the eejit planned on attendin' a fight club, ya'd think he might o'taken his head out o'his arse for a minute and realized that havin' a bone-breakin' hard chaw like meself by his side would have ensured his safety.

I was right pissed, but at the moment the priority was me cousin's health. No matter what, that mad chancer was forever me blood. I loved him as much as I have anyone on this twirling cesspool o'a rock we call a planet, and I'll be goddamned if there ever came a moment in this shiteshow we call life when I didn't have his back, or vice versa, despite what a bloody langer he was capable o'bein'.

Some runt with a name from the Archie comics—Moose or Jughead or some shite—accompanied Jed on his ride to St.

Paul's Hospital in Downtown Vancouver, but the wee bastard buggered off before I had a chance to question him proper about what exactly me cousin had been up to. The pint-sized runt also left no contact info behind. I was grateful to Jughead for gettin' me cuz medical attention *tits sweet*, but aside from sayin' Jed had taken a tumble off o'a buildin' durin' a fight club scrap the squirrelly li'l shite all but vanished into thin air.

I had smuggled some Red Racer tallboy IPAs into me cousin's private hospital room, a location where he had been moved after bein' discharged from the ER. They were no pints o'the black stuff, but did the trick, and I was grateful for a tolerable brew durin' such an emotional time. Once I crushed me second can while sittin' bedside as Jed remained unconscious, me Uncail Frank stormed through the door like King Kong with his arse on fire.

"Jesus jumped-up Christ! What happened, Declan?"

I explained to Frank what little I had learned from Jughead before he bolted, and how it tied into Jed's investigation o'Elijah Lennox's death. "He's stable, ya big ape. A concussion, a few broken ribs, some scrapes, stitches and bad bruises, but all in all, the jammy bollocks lucked out. It could o'been a hell o'a lot worse."

I vacated me chair and let Frank sit next to his boy. He squeezed Jed's hand tightly and choked back tears. "I pressured him so much to join my detective agency, but I never anticipated anything like this."

I placed one hand down on me uncail's giant shoulder and handed him a can o'ale with the other. Frank waved it off. "Later," he said. I nodded and slipped the brew back into me chilled Galway United travel cooler before the nurse entered the room.

"How are we doing here?" she asked in a sing-song voice.

"My son was kicked clean off a building and nearly fell to his death, Lady. How in the blue hell do you think we're doing?" barked me uncail.

The nurse nodded politely and exited the room.

"It ain't her fault, ya old sack o'shite," I said, in her defence.

Frank still clutched Jed's limp right hand tightly and held it to his forehead. For a man I ain't never seen show any fear or worry, it was quite the sight. "I'm so sorry," he said to me comatose cuz, chokin' back tears. "This is my fault."

"Oh no, Unc. Don't beat yerself up. This one is on Jed. He chose to exclude us on somethin' dangerous. I love him to bits, would take a bullet for him, and he's gonna be okay—but he's got a lot o'explainin' to do when he wakes up."

Me uncail nodded in agreement, leaned forward, and kissed his boy on the forehead. "We're here for you, Son," he said.

Despite me festerin' rage, I could not o'agreed more.

TWENTY-EIGHT

(Frank)

I never thought I would see my boy like this.

I knew I had been hard on him over the years and pressured him to give up on all that silly sparkly spandex wrestling balderdash and join the family business, but the son of a gun denied my requests at every turn until finally deciding to do so on his terms. He eventually joined Ounstead Investigations—renamed Ounstead & Son Investigations—but it certainly wasn't worth this price. Watching him breathe slowly in a hospital bed, all bruised, battered, hooked up to an IV, and unconscious was difficult to say the least.

The kid was a natural. John Edward Ounstead, AKA "Jed," as his beautiful angel of a mother—God bless her soul—had nicknamed him, took to private investigator work like a fish to water. While only a licensed PI for less than a year, he had solved some of the biggest cases I have ever seen during my thirty-plus years in the VPD, or after. I have never been prouder of John than

I was at this moment. And we had never been closer. To see him in this state shattered my heart into pieces, and it was the worst hurt I had felt since I lost my beloved Linda to cancer when my boy was just a youngster.

My eyes were getting misty when two muscular tattooed arms snaked around my bulky frame and squeezed me tight. "'Tis gonna be okay, Unc," said Declan.

I nodded and patted his arm. "I think I'll take that beer now, Dec."

My nephew dug two IPAs from his backpack and handed me one, pulling up a chair next to mine. We drank in silence for I don't know how long. Soon both cans were empty, and before we could toss them, a high-pitched voice shrieked like someone being murdered.

"Baby! Oh my God, oh my God, oh my God!"

My son's girlfriend Stephanie ran into the room, her high heels clip-clopping on the tile floor. She gently cupped and stroked my boy's face. Tears poured down her cheeks as she kissed him over and over again. Eventually she rested her head down on his chest and sobbed quietly. It was agonizing to watch. I looked away.

After a little while Declan walked over and helped guide her to her feet. "Come, Love. Sit with us."

Stephanie put up no fight and allowed him to escort her to a third chair he had brought to John's bedside. She sat closest to my son, with me in the middle, and Declan on my other side. Stephanie managed to compose herself, wiping away the mascara that had run due to an abundance of tears, and held my boy's hand with both of hers.

I put an arm around her shoulder. "Hang in there, Sweetheart. He'll pull through," I said, my voice sounding more confident than I felt. Stephanie sniffled and nodded, leaning into me and resting her head on my shoulder. We sat together quietly, listening to the repetitive, steady beep of the heart monitor, united by our concern for John. My son was a lot of things, but in that moment, nothing else seemed to matter other than the fact he was surrounded by so much love.

TWENTY-NINE

(Rya)

I've witnessed a lot of things in my line of work, but seeing Jed Ounstead unconscious, bandaged, and laid up in a hospital bed was something I never imagined I'd see.

My stomach was in knots and my distress only got worse when I saw the pain in my mentor's eyes, not to mention Jed's fraught girlfriend and cousin Declan, a guy I pretty much believed had never been concerned about anything. The game had changed, but knowing Jed as I did, I was willing to hedge my bets that he had done something either impulsive or stupid—most likely both. I had no doubt his heart was in the right place, but sometimes the loveable oaf just didn't see the big picture.

"Rya," said Frank, before giving me a mammoth hug that nearly squeezed all of the air out of my lungs. I followed that up with an embrace with Declan and even one with Ms. Stephanie Danielson AKA "Stormy Daze."

I opened my mouth to ask a question, but didn't even know where to start. Declan read me like a book. "Fancy a word in the hallway, Detective?"

I nodded and followed him out of the hospital room. Once we were alone, he recounted what was known about what had happened to Jed. I sighed and shook my head. Of course he would try and infiltrate an underground fight club on his own. When things got tough, Jed had a dangerous habit of trying to take on the world all by himself in some misguided attempt at chivalry. I had reprimanded him about such actions numerous times and tried to warn him that one day his luck would run out, but nothing I said ever stuck. And now here we were. With a man I … deeply cared for, probably in ways I have not ever fully processed. Seeing the fallout of him being pummelled to a pulp was difficult, although it was hard not to feel exceptionally fortunate that he had survived.

Declan left for the cafeteria with a backpack, but knowing him, I figured he was probably making a run to the beer and wine store across the street. I re-entered the room and found Frank sitting in a bedside chair, his elbows on his knees, and head in his hands. Ms. Danielson's eyes were puffy and red, but she was distracting herself by texting someone.

I took advantage of the moment and walked over to the other side of Jed's hospital bed. I gently brushed back his bangs, before giving him a soft but lingering kiss on his forehead. A moment later he inhaled deeply and his eyes fluttered open. He was dazed, but after about ten seconds his eyes focused on my face.

"Rya," he croaked, weakly.

I grinned and grabbed his hand with one of my own. "Hey there."

"Wha …where am I?"

"St. Paul's Hospital. You're going to be all right."

Jed grunted and tried to sit up, but I put a hand on his shoulder, gently pushed him back down, and shook my head. "Rest, Big Guy. Just rest."

He looked at me and feebly squeezed my hand. "Rya?" he said, hoarsely.

"Yes?"

"I … I need to tell you something."

My heart skipped a beat. I wasn't sure what he was going to say. Given the combination of the cocktail of painkillers he was on, in addition to the emotionally charged nature of our relationship, I was worried he might let something intimate slip. That would not go over well given our current audience.

"What is it, Jed?"

"You look terrible."

We held each other's gaze for a moment until we both started laughing despite ourselves. Jed quickly coughed, groaned, and clutched his side.

"Baby," said Ms. Danielson, springing out of her chair and not-so-subtly pulling his hand out of mine and holding it herself. "I'm here."

She hugged Jed and I took the hint and backed away. I made eye contact with Frank, who nodded, understanding I was making an effort to try and diffuse any tension I had inadvertently caused. Despite Ms. Danielson stroking his face and kissing his cheeks, Jed turned his head to look at me and reached out his other hand. Ms. Danielson was not pleased.

"I'll see you soon," I said, then turned my back and walked out the door.

THIRTY

Beep. Beep. Beep.

Those were the only sounds I remembered. Occasionally my body flooded with white-hot pain, but the spells were so brief and intermittent I was barely able to recall them. My first real memory—or was it a dream?—after my epic beatdown was of Rya looking down at me like an angel. Whether it happened or was only what I wished had happened, this was not the time to try and figure it out, especially since Stormy had crawled into the bed and was spooning me while weeping softly.

"Don't cry, Stormy. I'm okay."

She placed her head down on my shoulder. "I was just so scared, Jed. I thought I'd lost you."

"Shush, now. I'm fine."

Stormy lifted her head and kissed me softly on the lips. "I just love you so much."

I smiled and opened my mouth to respond—not even certain what I was going to say in return—when I was saved by a familiar Irish brogue.

"Well, slap me arse and call me Moira!" said my cousin. "Look who decided to rejoin the land o'the livin'."

Declan strutted into my hospital room with an open Styrofoam takeout container that contained an abundance of jumbo-sized beef ribs slathered in BBQ sauce, and he was gnawing on a bone so big Fred Flintstone himself would have approved. Declan flopped into a chair next to my bed and pulled a tallboy can of Kilkenny Irish Cream Ale from his pocket. He popped the top, took a big slurp, smacking his lips and licking the combination of BBQ sauce and foam from his upper lip.

"Nice to know some things are still the same," I said. "How long was I out?"

"Almost two days," said Stormy, squeezing me tight. A spiderweb of pain shot through my bandaged ribs and I yelped. "Sorry!" she exclaimed, before pulling back from me.

I sat up in bed, only then discovering my tightly wrapped right forearm was bandaged and in a sling. My shoulder was throbbing. I put my good arm around Stormy and kissed her on the top of her head. "It's okay. I'm just happy you're here. You too, D."

"You forgetting someone?" boomed a deep voice. My father stood in the doorway, his bulk taking up most of the frame.

"Hey, Pop," I said.

"You gave us quite a scare there, Boy," he replied.

I nodded. "Yes, Sir. And for that I'm sorry. It's kind of a long story—"

"And there will be time to get into it. But right now, let's just count our blessings."

"Fair enough," I said, relieved that the pressure of explaining exactly what I had been up to was postponed for the time being.

Stormy slid off my hospital bed, and she, Declan, and my old man each took a seat in the chairs next to me. There was an awkward silence, save for my cousin chomping meat and slurping ale. I tried to break the tension.

"Have you guys ever heard of goat yoga?"

They all looked at me as if I had announced I could shoot laser beams from my nipples. I told the story of how while meeting with Sykes to connect with the rooftop fight club, I had also been introduced to Brutus the baby goat and described his incredible vertical leap.

Declan laughed so hard he started choking on one of his BBQ ribs. "Are you takin' the piss?" he asked, pounding his chest a couple of times with his fist and coughing.

"I am not."

"Sounds adorable," said Stormy.

My father scratched his head and then stroked his moustache. "I don't get it. How can goats do yoga?"

"No, Pop. The goats are present while the people do yoga. It's a Zen thing."

"I'm getting too old for crap like this," he lamented.

We spent the next half-an-hour chatting, telling lighthearted stories, and laughing until the nurse came in my room with some meds and my lunch. My father, cousin, and girlfriend all took the hint.

"I'll see you soon, Son," my father said, before he hugged me so hard it caused agony in my bandaged arm and sent striking pain shooting across my broken ribs.

"Easy, Old Man," I said, patting his massive back and hugging him in return.

As soon as my father took a step away from the bed, Declan was on top of me for an embrace of his own. "Ya ever pull somethin' like that again without me by your side I swear to Christ I'll snip off yer nuts with a pair o' rusty hedge trimmers, ya banjanxed gobshite."

I wrapped my good arm around Declan and squeezed. "I love you too, Brother."

Satisfied, both my father and cousin exited the room, leaving Stormy and me alone. She sat on the side of the bed and gently cupped my cheek.

"Jed?"

"Yes?"

"I'm not trying to upset you."

"I appreciate that."

"But what the hell were you thinking?"

I took a deep breath and exhaled. "Elijah's mother." I explained how the kind, elderly woman was hurting so bad she'd hired me to find the truth about her son's death and was desperate for an answer to why her only child might have taken his own life.

"I get it, Jed. I do. But why not take Declan along? He's basically a commando. You would have been safe if he was there."

"You're right, of course, but you also know how reckless he can be. My intention was to win a quick fight, earn some street cred, then learn as much as possible about Lennox's connection to the club. Clearly, I made an error in judgement."

Stormy nodded. "Will you make me a promise?"

"Sure."

"Next time please at least talk to me or Declan or your dad before cooking up one of these hare-brained schemes?"

"That sounds fair."

Stormy gave me a kiss and rested her head on my lap. Before I knew it, I fell back asleep, my unconscious mind reliving what had happened to me over and over. The only difference was that every time, before I fell off the roof, I managed to catch Cassian's roundhouse kick, twist his foot into an ankle lock, and snap the bones in the joint. Cassian would scream out in pain and collapse on top of me, as the two of us plummeted to our deaths together. Given the circumstances, it was the closest thing I had to sweet dreams.

THIRTY-ONE

My recovery took longer than I anticipated.

After a week of convalescence, I was sick of being laid up and eating hospital food and found myself desperately counting the minutes until I was set to be discharged from the hospital. Despite her loving efforts to care for me, Stormy's repeated visits often left me feeling smothered, and I was losing patience. I felt like a complete jerk for harbouring resentment while my lovely girlfriend was only trying to be there for me. However, I also came to realize that the incident that landed me in the ER had been a lot more traumatic than I initially thought. While my body was healing, my spirits were not.

I was "Hammerhead" Jed Ounstead, for Christ's sake. Former WWE superstar and Tag-Team and Intercontinental Champion, expertly trained in multiple styles of wrestling and mixed martial arts. I had sparred with some of the world's best fighters over the course of my career. Yet here I was, laid up in a hospital bed like a pathetic chump who had his clock cleaned on a scummy rooftop in the middle of the night in Vancouver's Downtown Eastside. My confidence in my ability to handle myself in fights had always been a significant asset and influenced how I carried myself, but after having received my first ever legitimate ass-kicking, I felt shaken to my core. I was also full of anger, guilt, and regret, especially since I had let down both my clients Elijah and Alma Lennox.

Rya had texted to tell me a VPD officer would be coming by to take my statement, but I put the kibosh on that.

"Don't be stupid, Jed," she responded, *"You need to press charges."*

"For what? It was an accident. I was just partying with some friends on a rooftop and tripped and fell."

"You don't have any friends!"

"I've got nothing to say, Rya. Without a statement, the only thing your officer pal can do is give me a slap on the wrist for trespassing and you know it."

I knew Rya was ticked and she didn't bother to respond. On my last day in the hospital, I was awakened from a nap by a shrill voice. "Yo, Bro, you gonna Bogart that Jell-O or what?"

I looked around for a moment before glancing downwards and seeing Pocket, dressed in his signature white blazer, khakis, sockless loafers, and neon green shirt, holding up his tiny hands in anticipation. I sat up, peeled off the foil top, then handed the him the Jell-O cup and a spoon. He grinned, ran a few steps, and grunted as he leapt up and onto the bedside chair. Pocket gobbled up some gelatin dessert and licked his lips.

"You don't look so bad for a guy who fell off a roof."

"Kicked off a roof," I corrected. "Where's Tubbs?"

"He's parking the van."

As if on cue, thunderous footsteps grew louder as they came closer. Then Tubbs squeezed himself through the doorway and lumbered into the room carrying a huge gift basket that he placed on the tray at the foot of my bed.

"'Dis was at the nurses desk for you, Brah."

Pocket and Tubbs looked back and forth at one another, then at me. Their anticipation for what was inside the basket was palpable.

"Go ahead, open it," I said.

Tubbs dug into the basket with his fish stick-sized fingers faster than it took Pocket to scarf down the remaining Jell-O. "No card," he said, confused. He kept peeling back the plastic wrap until he withdrew a small, plush white goat.

"What the fuck is that?" asked Pocket.

Tubbs shrugged and tossed it to Pocket, who examined the stuffed goat, before tucking it under his arm. Knowing now who had sent the basket, I couldn't help but smile. Tubbs tossed Pocket a big bar of European chocolate, and the Samoan's face lit up when he came across a can of Hawaiian macadamia nuts.

"Ono!" he said, excitedly. The giant looked at me with puppy dog eyes.

"Go crazy, Bub."

Tubbs popped the lid and was able to only partially squeeze his rotund body into a chair near the foot of the bed. The hospital room fell silent save for the sounds of Pocket and Tubbs munching away. Pocket petted and straightened the stuffed goat's fluffy white beard with one hand while chomping on his chocolate bar with the other.

"Damn, Bro," he said. "This Belgian chocolate is da bomb."

"How are things at XCCW?" I asked, desperate to distract myself from Pocket's loud chewing and cocoa-bean musings.

Pocket and Tubbs shared a knowing look. "Morale is low, Bro. Sales for *WrestleFest* pretty much screeched to a halt once they took you off the card and your championship match was postponed."

"Seriously? What about your big fatal four-way tag-team TLC title match?"

Pocket shrugged. "I guess fans really wanted to see you finally take the strap off of El Guapo."

"Rajah, Braddah. Crowd 'tis gonna be tiny now."

"Grasby's stressing out and already scrambling to switch to a smaller venue. Speaking of Captain Velvet ..."

Pocket dug an envelope out of his back pocket and flung it toward me like a frisbee. I snatched it out of the air and opened it. Inside was a thoughtful, albeit generic, *Get Well Soon* card alongside five hundred dollars in cash. Grasby had signed his name and written a message.

"For your favourite charity."

I shook my head, pleasantly surprised. Say what you will about that hustler, but when the chips were down, Grasby always had my back. I tucked the card and cash back into the envelope and placed them underneath my phone on my bedside tray. By the time I looked up, Tubbs had moved on to a can of candied almonds and Pocket was greedily stuffing his face with so many rainbow-coloured jelly beans his cheeks started puffing out like a chipmunk hoarding acorns.

"Aznuts!" exclaimed Tubbs, with his mouth full. "What be dis?"

Both Pocket and I watched as Tubbs pulled out a bunch of bananas and retrieved a paper flyer from the bottom of the gift basket. Attached to it with a paperclip was a single ticket. The big man looked at it curiously and handed me the document. I plucked the ticket free and flipped over the sheet of paper to find an advertisement for an upcoming MMA bout between Collins and Robinson, two fighters I had never heard of. The match was set to take place at the Ironclaw Boxing & MMA facility, a ten-thousand-square-foot sanctuary of all things combat located in Richmond, a coastal city adjacent to Vancouver.

The fight was scheduled for late September, almost a month away. I was still taking in the advert when I noticed the peculiar handwriting strategically scribbled across the document. The "*C*" in "*Collins*" had been circled, while above it was written "*Mr.*" in black ink. Using the "*R*" in "*Robinson*," underneath the second fighter's name was a single handwritten word—"*Recruiting.*" So that's where I could find Cassian again. That son of a gun Sykes knew that despite the pounding I took I wasn't about to let things go. And, as always, he was one step ahead.

"Just an inside joke," I said, by way of explanation. Tubbs nodded and kept inhaling the candied almonds. Pocket had a kaleidoscope of colours around his lips from the jelly beans. My head was still spinning having now learned when and where I could find Cassian, but would I be ready in a month's time? Given the extent of my injuries, I wasn't exactly relishing the idea of being near the man who had nearly killed me. Before I could give it any more thought, my chest tightened up and my heart rate increased.

"You okay, Bro?" asked Pocket.

I folded the flyer, tucked it and the ticket away in my wallet, and took a deep breath.

"I'm good, Pocket. Thanks."

"Yo, so, uh, it ain't like you need this goat toy, right? I mean, maybe you could let me have it?"

"What?"

"This stuffy, man. I thought if you didn't want it …"

"Consider it yours."

"Sweet! I mean, uh, my niece will love it. Thanks a lot."

I did my best to force a smile. I was less concerned about my little friend's sudden obsession with a stuffed goat and more worried about just what the hell I was going to do about the Cassian bombshell that Sykes had just dropped into my lap.

THIRTY-TWO

I didn't say a word on the ride home.

Declan picked me up from the hospital after I was discharged, and as always, innately sensed my mood—which wasn't a very good one. We drove without speaking and before I knew it, he had parked on the street in front of my townhouse. My cousin knew better than to try and assist me out of his muscle car, despite the fact I was walking with a limp and clutching my bandaged ribs. Declan used his own key to open my front door. I leaned on the handrail and slowly made my way up the stairs to the main floor, grunting in pain, and eased myself into my La-Z-Boy recliner.

Without a word, Declan fetched my bag from his car. Once inside the kitchen, he set about fixing us turkey, cucumber, and Swiss cheese sandwiches. He served lunch, accompanied by pints of Guinness, and took a seat on the couch next to me. Declan cracked his can of stout, turned on the television, and channel surfed until he came across the action movie *John Wick*. Because visions of vengeance filled my idle thoughts, seeing Keanu Reeves doling out punishment to those who had wronged him soon put me in better spirits.

I unfolded the flyer for the MMA match Sykes had sent me, flipped it over so the blank side of the paper was facing up, and tucked it underneath my phone on the end table beside my chair. I was too tired to give it any further thought, so for now, out of sight was out of mind. As I was dozing off, my phone rang. It was Stormy. I sent the call to voicemail and texted *"Just settling in after Declan drove me home from the hospital,"* hoping that would be the end of it. But it wasn't.

She responded. *"When can I come over?"*

I hesitated before responding. *"I'll let you know in a bit, okay? I just need some time to adjust."*

"Of course," she responded. *"I love you."*

My finger hovered over the icon button that tags a message with a heart. I hesitated, took a deep breath, and clicked on the emoji. That was three times now that Stormy had told me she loved me. And each time I did not reciprocate. If anything, I was so upset with myself just the thought of a wonderful woman saying she loved me made me angry. It wasn't Stormy's fault— she was amazing, but I simply wasn't in a place to handle her endearing devotion.

I replaced the phone and it buzzed again. Picking it up, I was surprised to find a text from Rya.

"Maybe lay off the banana milkshakes until you're able to exercise again, you goddamn glutton. Otherwise you'll wind up looking less like Goldberg and more like John Tenta's Earthquake."

The late John Tenta was a Surrey-born sumo wrestler, who became a professional wrestler in the WWE in the early nineties. He was also a friend of one of my old man's coworkers in the VPD. Even though my father probably regretted arranging a meet and greet with him back in the day, since it only fanned the flame of my desire to pursue a pro-wrestling career, it was still one of my most cherished childhood memories. I couldn't help but laugh out loud at Rya's text message, which perked up Declan at once.

"There we go, Boyo. Nice to finally see a smile on yer ugly mug."

I texted Rya back "*Sound advice, Detective*," then switched my phone to silent and took a big sip of Guinness.

"Stormy?" asked Declan.

"Rya," I replied.

Declan rolled his eyes. "O'course."

"What's that supposed to mean?"

"Nothin'. C'mon, let's watch Keanu do some gun-fu. He's about to shoot up a bunch o'arseholes in a posh nightclub and it makes me nostalgic for the old days."

I didn't take the bait as I was not interested in hearing about any of my cousin's IRA exploits at the moment, despite the fact that he was usually quite cagey and selective of the tales he would tell. Instead, I simply nodded and took another bite of my sandwich and a sip of stout. A wave of guilt washed over me for brushing off Stormy and immediately responding to Rya, but I couldn't help myself. I needed to have a reason to chuckle again and Rya had made me feel better.

I zoned out of the movie, and my mind started to wander. How had I allowed things to get to this point? When I tried to move my arm in the sling, or shifted in my seat with my bandaged ribs, I winced in pain. I ran my good hand over my bruised temple and cheekbone, where Cassian's foot had struck me, but doing so only brought back visions of me plunging off the rooftop.

I had never lost an actual fight before, whether in an athletic competition or on the street. I put down my sandwich as my stomach twisted into knots. I realized that I didn't exactly have a frame of reference for how to deal with the feeling of complete failure that was consuming me. Thinking back to that night, not only was it foolish of me to enter the fight club solo, but not once did it even occur to me that I wouldn't come out on top. I just naturally assumed I would handily defeat my opponent and then would be given some leeway to question the other club members regarding Jerry Cripps and Elijah Lennox.

Elijah. I had forgotten thanks to the concussion, but it came flooding back to me. How I had taunted Cassian with his name, which pissed him off so much a split second later he sent me flying. It was clear I had touched a nerve. But how? What was Elijah's history with this fight club, and why did the mere mention of his name cause Reggie McIntyre's face to drain of colour and Cassian to try and kill me?

There was also something else about Cassian that bothered me, and it was more than his alpha male act. I sensed a deeper degree of menace in the man. And why wear so many dog tags? I had known some vets in my time and knew wearing tags was not uncommon, but soldiers only ever wore their own. To wear another's was stolen valour, and unforgiveable. Finally, what language was Cassian speaking when he yelled at the combatants to begin and end their fights? The man was a riddle wrapped in mystery, and the only reason I had learned what I assumed was his first name was because Reggie had blurted it out after my beatdown, when trying to diffuse the situation. Calling himself and his war amp partner "Mr. C" and "Mr. F" clearly conveyed the importance of anonymity on their part, and I found myself very curious about Cassian's motivation to continue to run the underground club after its direct connection to a battered and comatose Cripps and deceased Elijah Lennox. And those were just the questionable links that I knew about. My head started throbbing from too much thinking. I sat forward and clutched my temples with both hands.

"Ya all right, Mate?"

"I think I need another painkiller."

Declan fetched a Tylenol 3 and a glass of water and I quickly gulped it down before I put my almost-full can of Guinness down on the table next to my recliner and pushed it aside.

"Switch that bloody brain off, ya turkey-tit," Declan chastised. "Just empty yer head and enjoy the carnage."

I took my cousin's advice and returned my gaze to the television, just as John Wick slipped around a corner of a bathhouse, stabbed a man in the abdomen, chopped him in the throat, covered his mouth, then stabbed him again, upwards under his jaw. As the poor henchman slid down the brick wall behind him, the lethal hitman slowly watched the life leave his victim. Wick's cold-blooded assassin's eyes were somehow both dead inside and filled with rage.

A shiver ran down my spine and all I could think of was how Cassian's face had a similar expression before he nearly killed me. I reclined fully in my chair and closed my eyes. I hoped that if I dozed off, I wouldn't wake in a sweat with my heart pounding as the helpless feeling of falling to the ground consumed me.

I had no such luck.

THIRTY-THREE

I awoke in darkness.

My entire body was clammy. The TV was off. Declan had slipped out of my place in the night. He had covered me in a blanket and left me to sleep and even to drool a little on my black leather recliner. He locked up after letting himself out.

I wiped the corner of my mouth on the blanket, sat up in my chair, and reached for my phone on the end table beside me, trying my best to ignore the aching everywhere in my body. I had missed four calls and three text messages from Stormy. I got up and out of the recliner. My left hamstring seized up and cramped hard, sending me stumbling forward across the room. I managed to get a hand up to stop myself from falling into the wall. I cursed to myself. That's when the rage took over.

I slammed my palm against the wall and swore louder. It only made me more furious. At that point I lost it. I roared at the top of my lungs and punched a hole in the wall. Drywall dust floated around my face as I slowly withdrew my fist. Before I knew it, I had yanked my injured arm free of the sling, and, despite pain shooting up my arm like fire, I started pounding holes into the wall with both fists, over and over, and screaming in anger.

I'm not sure how long that went on until the lights flicked on and I was no longer alone.

"Jed!" Stormy shrieked, horrified by the scene she'd come upon. "Stop it!"

My shoulders sank and I hung my head, breathing heavily, and drenched in sweat. Stormy came up behind me and held me tight. She led me away from my trashed wall toward the bathroom. She sat me on the toilet and went about cleaning and dressing my bruised and bloody knuckles, rinsing my torso with a warm damp towel, and gently washing and drying my hair. Neither of us spoke. Hell, I couldn't even look her in the eyes.

Once I was bandaged well enough, she led me to the bedroom, stripped me down to my boxers, and tucked me into bed. She opened a top drawer, retrieved a pair of her pajamas and changed into them, then slipped underneath the covers next to me. We lay there together in the dark, with nothing between us but utter silence. Eventually, I heard a rustle and felt hesitant fingertips gently touch my shoulder, and before I knew what I was doing, I rolled onto my side and turned my back to her. Another ten minutes ticked by before Stormy spoke.

"It's going to be okay, Jed."

I tried to ignore her comment, but in my gut, somehow, I knew that the words were false.

THIRTY-FOUR

I couldn't sleep.

Stormy had drifted off to slumberland beside me, breathing slowly and deeply, with just a hint of a snore at times. I brushed back her hair and looked fondly upon the woman who wouldn't give up on me, even though in some ways I already had. I felt the familiar ripple of regret rising within me for pushing Stormy away. I got out of bed, changed into a pair of gym shorts and a tank top, and slipped out of the bedroom. I made my way up the stairs to my office, and closed the door behind me. I booted up my iMac and surfed the web aimlessly. I read sports recaps and professional wrestling rumour roundups until I reached a point where I was no longer able to distract myself.

I opened the liquor globe adjacent to the desk. Retrieving a fine crystal tumbler, I selected a bottle of eighteen-year-old Glenlivet and poured myself a generous three fingers' worth. I slowly spun around in my chair, sitting alone in the dark, sipping the expensive whisky, savouring flavours of honey and caramel, of cocoa and coconut. I glanced at the clock. It was almost one AM. *Still time to call*, I thought to myself. *He's a night owl.*

I finished my drink and placed the empty tumbler on the desktop. My hand hesitated, hovering between my iPhone and the Glenlivet. After a moment, I chose the glass. I poured myself more single malt and drank it way too fast. At this point any interest in the whisky's tasting notes were long gone. Now I was simply trying to take the edge off before what I was about to do. I placed the tumbler down, picked up my phone, and scrolled through my contacts until I found the number. Many a night I had tried to work up the nerve to make this particular call, and every single time I couldn't go through with it. But not tonight. This time it was different. I cleared my throat as the phone rang three times. Then a voice from my past answered.

"Hello?" he said, groggily.

I hesitated before speaking.

"Hello? Who is this?"

I swallowed hard and collected what little courage I had left. "Max. It's Jed."

There was a long pause on the other end of the phone. Each second I waited felt like an eternity.

"I know I'm probably the last person you want to talk to," I continued. "But I'm calling because ... well ... honestly, I don't know where else to turn."

More silence. I bit my tongue. Twenty seconds later he responded. "Okay. Let's talk."

And with that, I began the first real conversation with my former best friend and tag-team partner turned pro-wrestling rival "Mad Max" Conkin since the day I accidently paralyzed him while we were prepping for a non-televised WWE house show match in upstate New York.

THIRTY-FIVE

"Breathe."

"What?"

"I can hear you holding your breath, Jed. Just breathe. In through your nose, out through your mouth. Slowly."

"Okay."

I did as instructed until Max decided to continue. "What happened?"

I didn't even know where to start. "I'm going through some shit, Max. Nothing like you did, of course, but … I'm not doing well."

I heard a rustling as he shifted his phone around. After a few moments, Max said "Tell me about it."

I began to recount how becoming a private investigator had changed me for the better, and how helping people in need had given my life purpose. I quickly summarized the Elijah Lennox case and mentioned how both the late former UFC fighter and his mother had hired Ounstead & Son Investigations, albeit for very different reasons. I ended my recap with how the trail had led me to the rooftop fight club, the brutal beating and fall I had taken, and how I had felt like a shell of myself ever since.

My words hung in the air as Max processed my diatribe. "You've had a rough go of it," he said, finally.

I shook my head, disgusted with myself. "What am I even doing calling you? This is peanuts compared to what you've been through. I'm sorry, Max, this was a terrible idea. I never should have—"

"Shut up, Jed," he snapped.

"What?"

"Shut up."

I immediately zipped my mouth and hung my head. Neither of us spoke. After about a minute, Max broke the silence.

"You remember the first time we met?"

I leaned back in my chair and took a sip of Glenlivet while I racked my brain. "Bakersfield, right? For, uh, M … MW—"

"MWF. Mayhem Wrestling Federation."

"That's right. Shit, we didn't know it at the time, but that was one piss-poor, low-budget operation."

"Low-budget? The owner's wife sewed stuffing into stitched-up pillowcases to make the goddamn turnbuckles."

That memory broke the ice and we both shared a hearty laugh. "We weren't even on the card that night," I said. "We were just a couple of wet-behind-the-ears, wannabe-wrestler roadies desperate to be around any in-ring action we could find."

"But they found a spot for us, remember?"

It took me a second before the memory came back to me. "That's right!" I said, excitedly, slamming a palm on the desktop. "They threw us in the Battle Royale last minute."

"We didn't even have gear," he said. "We just wrestled shirtless in jeans and sneakers."

I laughed some more. "I don't think what we did was wrestling."

"Sure it was. We both lasted a couple of minutes before tossing each other out of the ring at the same time."

"What a glorious debut," I scoffed.

"Hey, at least you got to eliminate a guy."

I almost choked on my whisky. "I'd hardly call it that."

"He went over the top rope because of you, didn't he?"

"Max, the dude's name was 'Manther.' He looked like Homer Simpson if he got his hands on a knock-off, dollar-store Black Panther costume."

"How'd you get him out of the ring again?"

"I dangled a squeaky mouse toy in front of his face then chucked it out of the ring. Son of a bitch dove over the ropes after it."

"Fucking 'Manther!'" exclaimed Max. "Say what you will about that guy, but he committed to his character."

After a good deal of cackling, we eventually composed ourselves.

"Why'd you bring up that story?" I asked.

"Because I'll never forget what happened after."

I thought hard but was at a loss. "I don't recall."

"We hit a shitty dive bar post-show for beers with some of the other guys then walked back to our motel. I only had a T-shirt on and was cold so I was ahead of everyone. I had my hands shoved deep in my pockets and was looking at the ground. Next thing I know, you're screaming my name at the top of your lungs. I stopped dead and before I could even turn around to see what your problem was, a huge gust of wind whooshed over me and a Greyhound bus sped by my face, less than a foot away."

I leaned forward in my chair. "Holy crap, that's right. I forgot about that."

"You saved my life that night."

"You would have seen the bus."

"No, I wouldn't have. But you did. Because you're a guy who sees all the angles."

I pressed my phone closer against my ear. Max was driving at something. "What are you saying?"

"I'm saying you didn't see the angles this time. And you're punishing yourself because of it."

I hesitated before responding. "Nah, I've just been—"

"Don't discount this, Jed," he said, cutting me off. "If you do, you will never heal. After my neck ... well, let's just say my physical recovery turned out to be the easy part. It's the mental anguish that you need to come to terms with. Otherwise, it will eat away at you until you're just a husk of who you used to be."

"This is different."

"Is it? So you didn't see this one coming. It was always going to happen sooner or later. The question isn't why did it happen? The question is what do you do now?"

I swallowed hard. "I can't just flick a switch in my head, Max. I've tried."

"I get it. And I'm sorry to say, old friend, moving forward is not going to be easy. You've been through some serious shit. And you're going to go through more."

"I ... I just don't think I have it in me."

"Listen. Despite whatever differences or distance we may have between us, I know you, Man. You've got the heart of a lion. Always have. And I've seen the headlines from afar. Your work with your father as a PI helps people. Which is why you've got to get back to it. You're good at it. It's what you're meant to do. And even if you don't want to do it for yourself ... then you goddamn well do it for me."

My heart skipped a beat, my stomach twisted into even more knots, and I choked up so fast I'm surprised I didn't make a sound. A couple of tears trickled down my cheeks. I tried to wipe them away as fast as possible. It must have been close to a minute of silence while we both remained on the call. I heard Max clear his throat before he spoke.

"Not once have I asked you for a single thing since what went down between us. But I'm asking for something now. I'm asking you to pick yourself up, dust yourself off, be a detective again, and help that poor old lady find the peace she deserves. Because you're the only one who can give it to her, Jed."

Tears were streaming down my face. I did my best to collect myself, before mustering three words.

"Thank you, Max."

With that, the line went dead. I leaned forward on the desk, put my head in my hands, and cried for the first time since I was nothing but a naïve teenager whose world had been shattered by the loss of his mother.

THIRTY-SIX

I had never been to Annacis Island. Despite having spent most of my life in the Lower Mainland of British Columbia, one of the city's less than glamorous isles had always eluded me. Over time the island had become mostly industrial, as well as offering a permanent home for one of Greater Vancouver's biggest wastewater treatment plants, so there really wasn't much to see other than an abundance of smog, grey-slab buildings, tugboats, and log booms chugging along the Fraser River.

I stayed on Highway 91, curving away from both Annacis Island and the concrete monstrosity known as the Alex Fraser Bridge, one of the longest cable-stayed bridges in North America that connected Richmond with North Delta and New Westminster. The 91 straightened out and it was then a straight shot through wide open fields and an abundance of farmland. Black-and-white Holstein cows chewed cud almost in slow motion as the potent scent of manure filled the inside of my truck. I switched off the air circulation fast, clearing my throat and breathing through my mouth.

It had been three weeks since I had spoken with Max. Despite it having been such an intense conversation—some of which I was still processing—his call to arms had provided me with clarity and purpose. I knew what I needed to do. My recovery from my beating had gone well. My right arm was out of its sling and my forearm and shoulder had returned to full function. The bruises on my body were either gone or nearly healed up, as were the lacerations on my face, save for a few faint and fading scars. The only lingering injury I was dealing with was that of my broken ribs, although the more I could limit my movement the less pain coursed through my torso like radioactive electricity. I had begun taking brisk walks along the seawall in Vancouver and felt good enough that I started jogging. However, after my walk with Sykes and Brutus, I found myself keeping a lookout for piles of poop pellets on the pavement. I had even resumed hitting my local gym for a few lightweight workout sessions.

While physically I was feeling much better, how I felt emotionally was a different story. I had pretty much withdrawn from those I was closest to, especially Stormy, my old man, and Declan. The latter two seemed fine with giving me space, but I knew shutting my girlfriend out of my life was hurting her feelings. I did it anyway. Max was right. I was a guy who saw all the angles, until I didn't.

Aside from an abundance of banana milkshakes topped up with Torani Crème De Banana Syrup, the only comfort I took was in doing the job. Helping people is what kept me going. Somehow, it centred me, and it also helped me keep the promise I had made to Max, which made me feel good about myself for the first time since my merciless beatdown.

Reaching the exit for Number 3 Road, I turned off the highway onto the flattest roadway I had seen since working as a jobber for Prairie Pro-Wrestling Academy in Saskatoon many years ago. I made my way down the road toward the gigantic boxing and MMA sports complex. I knew my old man, Declan, Stormy, and especially Rya would be livid with me for even entertaining the thought of attending such an event without backup. But this was something I had to do on my own. I needed to address what went down with Cassian, and had to do it by myself. The Man-Beast had gotten the better of me. While I had come to terms with that, I wasn't about to let anyone else fight my battles, for better or worse. I was also hoping that this evening's events would be a strict exercise in reconnaissance, as I had no interest in interacting with Cassian so soon after he had nearly pulverized me into oblivion.

I pulled into the oversized parking lot and found a stall. I had tucked my bangs behind my ears underneath my Vancouver Canadians baseball cap, popped up the collar on my light jacket, and sported a borrowed pair of Declan's amber-tinted aviator sunglasses in order to blend in among the fight fans who were already lined up at the entrance to the venue. The only thing that made me stand out was the banana milkshake in my hand, which I made an effort to keep covered by holding the cup inside my jacket. My disguise seemed to be working and so far I was incognito.

I showed the ticket Sykes had given me and was granted access to the gym. I walked past a dozen heavy bags, slowly creaking as they swayed back and forth from the chains on which they hung, their leather covers patched up at different angles with strips of duct tape. I found an empty chair in the back row of the unassigned seating in the spectator section. I tried to shrink my bulk into my chair as the other fight fans made their way into the building. The buzz for the evening's fisticuffs built audibly as the attendance reached maximum capacity.

The card was solid. I sat quietly, stealing sips of my shake from under my coat, and watched the half-dozen matches before the main event. The fighters were okay, but one was outstanding—a wiry and very nimble young South Asian man who fought while wearing his turban. He buzzed around the ring like a bumblebee, making short work of his opponent with strategic strikes. When the opportunity presented itself, the young man followed up his assault with a devastating jumping knee to the face that had the ref calling the match before his unconscious opponent hit the mat. It was an impressive display.

Finally, the main event between Collins and Robinson started. I was surprised when Cassian himself made an appearance in the ring, whispering in the ring announcer's ear and walking to both corners and fist-bumping the combatants. Cassian, AKA "Mr. C," was dressed in black jeans and a matching Henley shirt, but his necklace of dog tags still jangled loosely outside of his tightly-fitted top. The big, bald bastard hopped out of the ring and gave the ref a thumbs up for the match to begin.

It was a solid contest for a couple of rounds, although Collins did score a few clean and deadly jabs that stunned Robinson. Nevertheless, it was a mediocre fight at best, until Robinson's stamina failed him in round four. Collins capitalized on his opponent's poor conditioning and finished him off with a well-timed flurry of hooks and uppercuts.

The audience applauded wildly, and just like that, spectators began heading toward the exit. I lingered in my seat, watching as Cassian hopped back in the ring to console Robinson and congratulate Collins with a handshake and a bro hug. Whatever he said to the victor seemed to make the young scrapper happy, as he wiped his sweaty brow with the back of one of his leather MMA gloves and grinned from ear to ear.

Most of the fight fans had left, and not wanting to stand out, I headed toward the exit. I made a slurping sound as I polished off what remained of my banana shake, tossing the cup in a garbage can beside the doors leading to the parking lot. Unfortunately, my escape plan was cut short when two large goons with necks nearly the size of monster truck tires slammed the doors shut and blocked my path.

"He wants to see you," grunted the first man, who with his bulbous nape and shaved head resembled a giant, talking, human thumb.

I turned around to see Cassian standing in the middle of the now empty ring, next to a couple of folding chairs facing one another. He spread his arms wide in a welcoming gesture and motioned for me to join him. Resigned to my fate, I took off my ball cap and clipped my cousin's sunglasses to my T-shirt. I climbed into the ring, just as I had done so many times before, and took a seat across from the man who had kicked me off a building and left me for dead. After staring at each other eye to eye for twenty seconds, Cassian smiled.

"Good to see you again."

THIRTY-SEVEN

"You're looking a little stressed, John. And you're surprisingly quiet."

"It's Jed. Not John."

"Potato, poh-tat-toe."

"So you say."

"I know much more about you than you realize, my friend."

"I'm not your friend. And if you keep calling me *John* you'll learn something new about me. I guarantee it."

Cassian chuckled. "You've got balls, I'll give you that. Colour me impressed." After a moment, he extended a hand. "Let's try this again. Cassian. Cassian Cullen."

I hesitated before shaking the hand of the man who had nearly taken my life.

"John Edward—'*Jed*'—Ounstead."

"Oh, I'm well aware. You and your father have earned your-selves quite the reputation over the past year."

"Is that so?"

"Taking down Hector Specter and the Steel Gods? Most definitely. Quite impressive."

"They were murderers. And real assholes to boot."

The giant man nodded approvingly. "How is it you're any different?"

"Excuse me?"

"I'm not an idiot, *Jed*. Do you really think for a moment that I buy your handcuffed sexagenarian father single-handedly taking out five of the most badass bikers I've ever known while being held hostage in the back of a van? All while a 'random' SUV with air bags just happened to smash into their motorcade? Sorry. No goddamn way. I don't know exactly how you did it, but you foiled their plan, saved your dad, and took those motherfuckers down."

I tried not to gulp, but my Adam's apple betrayed me. Only one other person figured out what actually went down on the Lion's Gate Bridge that fateful night—*Rya*. And she had warned me then, and many times since, that despite having the best intentions, my detective work was quickly taking me down a dangerous path. She had been right. I saw that now, clear as day.

"You don't seem too choked up about their absence," I said.

"I'm not."

"You knew the Steel Gods?"

Cassian smirked. "Oh, yes. And they were definitely pricks who had it coming. Kendricks in particular was a smug bastard whom I've enjoyed no longer having to deal with. I suppose I should thank you for that."

"Seems like a good start given the extent of my injuries."

"Yes, well, I'll get to that. But first things first. What you don't know is that several of the Steel Gods were eager to join my fight club as it was getting started."

"Is that so?"

"Hundred percent, Brother. They were particularly motivated and eager for combat. The heavy-set one in particular."

"Don't call me 'Brother.' And I know exactly which one you're talking about."

"You do?"

"Yep. You see my cousin blew his head off with a shotgun before the other bikers shot him, kidnapped my father, and burned my family's pub to the ground."

"Well, we weren't exactly close. Just associates. I do remember that the portly fellow was quite enthusiastic about my new business venture and wanted in."

I had had enough. I waved my hands in the air in exasperation. "What is all of this, Cullen? Middle of the night rooftop fights, leaving me for dead, scouting MMA events, post-fisticuffs recruiting, and in-ring *tête-à-têtes*? Help me understand. What is it you're trying to accomplish here?"

Cassian linked his fingers together and cracked his knuckles. He leaned forward in his chair and rested his elbows on his knees. "I'm glad you asked me that, Jed. Most people don't. Especially nowadays, when my success has left me surrounded by mostly yes-men. I do miss having my point of view questioned from time to time."

"Enough bullshit. What's your angle?"

"I beg your pardon?"

"I infiltrated your fight club, with suspicions about foul play with regards to Lennox and Cripps, yet here you are acting like we're buddies and avoiding the fact that you all but killed me."

As if on cue, one of Cassian's bald, thumb-head goons provided us with a couple of bottles of ice-cold Granville Island Infamous IPAs before returning to their duties of collapsing the metal folding chairs that surrounded the ring. I crossed my arms, refusing the drink. Thumb Head looked at Cassian, who nodded, before he placed the beer by my feet on the canvas mat. Cassian took a swig and licked the froth from his lip before continuing.

"I won't lie, you name dropping Lennox like that rattled me. It's possible that I may have overreacted."

"It's *possible*?" I said, dumbfounded.

"Lennox and I weren't on the best terms before ... he expired."

"You referring to his staged suicide?"

A smirk crept across Cassian's face. "You're a lot bolder than I anticipated, Jed."

"I'm just full of surprises. I'm also not an idiot. Elijah had no reason to off himself. You see, what I can't figure out is why he would fake the theft of his championship belt and then hire me to find it. Something tells me you might have some insight into that."

Cassian took another pull of his beer. "I'm afraid I can't help you there."

"Yeah, big surprise. Tell me, Cassian. What's the point of all this? What's your end-game?"

"There is no end-game, Jed. There's only the fight."

"So why is a rinky-dink rooftop fight club so important to you? How did you even entice a guy like Lennox to join in the first place, and what went down between him and Cripps that left one dead and the other comatose?"

That question appeared to hit Cassian hard. He reclined in his chair, placed his beer between his massive thighs, and steepled his fingertips together.

"Again, I don't think I can be of help."

"I wish I could say that caught me off guard."

Cassian tugged on his necklace, clanking his multiple dog chains together. "You see these?" he asked.

"Kind of hard to miss," I replied.

Cassian stifled a smile. "You ever have the honour of serving our great country in combat, Jed?"

I shook my head. "Dropping out of university for professional wrestling school kind of got in the way of that."

"Fair enough. But let's face it, you grew up with a certain degree of privilege. No shame in that. Those were the cards you were dealt." Cassian drank more of his beer and continued. "I, however, received a different hand. Grew up with nothing. Just like Lennox. Joining the military was an escape. A vacation from the misery of my youth."

"You couldn't have just run off to Disneyland and enjoyed a breakfast buffet with Beauty and the Beast? Something tells me you and that horned brute would have hit it off."

Cassian chuckled. "I did two tours post 9/11, Jed. I don't regret it, but it was ugly. I was taken hostage and held as a POW in Afghanistan for nearly two years. When you're stuck in the middle of nowhere, with nothing to do, it stops mattering whether you're the captive or captor. At some point you start to lose your mind. That's when the fights began."

"Afghanistan, eh?" I asked. "Is that the language you were speaking when barking at the combatants to start and end the fights?"

He nodded. "That would be Pashto. I learned to speak it while fighting in the pits."

"The pits?"

"Pit fighting. Battles to the death. Tell me, Jed. What choice do you think you have when there's a gun barrel pressed against your head?"

"I assume not much. But you're also saying you killed your fellow soldiers to survive? Your brothers-in-arms?"

Cassian glared at me with an intensity that was almost impossible to describe. "Would you have done any different?"

I considered Cassian's words before responding. "I suppose that's one of those things you just don't know about yourself until you're tested."

"Exactly!"

"May I ask another question?"

"Fire away."

"Those dog tags," I said, nodding toward the chain around his neck. "I don't know much about the military, but I'm pretty sure you're only supposed to have two."

"These are my trophies. Taken from the corpses of those I've vanquished."

"In the pits?"

"Mostly," he said, touching his stainless steel ID badges. Each represents a life and death clash to the bitter end. Friends, foes, strangers—if you were facing me it didn't matter. Your number was up. But these were all earned before my dishonourable discharge."

"So the Canadian military kicked you out, but didn't lock you up despite what you did?"

"Bad optics to imprison a hero, Jed."

"You? A hero?"

He nodded. "That's why I'm not doing time. I single-handedly orchestrated an escape from the POW camp and saved most of the guys in my platoon."

"You mean the fellow soldiers you didn't murder."

"That's a matter of perspective."

I took a moment and let Cassian's revelation sink in. He sipped his beer and waited for me to respond. "Boy, we're really having a moment here, aren't we?" I said, cheerily.

That elicited a laugh. "I will say that you're pretty good company."

"Tell that to my girlfriend."

"Why's that?"

"Because I've kind of been a hot mess since you thrashed me."

"It's our failures that define us, Jed."

I kept my mouth shut as Cassian's words hit a little too close. Hit home, in fact. The Man-Beast ran his thumb gently across the mass of dog tags that hung from his neck with the same amount of pride a brand new father would have touching his child's fingertips for the very first time. "I've never relished killing, Jed. But the world is what it is. And if I'm one thing, it's this."

"Which is?"

"A survivor."

I gritted my teeth. "Is that why you created a fight club? To provide a place for flaccid punks in a state of arrested development to pound out their rage?"

"I suppose, in a way. But that's an oversimplification. It's much more than that."

"How so?"

"What do you know about anger?"

"Once I would have been inclined to say *not enough*. Then I was swiftly roundhouse kicked off of a building."

"Touché."

"Give it to me straight, Cassian."

"After our ... encounter ... you were left with a malignant tumour of rage that will rot you from the inside out. Just like I can see it's doing to you now. Sure, my club might earn some bucks from wagers here and there and provide up-and-comers with a chance to blow off some steam and make connections, which could potentially open doors for their fighting careers. But it's not why I do it. What I do is give damaged men like me a platform to beat out their indignation, their repressions and displeasures. To embrace and discover who they are. Not for money. Not for fame. For self-respect. And it works, Jed. It's the only thing that kept me alive when I was held hostage in Afghanistan."

"When you were killing people," I said, nodding at his dog tags.

"I saved more lives than I took. Are you able to say that?"

I considered Cassian's words carefully. It didn't matter if I agreed with him because things were escalating quickly, and I was outnumbered three to one. I had already had my ass handed to me the last time we had gone toe to toe. So, as a result, I played nice.

"Not yet."

"It's nice to see you coming around to my way of thinking," said Cassian.

I knew what I was about to say was a bad idea. But I just couldn't help myself. "Yeah, well, I'm not. But I want you to know I'm going to take great pleasure in taking you down."

Cassian responded without missing a beat. "Really?" he asked.

"That's right. And when I do, I'm taking your precious dog tags and giving them back to the families of all the poor bastards you murdered. Yours I'll just flush down the toilet."

Cassian gritted his teeth hard and his face reddened while he held in his breath and his festering anger.

"You're looking a little stressed, Cassian. And you're surprisingly quiet."

THIRTY-EIGHT

To say I was shown a courteous exit after lipping off to the big man would be putting it nicely. After Cassian nodded his approval, the two Thumb Heads escorted me out of the ring and dragged me from the combat gym before tossing me unceremoniously onto the sidewalk on the edge of the parking lot. I got to my feet, dusted myself off, and made my way back to my truck.

Cassian had been in a chatty mood. I begrudgingly realized that had I played my cards better he might have revealed more. Real assholes always liked to hear themselves talk. Once in the truck, I started the long trek back downtown. My mind was consumed with replaying my conversation with Cassian. I had been taken aback to learn that the Man-Beast had a relationship with the Steel Gods biker gang. It had been a while since I had even thought of those bastards. I was also surprised by his awareness of my work as a PI and the showdown with Hector Spector. Not to say that any of that was private, but it was very apparent that Cassian had done his due diligence and knew more about me than I did him. It was clear he was acquainted with both me and Ounstead & Son Investigations. This only made his cavalier attitude more concerning. Perhaps what rattled me most was how astutely Cassian deduced that I alone had taken down the Steel Gods, the violent biker gang that nearly killed my cousin and father. Rya Shepard had done so as well, but otherwise, it was a well-kept secret. Like it or not, Cassian had my number better than the Steel Gods and Hector Spector combined. Just the fact that he had run with some of the baddest men I had ever known made him dangerous.

Yet here I was, left with nothing. There was no tricking him into a confession. No epic takedown. No evidence I could pin on him either for Lennox's suicide or the shady fight club shenanigans. Whatever went down between Cassian, Cripps, and Lennox appeared to be something I was not going to learn about any time soon. I ignored a text message from Stormy on the drive home, my mind swirling until I stripped down to my André The Giant underwear and crawled beneath the bed covers to sleep alone.

THIRTY-NINE

"Cuff him."

"This isn't a heel turn, Detective. You know me. I'm not a murderer."

"I hope you're right, Jed."

It had been almost a year since I had been in a VPD police interview room as a potential suspect. I had not missed it. Rya and her coworkers were content to let me sweat, but I had to think that she was wise enough to know it would be a useless tactic.

I spent my time in solitude pondering my encounter the previous night with Cassian Cullen, being relieved that I had a pair of track pants and a T-shirt on standby before the arrival of Rya and the VPD officers, and wondering if my old man's protégé had bothered to give him a call to let him know that his one and only child had been arrested under suspicion of murder. If so, I figured my father would shortly be kicking down the door to the room where I was trapped.

I didn't have many facts to work with and knew I had to stay cool until the VPD played their hand. But there was no doubt something significant had gone down. Otherwise I wouldn't have been handcuffed to a metal bar on a desk in a drab eggshell-coloured room waiting to be grilled like an Arctic char.

The door opened and Vancouver Police Inspector Richard "Dick" Cornish entered. Cornish and I had history, and it was safe to say it wasn't the good kind. He hated my guts and resented the perks I often benefited from due to my father's former position on the force. And I couldn't stand the smug son of a bitch because he was such an officious tool. He reminded me of a power-hungry vice-principal who had a large stick permanently lodged up his ass.

Cornish slapped a thick manila folder down on the table and took a seat. He was still rocking the same flat-top haircut, moustache, slim black tie, and white, short-sleeve shirt combo that I remembered so fondly. He crossed his arms and glared.

"Howdy, Dick!" I said cheerily. "Still rocking the seventies out-of-work porn star look, I see. I respect the commitment."

"Fuck you, Ounstead."

"I guess the pleasantries are out the window then?"

"Why Shepard puts up with your dumb-ass I don't under-stand. I know she's loyal to your old man, but her devotion to you at this point is ludicrous."

"I'm surprised you didn't try and have her booted from the case when this supposed *incriminating* bullshit on me surfaced."

"Don't think I didn't try. But she's got friends in high places and insisted that she be the one to bring you in."

"Probably to ensure that I wouldn't be shot."

Cornish slammed a palm down on the table. "You arrogant prick. Like you know what this job entails."

"You know who I am."

"I'm going to get a hard-on when we throw the book at you, I swear to Christ."

"All right, now we're cooking! Let it out, Bub. And please, don't hold back."

At that moment the door to the interview room swung open and Rya marched in with a leather briefcase under her arm. "Richard!" she exclaimed. "Five minutes. *Now!*"

Cornish flipped over his chair in frustration before giving me the stink-eye, and declaring, "We're not done here, Shithead."

"Look, Dick … if you want a hug, all you have to do is ask."

Cornish stomped out of the room and slammed the door behind him. Rya rubbed her tired eyes before flipping the chair back over and sitting down across from me. She placed the briefcase on the table. We stared at one another, neither of us giving an inch. After a long silence she finally spoke.

"It's Darren's birthday today, you know."

"That handsome devil. What is the Rocket now, thirty-two?"

"Thirty-five," she responded, matter-of-factly. "And he wasn't even angry when I had to cut his birthday brunch short thanks to your latest reckless antics. He likes you that much."

"I love that guy."

"Do you know what he said? '*Go help Jed, Honey. We can grab a bite anytime.*'"

"That's a good man you got there. Does he like bowling? I'm thinking it's high time for us to have a man-date."

"Shut up, Jed."

"Shutting up." Rya was exasperated. I started to get the feeling I was in hotter water than I realized.

"Would you like to know why you're here?" she asked.

"Well, I'm pretty sure it's not to cuddle with Cornish."

Rya opened her briefcase, withdrew a plastic evidence baggie containing an empty Dairy Queen milkshake cup, and flopped it down on the table.

"Does this look familiar?"

"Is there any left?" I asked, trying not to lick my lips.

"They found this at the scene, Jed."

"What scene?" I asked.

"Next to Reggie McIntyre's corpse. He's dead. Murdered in his apartment. And your fingerprints are all over this," she said, nodding toward the cup. "You wouldn't have anything to say about that, would you?"

It took a moment for the reality of what Cassian had pulled off to set in. The rat bastard had swiped my empty cup from the garbage can at the MMA fight and set me up.

"I do like bananas," I said, quietly.

"This isn't a joke, Jed. They've got you dead to rights."

"Hell of a way to go out, I guess."

Rya smashed a fist down on the table. "Goddamn it! Do you realize the shit you're in?"

"Even if that is my cup how did you get the prints back so fast?"

"Let's just say I called in a favour with the boys in the IDENT crew the second I realized it was the remnants of one large banana milkshake. I mean seriously, Jed. You may as well have taken a selfie with the body."

"You of all people know I didn't do this."

"What I believe is irrelevant. This evidence is not."

As if on cue, Frank Ounstead smashed open the door to the interview room and stormed inside. "This is over!" he bellowed. "What are you even thinking, Rya?!"

She leapt to her feet and stabbed an accusing finger at me. "*He* left me no choice, Frank!"

My old man snorted like an enraged bull and jabbed a thick thumb over his shoulder. "We're out of here, Son. I've cleared it with the brass."

That's when things escalated. Dick Cornish charged through the open door and pushed my father on his chest with both hands, which had the same effect as if my little friend Pocket tried to move a Buick. It was a bad decision.

"You fucking Ounsteads!" snapped Cornish. "You think you can get away with this?"

Rya and I stayed silent as my father grabbed Cornish by the throat with one of his bear-paw hands and squeezed so hard the Inspector's face turned redder than a radish. "Don't you *EVER* come after my boy without telling me first, you gutless worm."

Bits of white foam began to dribble from the corners of Cornish's mouth as he gasped for air. My father let go of his chokehold. It was only then that I realized he had been lifting the man off of the ground with one hand. Cornish collapsed on the floor in a heap.

My pop nodded toward the exit. "Let's go, Son." Rya uncuffed me, and moved to help Cornish regain his feet. I kept my head down and followed my old man's lumbering footsteps out of the interview room and into the VPD bullpen, where over a dozen cops and office staffers moved aside and cleared the way for us, much as the water of the Red Sea had done for Moses.

"Text your cousin," barked Frank Ounstead.

"About what?"

"Tell him to have some of the black stuff ready."

"Yes, Sir."

We didn't speak at all on the ride to our pub. Once seated at the great mahogany bar of the Emerald Shillelagh, my father and I only engaged with my cousin after we were halfway through our pints of Guinness and Declan deemed it high time to start grilling us about what had gone down.

FORTY

"He shoved yer arse?" Declan asked, dumbfounded.

"He did."

"Did ya twist off his nuts and stomp on 'em like a couple o' cock-a-roaches?"

My old man fought back a smile. "Not quite."

Declan scowled. "Ya disappoint me, Boyo."

"I lost my cool and choked him out for a few seconds. If I didn't let go when I did, I think he probably would have crapped himself."

That made my cousin happy. "Now we're talkin', Frankenstein."

"That's Uncle Frank. And it's probably not going to go over very well in the department when word spreads of what I just did."

"Are you kiddin'? That Cornish gowl is gonna be so scarlet he won' breathe a word o' it to anyone."

"Maybe," my father replied, before he and Declan drained what was left of their pints of Guinness. The pub was quiet and Declan had shut down the karaoke machine for the day. I don't think at that moment any of us was in the mood for music.

Declan cleared his throat. "So, Jed made bail then?"

"Not exactly. Let's just say the Chief made the charges pending for now. They're not official yet … but they will be if we don't figure this out."

"Jaysus," muttered Declan.

"They found my fingerprints at a murder scene. How are we supposed to get around that?"

"You were set up," said my father assuredly. "And they know Cornish has a chip on his shoulder and has been suspicious about you since everything that happened with the Steel Gods. He's been waiting for something like this."

"What about Rya?" I asked.

Frank Ounstead stifled a burp and grimaced. "She did what she had to do. That being said, you better keep your nose clean and not leave town for a while. You're still their number one suspect."

Declan shook his head. "Me own bloody cuz wanted for murder. An' you," he said, nodding at my father, "stompin' around the cop shop like a sasquatch who stepped in his own shite. If our business takes a hit it's on yer arses ya hooligans."

"Watch that tongue, Dec," cautioned my father.

Declan ignored him. "Ya know, back home, there's two types o'tossers, an' that's bloody well it."

I scratched my head. "And those would be?"

"The gobshites that are killers and the gougers that aren't."

I decided it was high time for a healthy pull of my pint. "Cousin, I love you, but I have no idea what the hell you just said."

Declan waived a hand at me and told me to "sod off" before meandering down the bar to tend to a dishevelled, middle-aged, surly-looking son of a bitch slowly sipping a scotch.

My old man and I sat in silence for a while until I finally spoke.

"Thank you, Pop."

He waved the comment away. "Forget it."

"No, I won't. You put your entire reputation on the line to get my ass out of a jam, and we haven't even talked about if I did what they think I might have."

"Don't need to."

"Just like that?"

"Just like that."

I nodded and returned to my Guinness, while Declan reappeared to provide my father a fresh pint. "So what do I do now?"

"You find out who bumped off this McIntyre fella, why Cullen tried to frame you, and clear the Ounstead name. And you finally figure out the truth about what went down with Lennox and Cripps."

My old man took a big sip of his Guinness, his hand trembling ever so slightly. The great Frank Ounstead was nervous, and I couldn't remember the last time I had seen him imbibe so much so quickly. I opened my mouth to reply, then thought better of it. We drank our pints in silence.

FORTY-ONE

My father's old uniform fit loosely, despite my best efforts
to tighten up the excess. I had borrowed it—with permission—
from his closet in my childhood home in Kerrisdale, Vancouver,
for which I still had a key. The neighbourhood was well-known
for low and mid-rise apartment buildings housing an ethnic mix
of Caucasian and Asian Canadians. That might explain why my
first love was a young girl named Lucy Chen, a Eurasian beauty
who had stolen my heart until Rya Shepard came into my life.
Naturally, I had not once shared any of this with my current
girlfriend.

Stormy.

She must have been furious with me for pushing her away,
over and over, but I just couldn't help myself. Between the Lennox
investigation, my brutal beatdown, and now my troubles with
the law, I couldn't bring myself to look her in the face. I was
filled with self-loathing and knew on some level she deserved
better. Yet she still wanted to be with me. I didn't even know
why anymore. I was at the point that when I caught a glance

of my reflection in a mirror I was overcome with disgust. I felt like a failure.

Yet here I was, dressed like a poor man's rent-a-cop trying to sneak into a dead guy's apartment—a man I was accused of murdering—in hope of finding evidence to exonerate me from a bogus murder rap, let alone provide the beginnings of a plan for dealing with Cassian. The Man-Beast may have been a bastard, but he was also smart and cunning. I had gone toe to toe with some formidable opponents, but neither Kendricks and his badass biker buddies, nor smarmy narcissist Hector Spector ever boxed me in like this. They all had exploitable weaknesses. But if Cassian Cullen had an Achilles heel, then I was still in the dark. The man had been two steps ahead of me the entire time.

I complemented my cop uniform with Declan's sunglasses and my old man's police badge. Upon closer inspection, my police duty belt was clearly dated by its antiquated black baton and lack of a holster for a sidearm, so I had to hope no one else would take notice. It wasn't lost on me that I was impersonating an officer of the law right after my old man had temporarily taken me off the hotseat with the VPD, just so I could pursue what many would consider a fool's errand. Unfortunately, it was the only lead I had at the moment.

I parked a couple of blocks away from Slocan Park in East Vancouver and stole a quick glance at myself in my truck's tinted mirrors. I looked okay for the most part. While to the trained eye I might not look exactly like a VPD officer, it would be enough to get me in and out of Reggie McIntyre's apartment without a hassle.

The sun burned the back of my neck as I walked past the park, with its lush green grass and wading pool full of laughing children, who were spraying each other with Super Soakers to beat the heat of the muggy, late-summer day. I remembered my mother bringing me to this same park when I was a child, while my father was first starting out as a patrol cop. I used to love climbing up and inside an oversized, concrete igloo on the playground, and was sad to see it had been removed.

I did a lap around McIntyre's drab apartment building, the colour of which I could only describe as lima-bean green. It was in desperate need of another coat of paint. There were no signs of squad cars or a police presence. The front door to the complex was open, held ajar by a dusty black rock. I headed inside and turned left toward Reginald McIntyre's first-floor unit, an address obtained by my father before my less-than-legal intrusion. I walked past an old man in a tattered bathrobe carrying a shabby-looking grey cat. He gave me the once-over, and I nodded as professionally as I could. He huffed under his breath.

"McIntyre?" he asked, regarding my outfit.

"Yes, Sir."

"Apartment 1-F."

"You a neighbour?"

"Landlord. Always trouble, that one. And he hated cats."

"How could you hate this little guy?" I asked, reaching out to pet its straggly haired head.

As if on cue, the feline hissed and flung out his claws at me. No contact was made, but it was unnerving nonetheless.

"Just ignore Floyd, Officer. He can be a real cranky bastard."

"Appreciate the heads up." That seemed to please the cat-loving, octogenarian quite nicely and he saluted me in return before turning to leave.

"Just one more thing," I said. "Do you know how he died?"

"Somebody strangled him, thankfully."

"Thankfully?"

The old man nodded earnestly. "No blood to clean up after they removed the body." Then he moseyed off down the hall without looking back.

I reached the door of unit 1-F and retrieved a pair of latex gloves from a leather pouch on my duty belt. Rows of yellow police tape stretched across the door frame. Once I'd worked the deadbolt with my lock picks, I ducked under the tape, slipped on the gloves, closed the door quietly behind me and sized up the place.

Reggie had been a music lover, and his bright orange furniture contrasted with the collection of framed album cover posters that adorned the walls of the living room. Pink Floyd's *Dark Side of the Moon*, Prince's *Purple Rain*, The Sex Pistols' *Never Mind the Bollocks*, and more brightened up the apartment with splashes of colour. I slipped into his bedroom, where I found nothing but a rumpled futon, a bedside dresser, and a closet filled with clothes and workout gear. I returned to the living room to do another pass hoping that something—anything—useful would jump out at me.

Nothing did. I sat on the orange couch and sighed. What the hell was I even doing? This was leading nowhere. I'd been grasping at straws. Why did Cassian have Reggie McIntyre murdered? And why try and pin it on me? If he were so at ease with rubbing someone out, wouldn't that have been a more efficient way to keep me from sniffing around? Why bother setting up the frame job? And, of course Cassian would ensure that the crime scene in McIntyre's apartment would be clean except for the damning evidence that pointed directly toward me. Cassian was smart, cagey, and cautious, not stupid and sloppy.

I had been chasing my tail and deluding myself that I could find some way to take him down. The truth was my heart wasn't in the investigation since the brutal beating he gave me. I had never worked anything like this before. I'd always solved the case and got my man.

I couldn't deny it anymore—I just wasn't the same guy I used to be. I sat there for a few minutes until a phone in the kitchen rang. I ignored it. The phone stopped after four rings. Ten seconds later it rang again. By the third set of rings, I walked over and answered the call.

"Get out of there now, Ounstead," snapped an urgent, garbled male voice.

"How do you know my name? Who is this?"

"I'm the person saving your life."

FORTY-TWO

"Who is this?" I demanded again.

"There's no time. They're coming."

"Who's coming?"

"Go now! And wait for my call."

Click.

I hung up the phone and tried to process what had just happened. Snapping out of it, I went to the door and inched it open to peek into the hallway. Fifty feet down the hall I saw the old man, still holding Floyd the cat, and talking to Cassian. Mr. F, Cassian's right-hand man with the prosthetic leg, stood nearby. The old man turned around and pointed a finger toward McIntyre's apartment. That's when it happened. I pulled my head back from the door and the room started spinning. Sweat broke out all over my body, and I felt a wave of nausea rising. I took a few unsteady steps backwards and looked at my latex gloved hands. They were shaking. What was happening to me?

I tried to compose myself and stole another glance out the doorway. Cassian and Mr. F were marching straight toward the apartment door. As they approached, Cassian withdrew a pair of the biggest brass knuckles I had ever seen. He slipped them onto the meaty fingers of both his hands as his combat boots thumped with each step he took down the carpeted hallway. I pulled further back from the apartment's door, and started hyperventilating. I did my best to slow my breathing, which was coming in jagged gulps. Looking frantically around the room, I noticed a window behind the orange couch. I stumbled toward it, slid the sash open, climbed out, and landed on the grass below with a thud. Still fighting off dizziness, I heard the door to McIntyre's apartment smash open.

My heart pounded and my head cleared a bit as I bolted toward my truck, too afraid to even risk a glimpse backwards. Reaching my Ford F-150, I leapt into the driver's seat, slammed the door shut, and sped off as fast as I could. By the time I was three blocks away, I had worked up the nerve to look in the rear-view mirror. It didn't appear that I was being followed, but I wasn't going to take any chances.

I peeled onto a random side street before turning into half a dozen more, with no direction or destination in mind. I used a couple of other tricks my father had taught me to lose a tail until I was finally able to catch my breath. I rolled down my windows to get some fresh air. It wasn't until I heard the collective shrieks of passengers secured in their seats and dropping with the force of negative 1G from the top of the HELLEVATOR ride's two-hundred-foot vertical tower that I realized I was zooming past Playland Amusement Park on Hastings Street. I drove another couple of blocks before parking haphazardly and hurrying inside the building. I bounded up the stairs to the second floor, pulled out my keys as I reached the door, inserted one into the lock—but hesitated to turn the key.

After a few moments the door swung open. Stormy stared at me, her expression betraying no emotion. We looked at each other for what felt like an eternity, my chest still heaving, and the collar of my police uniform soaked in sweat. Stormy looked at my hands, and it was only then I realized I was still wearing the latex gloves I had put on to search McIntyre's apartment.

She slammed the door in my face.

FORTY-THREE

I knocked on the door.

I slipped my keys back in my pocket, snapped off the latex gloves, tucked them away in my duty belt pouch, and waited. After a minute had gone by, I rapped again. The door opened slowly. This time there was no mistaking Stormy's expression when she glared at me.

"The sailor and biker are parking the car," I said, jabbing a thumb over my shoulder. "Meanwhile the cowboy and construction worker are outside having it out over who has the better moustache …"

Stormy stepped aside and swung the door open. "Get in here, already. You look like an idiot."

I did as I was told and entered her apartment. I took a seat on the couch and undid the top few buttons of my police shirt, exposing some damp chest hair. Stormy went to the kitchen, grabbed a dishtowel, balled it up, and threw it at me. I caught it mid-air. "Don't sweat on my furniture," she ordered. I nodded and dabbed myself down while she poured herself a glass of red wine. She didn't offer me one. After a couple of big sips, she walked around the granite countertop and took a seat in the chair across from me. We sat in silence for I don't know how long. Eventually, she spoke.

"Why are you here, Jed?"

"I, uh … was working nearby."

"Impersonating a police officer. Does your dad know?"

"It was his idea. You see, I went to this MMA fight last night—"

"You what?"

"Sykes tipped me off that Cassian was going to be there."

"And you went to see him?" she asked, incredulously.

"No! I mean, sort of. I went undercover. Strictly recon. Or at least it was until the big bald bastard spotted me and made me sit down for a face to face."

Stormy just shook her head. I trudged on with my story.

"Anyway, I tried to get him to say something—anything—that I could use to help prove he murdered Elijah Lennox and staged the suicide, but—"

"I'm going to stop you right there," she snapped.

"No, Stormy, you don't understand. Cassian framed me for murder! I was arrested earlier today and interrogated by the cops before my old man was able to temporarily spring me."

"Daddy saved your ass again, eh?"

"He bought me time. But the clock is ticking. If I don't prove my innocence, I'm going to wind up rotting in prison for something I didn't do."

Stormy drank more wine as she considered my words. "Let me guess, your precious Detective Rya was in the interview room with you too, right?"

"*What?* Well, yeah. It is her job after all. Trust me, she wasn't pleased."

"Cut the bullshit, Jed! I'm not stupid. Don't think I haven't seen the way you two look at each other. Especially after you woke up in the hospital. You called out her name for Christ's sake. You didn't even give a shit that I was there."

"Stormy, come on, I was drugged up and just coming to after—"

"I don't want to hear it!" More silence. More sips of wine. I stared at the floor, not knowing what else to do. "I gave you everything I had, Jed. I would have done anything for you."

"I know."

"Then why did you push me away?"

"I ..."

"I was your girlfriend. In fact, I foolishly thought I may have been more than that."

Her words cut like a knife.

"Was?" I said softly. Stormy killed her remaining wine, walked back to her kitchen, and placed the empty glass in the sink.

"Yeah," she said. "*Was.*"

I rose from the couch and walked toward her. "Stormy, I'm sorry, okay? This case has got me all turned around. You know we're great together. Let's not throw it all away. I just need to see this thing through."

"And then what? We have a good month or two until something else comes along that allows you to pursue your death wish?"

"Hey, come on. I don't have a—"

"Stop talking."

I did as she asked. Stormy hung her head, her blonde hair cascading down in front of her face. She sniffled, turned to face me, wiped her eyes, and pushed back her hair. Her jaw was clenched and the look on her face was resolute.

"Goodbye, Jed."

I stood there, my stomach in knots, shell-shocked. As if my life wasn't crappy enough, it just lost one of its few bright spots. Stormy removed my house key from her key chain and placed it on the counter. Reluctantly, I did the same with hers and exchanged it for the key I had given her. With nothing left to be said, I left her condo for the very last time.

FORTY-FOUR

"Your milkshake is getting warm."

"What?"

"Enough with the pity party, John. I understand you've had a really rough go of it and that you lost your woman. Been there myself before, believe it or not. But now is not the time for you to rest on your laurels."

My father shoved a large DQ banana milkshake across my dining-room table. I was too tired to go to my kitchen and top it up with a shot of Crème De Banana Syrup. I simply took a sip and sighed. My old man stifled a burp and took a huge scoop of his seasonal Pumpkin Pie Blizzard, which in my humble opinion was an utterly profane, autumn-themed, dairy disaster. I focused on my banana shake and for a few moments my troubles melted away.

"Thanks for coming over, Pop."

My father nodded his head while devouring spoonfuls of his Blizzard as if he were in a competitive eating contest. "I wanted to see how you were doing."

With another sip of my banana shake, my taste buds came alive and pumped some much-needed endorphins into my body. "I didn't tell you everything that happened at McIntyre's apartment."

My father eyed me curiously. "Then tell me now."

I recounted the part I had glossed over, how when I'd peeked out the door, I'd seen Cassian, all brass knuckled up, with Mr. F, storming down the hallway toward me. I told him how I had frozen, became dizzy, started shaking, and that my heart pounded so hard in my chest I could barely make my escape out the first-floor window.

"Doesn't sound like much fun," he said.

I looked at him quizzically. "Isn't this the part where you're supposed to tell me a story about when you were back on the force you once seized up on the job too?"

My father licked some pumpkin pie bits from his bristly moustache. "Not today."

"So you never once …"

"Of course I did. Quite a few times over the years, in fact."

"How'd you deal with it?"

"Dairy Queen and beer, mostly."

"I gotta say, as far as pep talks go, this one's a stinker."

"The last thing you need is to hear stories about me going through the same thing."

"Why not?"

"Because you need to get mad. And fight back."

"Against Cassian?"

"Against your fear. Look, you got served a monster beating. I'm talking one for the books. But you're looking at it all wrong. Cullen went after you with everything he had. He most certainly thought you were dead, Son. But you took it. You took his worst and you not only survived, you got back on your feet and resumed nipping at his heels."

"What's to stop him from doing it again if we cross paths?"

"*When* you cross paths. This ain't over until he's out of commission and you've cleared your name."

"I can't even find the guy. No phone number or address on record. He's a ghost. I had one chance to confront him again thanks to Sykes and I blew it."

"That mystery caller of yours will see to it that you get another crack at Cullen. He gave you a heads up for a reason. We don't know exactly why yet, but something tells me it's because he wants or needs something from you."

"Yeah, but—"

"But nothing. You owe it to Lennox, his mama, and that poor bastard McIntyre to finish this. No one else can get justice for them except you."

I popped the lid off my cup and stirred what was left of my shake to ensure a couple of final sips. "I can't do it, Pop. He's too big. Too strong. Too smart. I've been running all over town trying to dig shit up on the guy and I've got jack squat."

My father shook his head. "Strength means nothing. Determination is everything."

I considered my father's words, but was still left with a sinking pit in my gut that was so intense I instantly lost my appetite and pushed aside what was left of my milkshake. Now I knew that I had been rattled to my core.

"You need to get your mind off all of this hoodoo, get your head straight, and remember just who the hell you are."

"And who is that? Because I'm not sure I even know anymore."

He furrowed his brow and slammed a boulder-sized fist down on the table with such force the oak reverberated and our DQ cups nearly tipped over.

"You're 'Hammerhead' Jed Ounstead, goddamn it! The best private investigator this city's ever seen. Present company excluded, of course."

In all of the years since my mother had lovingly shortened my given names John Edward into Jed, not once had my old man ever called me by my preferred moniker. Let alone prefacing it with my pro-wrestling identity.

Despite the ass-kicking, multiple failures, and now the loss of Stormy, I'll be damned if a big smile didn't creep across my face. "Thanks, Pop. And I know just the son of a gun to turn to for a little help."

FORTY-FIVE

"Okay, Boyo, let's rock!"

I walked forward, weaving in between nearly a dozen free-standing heavy bags as I made my way toward Declan. Once free of the maze of padded pillars, I stepped barefoot onto the open mat section of the kickboxing studio and joined him. I inhaled the swirling scents of sweat and new leather. My cousin and I were both dressed in workout gear and alone in the venue. Declan had a lady friend who owned this particular studio in Yaletown, which was just below his flat, and had charmed her into giving us free access after hours. We both wore MMA gloves, rather than the traditional red-and-black boxing gloves that hung on hooks on the wall, so our fingertips were free and we had more flexibility and control of our fists.

"On your toes!" barked Declan, and I followed his lead, bouncing back and forth on the balls of my feet.

"High knees!" he commanded.

We put our palms out flat in front of us and drove our legs so far upwards our kneecaps slapped loudly against our padded hands.

"Shadow!"

This time, I fell in line behind him, and we jogged around the perimeter of the open mat, bobbing and ducking, while popping up and snapping off alternating uppercuts in between a series of jabs, hooks, and overhand strikes. It wasn't long until we had worked up a decent sweat. My cousin grabbed a couple of gym towels from a folding chair and threw me one. We dabbed ourselves down before continuing.

"Fightin' stance!" shouted my cousin.

I tossed my towel aside, put up my dukes, slightly bent my knees, and resumed bouncing up and down on the balls of my feet.

"There we go, Laddie!"

I nodded, feeling pretty good as I was loosening up.

"Lookin' grand. Now let's see some strikes. And not them wee, warm-up ones. I'm talkin' 'bout some big ol' bombs that'll rattle his bollocks so hard he'll be waddlin' for weeks!"

Colourful description aside, I heeded Declan's instructions. I grunted with each strike, and my punches only got harder as I imagined Cassian's face on the receiving end of my charged blows.

Declan whistled and clapped his hands approvingly. "Good work, Mate! C'mon, let's do some sparrin' now, yeah?"

I nodded and my cousin sprung in front of me and attacked with a flurry of strikes and kicks. I immediately felt that familiar pang of anxiety by being thrown into a fighting situation so quickly. The confidence I had built up during the warm-up began to dissipate.

"Let's go, Fella," said Declan, coming at me ferociously again. I turtled up and backed away defensively. "Throw a punch, ya gee!"

I hesitated before telegraphing a couple of at best mediocre punches, which Declan swatted with ease.

"That's bloody shite! Again!"

I tried to put more power behind my blows, like when I was shadowboxing and feeling strong. But my heart wasn't in it. Both Declan and I knew it. He batted away my swings, furrowed his brow, then delivered a kick to my midsection and a hard fist to the side of my head, which knocked me down in an instant.

"Jaysus, Jed!" sniped my cousin in frustration. "Yer better than this!"

I stayed on the floor, one arm clutching my throbbing ribs, while I hung my head low in shame.

Declan sighed deeply and sat down cross-legged beside me on the mat. "Did I ever tell ya about me mate Fergal O'Brien?"

"I don't think so."

"He was somethin' else. A real tough nut and the funniest son o'a bitch I ever met. He could take the piss with the best o'them, pound pints like a champ, an' was as brave a bastard as I've ever seen."

"A friend from when you were in the IRA?" I asked.

"Aye. An' best friend ever. Except for yer big dumb arse, o'course."

"What happened to him?"

Declan traced a fingertip alongside the jigsaw edge of one of the many square mats that interconnected with the others. "One time we got an intelligence report. Said there might be a raid on one o'our headquarters by the UVF."

"What did you do?"

"Geared up. It was just me and Fergie. We were closest to the location and able to get there first."

"Go on."

"When we arrived, everythin' was fine. I went inside to check things out, while Fergie stood guard out front. But after I had cleared the HQ, I opened the front door to find me mate bleedin' out on the pavement. Fergie had put up a hell o'a fight. He kept the fuckers from comin' inside and sent 'em scurryin', but not before he took an absolutely brutal beatin' for his efforts. He was moanin' and spittin' out teeth, an' all I could do was call for help, hold him in me arms, an' tell him he was gonna pull through."

"That's horrible," I said.

"Aye. 'Twas indeed. But there's more to the story."

"Do I even want to hear it?"

Declan uncrossed his legs on the grey mat and stretched them out. "I think ya should."

I nodded and Declan continued.

"Ya see, after that day, despite everything me an' the lads tried to do for him, Fergie was never the fella he used to be. He became extremely depressed an' started drinkin' way too much, which is a feat, considerin' he was FBI."

"FBI?"

"Full-Blooded Irish."

"Oh."

He ended up movin' down south to Cork to live with his mum an' that's the last I ever heard o'him."

"Damn," I muttered to myself.

"I don' wanna see that happen to ya, Jed. I know ya took a thrashin'. A bad one. An' I'm sorry. I really am. But we gotta get yer goddamn groove back. That's what I'm tryin' to do here. 'Tis why I think this is so important."

I took a deep breath as Declan's words of wisdom resonated with me. He was right of course. I was tired of being haunted and humiliated by the defeat I had suffered. I owed it to my cousin, father, Reggie McIntyre, and especially my clients Elijah and Alma Lennox to pick my sorry ass up and get back to it. I pushed down the crippling fear that had haunted me of late and climbed to my feet. "Let's try again."

"Aye, there's the big ol' bugger o'a cuz I know an' love."

I slipped into my fighting stance as did Declan. He attacked me suddenly with some vicious strikes, but to my amazement I was able to block them.

"Bloody hell! That's what I'm talkin' about!" crowed my cousin. "You got this!"

Declan continued with more punches, which, again, I was able to defend against. I followed that up by scoring some blows of my own and even managed to land a forceful shot to his sternum.

Declan doubled over and clutched his chest. I took a step back. "I'm sorry, D."

Declan coughed a few times before laughing. "Are you kiddin'? That was brilliant! Well done!" I helped him stand up and he patted my back enthusiastically. "Yer lookin' great, Mate. But there's one more thing we need to talk about."

"Which is?"

"How ya fight."

"How I fight?"

"Aye."

"D, I fight the way I was trained. You know that better than anyone."

My cousin placed both of his black gloved hands on my shoulders and gave me a shake. "But at yer core, yer not a fighter, Jed. *Yer a grappler.* Ya went into that fight club thinking o'yerself as a different creature than what ya truly are."

"What do you mean?"

"I know ya have had trainin' in Judo an' Jiu-Jitsu an' other shite with fancy footwork. An' that's bloody well great. But we both know yer at yer best when ya think o'yerself as a wrestler. Takedowns, chokeholds, suplexes—that's yer bread 'n' butter. Don't fight it. Lean into it."

I took a moment to consider my cousin's words. They were a bit critical, but they also made sense to me and rang true.

"Do ya remember yer Five Moves o'Doom?"

I chuckled. "Of course I do. Headbutt From Hell, haymaker, Irish whip off of the ropes into a spear, then the Hammerlock DDT. I still use them in XCCW." That set of moves was how I often ended my pro-wrestling matches, a signal to the crowd that I was ramping up to a victorious finish.

"Aye, those."

"Why would you ask that?"

"Cuz even though ya use 'em for fanfare and theatricality, it's still a deadly set o'moves. Ya could bloody well take down pretty much any bloke if ya can deliver those strategically an' with a vengeance."

"You're suggesting I use my in-ring finishing routine to win real fights?"

"I am indeed. Yer a bloody Hoss, Jed. Ya land those blows in succession, for real, an' it's over."

I considered Declan's words, but not for long. A moment later he came at me hard and fast with lightning-quick punches. I blocked all of his blows efficiently, before performing a freestyle wrestling double leg takedown that drove my cousin to the mat with such force it knocked the wind out of him. Rather than transition into ground and pound mode, I rolled off of Declan, and we laid on our backs, both of us breathing hard before breaking into laughter.

"How was it for ya?" he asked, wheezing.

I chuckled. "Not bad. Not bad at all."

I was saved from any more roughhouse-sparring with Declan when my phone rang. I darted over to my workout bag by the edge of the mat, dug through a dishevelled mound of my clothes, and found my smartphone. The call was from an unknown number. I answered with a swipe of the thumb. "Hello?"

"We need to meet," said the same mystery voice that had called me at Reggie McIntyre's apartment and saved me from another vicious beating by Cassian.

"When?" I asked.

"Now."

FORTY-SIX

The rickety bridge swayed and bounced from the foot traffic of a hundred people, and the unsettling movement caused one of my hands instinctively to grab the railing. I peeked over the edge of the wobbling walkway to see the seventy-metre drop to the river below, the dark blue water cutting through the evergreen coastal forest with strong currents and white foamy splashes.

The Capilano Suspension Bridge was a historic Vancouver landmark built by a Scottish civil engineer and park commissioner in 1889. Originally constructed of hemp ropes and cedar planks, by the early 1900s the bridge was replaced with wires and cables until it was sold and completely rebuilt yet again in 1956. Amazingly, this simple suspension connector, crossing high above the Capilano River and slicing through a swath of Douglas Firs, was one of the most lushly verdant transportation arteries in all of British Columbia.

I breathed a sigh of relief when I reached the other side of the suspension bridge, since great heights had never exactly agreed with me. But this was where my mystery caller—someone who had saved me from either a brutal beating or death itself—had wanted to meet. It felt a bit silly to me, for any criminal worth his salt knew better than to schedule a meeting in such a public and potentially dangerous location. The moment I stepped onto sure footing, the alert tone on my iPhone began playing the opening guitar riff from Fleetwood Mac's "The Chain." I walked away from the jiggling death trap of a bridge into Capilano Park and checked the text message.

"*Treetops.*"

I located the signs for the different towers. Treetops was aptly named, for it provided a squirrel's-eye view of not only the Capilano Suspension Bridge, but also the Canadian West Coast's most impressive rainforest. My phone chimed again. I checked the new message and found that my mystery caller had chosen a specific location with the most succinct of instructions.

"*North.*"

Following the directive, I climbed the steps toward the Northern Treetops destination, keeping my head low as I walked past dozens of nature lovers and tourists making their way down through the centuries-old forest. I reached a semi-circular ramp, in the shape of a crescent moon, jutting out above the dense foliage. From the middle of this walkway, I could admire one of the most spectacular natural sights that British Columbia has to offer. I spent a few moments admiring the trees and leaned against a railing while awaiting the arrival of my mysterious caller.

"'Hammerhead' Jed,'" she said. "I've been looking forward to meeting you."

I turned to face a five-foot-three woman I estimated to be in her mid-to-late forties, whose long auburn hair was pulled back in a tight ponytail. She wore very little makeup and was quite attractive, but in a world-weary kind of way. I got the impression from the glimmer of sadness in her eyes that she had seen some unpleasant things in her time.

"I'm afraid you have me at a disadvantage," I said.

"Kate Roland," she replied, "with the *Vancouver Sun*."

"You're a reporter?"

"*Crime* reporter. I work the beat. And considering what your pals Elijah Lennox and Reggie McIntyre shared with me, I'm definitely someone you want to know."

I shook her hand. "Why did you call to warn me about Cassian Cullen when I was in McIntyre's apartment?"

"Seemed like a waste to let such a pretty face get mucked up a second time," she said, before tracing one of her knuckles gently alongside my lightly bruised cheekbone, which was still tender from the sparring I had done with Declan.

"You disguised your voice to sound like a man."

"Anonymity goes a long way in my business," she said coyly, pulling an electronic voice-converter from her pocket. "You know I paid a small fortune for this thing? That was before you could download one as a cheap app on your phone."

"What's your angle in all of this?" I asked.

"I won't lie, I've been keeping tabs on you for a while. You're a player, Ounstead."

"So you've been following me?"

"No. Just aware of the waves you've been making. The day I called you I had been staking out McIntyre's building. I had a feeling Cassian and Ferdinand might be doing the same, hoping the chump they pinned the murder on might come by."

"Ferdinand?"

She nodded. "Ferdinand Gonzales. Cullen's right-hand man."

"Mr. F," I said, connecting the dots. "And his leg?"

"Blown off in Afghanistan in 2011. Gonzales was a member of Cullen's special forces squad. Medevacked out of the shit just before the rest were captured. Losing that leg probably saved his life."

I said nothing while processing what Roland had shared. She patted me on the back.

"Let's take a walk, Big Guy."

I followed Kate Roland as she led the way down the stairs away from the high traffic Treetops location. A sudden breeze picked up a cloud of mist from the waterfall that trickled over jagged rocks into the Capilano River below, and the sprinkling of moisture was a welcome and cooling relief as it pinpricked my cheeks on such a humid night. Roland found a park bench in a quiet spot, with nothing but woods and wind behind us. I was a bit hesitant as we sat down since there had already been enough surprises, but I got the feeling that listening to her would be worth my while.

"Isn't this better?" asked Roland, as a cherubic-faced kid holding his mother's hand and a cone of cotton candy walked by. Substitute a banana milkshake and subtract twenty years and it was like catching a glimpse of my late mother and me.

"It'll do," I replied. "I have questions. A lot of them."

"I figured as much."

"Do you regularly disguise your voice?"

"Depends on the case, but I can tell you why I did for this one—Cullen is not a person whose radar you want to be on. Unfortunately for you, I'm afraid that ship has sailed."

"Thanks for the hot tip, Murphy Brown."

"Do you even know who you've been messing with, Ounstead?"

"You mean the ex-commando turned combat kingpin. One who would just as easily throw a jab as slit my throat because I was hired to find an ex-UFC fighter's missing championship belt? No, not at all. What have I missed?"

Roland chuckled. "You know, for a guy who breaks two-by-fours over his head on a regular basis, you're a lot smarter than you look."

"That's high praise, but why were you really staking out McIntyre's place?"

"When I got word of his murder, I knew something was up, and the apartment seemed like a good place to start. I just didn't expect you of all people to enter the fray. And that bullshit with the milkshake cup? I heard about that from one of my confidential VPD sources. Cassian is setting you up."

"I'm well aware of that. But why were you even sniffing around in the first place?"

"Because of Elijah."

"He contacted you?"

"He *confided* in me. Wanted Cassian gone. We were working on an exposé to take down Cullen and his fight club once and for all."

"How?"

"You have your former client to thank for that. Besides, after what he told me about Cripps, well, let's just say I was heavily invested in making sure justice was served."

"I've been running myself ragged trying to figure out the link between Lennox and Cripps. And you're telling me that you know what it is?"

Roland nodded. "They had a fight. On a rooftop."

"Lennox and Cripps?"

"Yes. Elijah regretted it, but he had been so stressed and stir-crazy with expanding his business that when he got word of Cassian's club he couldn't resist an invitation. And Cullen desperately wanted to beef up his roster of fighters with a celebrity. Elijah once told me, '*Going toe-to-toe with an opponent makes things simple. There's no distractions, no miscommunication, just combat. Pure and simple.*' He loved it. He missed it. But he still fought with honour. He was a good man."

"How do you know that?"

"Because he was racked with guilt over what happened to Jerry Cripps."

"You mean putting him into a coma?"

"No. I mean not doing enough to stop it."

I leaned back on the bench and absorbed Roland's revelation. Things were starting to fall into place. "Stop it?"

She leaned forward and put her elbows on her knees. "Apparently Cassian has a real hard-on about fights ending with one combatant either unconscious or incapacitated. I guess that was how it went when he was fighting for his life in Afghanistan."

"Yeah. I deduced as much," I said.

"Elijah told me he had a surprisingly challenging fight against Cripps, who managed to get in a few good licks of his own on the former UFC champ. Elijah lost his temper and went off on Cripps, but backed down after he knocked him clean off of his feet. Cassian ordered Elijah to finish him, but he refused. Cullen did not like that. Not one bit."

"So Lennox didn't put Cripps into a coma?"

Roland shook her head. "Not even close. Elijah had already stepped aside when Cassian stormed over and delivered a couple of piledriver-style right hands to Cripps's swollen face, the last of which knocked him out so cold apparently the poor bastard now has brain damage and may never wake up again."

"So *that's* why Lennox staged the theft of his belt."

"Yep. He was cash poor from opening more gyms and it was killing him that he played a role in Cripps's fate. The insurance money for the belt was supposed to go to Cripps's wife and children. It was Elijah's penance, until you went and screwed it up."

"By doing my job?"

Roland shrugged. "He just never expected you to retrieve the damn thing."

"Had I known what was going on, I wouldn't have."

"It was around this time when Elijah reached out to me. He wanted to take Cassian down. Bad. He was sick to his stomach that he had let his post-career melancholy get the better of him. He just wanted to make things right."

"Did Cassian learn that he was speaking to you?"

Roland sighed. "I think, maybe, yeah. I don't know how exactly, and thankfully Cullen doesn't seem to know of me specifically or that I was in cahoots with Elijah. The only thing I'm certain of is that the determined man who reached out to me never would have taken his own life."

I nodded. "So that's why Cassian had Elijah murdered and staged as a suicide. To shut him up and prevent exposure."

"Looks that way."

I leaned back on the bench and ran my fingers through my hair. "Cripps. Lennox. But why McIntyre?"

"Because he tried to pick up where Lennox left off."

"And Cassian found out. He took them out, one by one. And he's just going to keep leaving bodies in his wake."

"Unless we can stop him," said Roland.

"You said you were working on an exposé with Elijah and later McIntyre. What do you have?"

Roland huffed and crossed her legs. "Jack shit."

"Nothing at all?"

"I'm afraid not. Look, I know all about you, Ounstead. Even wrote a few pieces about your exploits. But Cullen isn't some grandiose narcissist like Hector Spector or a knucklehead like one of those bikers—he's devious, detached, and deadly. A guy like Cassian doesn't make mistakes. All I've got are some audiotapes of Elijah and McIntyre spewing theories and conjecture. There's no meat on the bone. Just hearsay."

"So how do we take him down?" I asked.

Kate Roland shrugged. "I don't know. You're kind of my last hope."

"How's that?"

"Given your history I thought perhaps you might have dug something up on Cullen that I could run with. My paper won't print anything without facts to back it up, regardless of Elijah and McIntyre's eagerness to talk."

I rubbed my face in my hands. "Look, Roland, if you're the real deal, then what the hell took you so long to reach out to me? I've been driving myself nuts trying to figure out what went down between Lennox and Cripps and Cassian's club to no avail."

"Hey, I'm here now, aren't I? What can you do for me?"

I silenced her with a look. "I think you mean what can I do for them." She nodded in silent agreement but stayed quiet, waiting for me to speak. "Cassian almost killed me the last time we tangled, but I suppose I could take another run at him."

"You're not going to outwit him or get him to fall for some parlour trick like a recorded confession. He's not Hector Spector. He's too crafty and smart."

The thought of my old nemesis Hector rotting in a jail cell while he awaited trial for a variety of charges that he had no chance of beating almost brought a smile to my face.

"You're right about Cassian. But I owe it to Elijah, and his mother, to at least try."

"His mother?"

"She's my client. Hired me to find proof that Elijah didn't off himself."

"Jesus," muttered Roland. "Forget what I said. Cullen has us beat. It might be best for both of us to just walk away while we still can."

"You should have led with that before telling me that Cassian put Cripps into a coma and confirmed he was responsible for Elijah's death."

"Why?"

"Because I *can't* let that stand."

"Is it worth that much to you?"

"What's the alternative? Quit so Cassian can continue to brutalize and kill more people at will? No. He has to go down. And at this point, it looks like I'm the only one left who can do it."

A pack of giggling teenagers walked by, making crass jokes and generally acting obnoxious. Roland and I waited for them to pass before resuming. She sat forward on the bench and turned to face me.

"If you do this, and if you can get me something concrete, I give you my word I'll bury the son of a bitch. My editor is absolutely chomping at the bit for this story. He just can't publish anything that's so paper thin."

"I hear you."

"Any ideas on where you're going to start?"

I nodded. "I need to find out when the next meeting of Cassian's vicious fight club is taking place."

"That, I think, I can help you with," she said, smiling.

FORTY-SEVEN

If Declan was surprised to find me searching through the escort ads in *The Georgia Straight* newspaper then he certainly didn't show it.

I was at the bar of the Emerald Shillelagh, which was quieter than usual since my cousin had shut down the karaoke machine for the night. I enjoyed the muted environment as I double-fisted a pint of Guinness and large DQ banana milkshake topped up with Torani Crème De Banana Syrup in between circling the adverts that caught my eye with a red pen—although I was doing so for a very specific reason.

I jabbed a thumb into the tightening waistband of my cargo shorts, and for the first time considered that the sugar content of my newly beloved Italian syrup might be throwing my already dairy-heavy metabolism out of whack. It suddenly occurred to me that I might have let my sugar-and-banana-loving taste buds get the better of me.

Roland had explained to me how Cassian stealthily advertised his upcoming fight clubs through disguised escort ads in *The Georgia Straight*, Vancouver's premiere news and entertainment guide for all things music, arts, and … nightlife. It was an under-the-radar measure, but also gave the combatants and invited clientele a notice that was for their eyes only. Leave it to yuppies to get off seeing what a real fight was like without getting their hands dirty.

"Don't waste yer time with Elegant Emma, Mate," said my cousin, interrupting my thoughts and tapping the black-and-white paper in front of me.

"What?"

"She's too mechanical. Not to mention that she's paler than a banshee an' just sort o'lies there while ya do yer business. Dazzlin' melons, though."

"I'm not looking for a—"

"Zip it. I know me brassers, Boyo."

I sighed and sipped my Guinness, without bothering to explain to my cousin why I was looking at the ads. Eventually, I found what I thought was the one—an advertisement by an escort by the name of "Cassie," who had a distinctive way of trying to lure clients. "Cassie" mentioned in her ad that she preferred in-person interactions, specializing in "incall" meetings over "outcalls," and that her upcoming location for appointments this week would offer "high-altitude insight" during the hours of midnight and two AM this coming Friday.

Insight.

The capacity to gain an accurate and deep understanding of someone or something.

Which sounded a lot like the preachy, high-horse bullshit Cassian slung when trying to romanticize two guys fighting each other on a rooftop to the point of incapacity or death. Battles that took place exclusively in and around the Downtown Eastside.

Insight.

Of course! I felt like an idiot for not seeing it sooner. Insight—spelled *InSite*—was also the name of Vancouver's safe injection site for drug addicts. This service just happened to be located

in the core of Vancouver's famously downtrodden neighbourhood, only a stone's throw from The Emerald Shillelagh. Toss
in the "high altitude" reference and that the phone number in
the ad matched the one Roland had received from Lennox and
McIntyre, and it was pretty clear the next location for a night
of combat would be taking place on the rooftop of the InSite
building. I circled the ad several times before placing my pen on
the bar and finishing my milkshake. My cousin sauntered his
way back toward me.

"Let me set yer sexy arse up with Curvy Camilla. She's a
redheaded doll, kind o'got some chompers on her, but is still a
looker an' has a delightfully effervescent personality."

"Chompers?"

"Aye, ya know, big teeth. But trust me, a little friction is a
good thing. Plus, she's got a killer dragon tattoo on her back as
well, which looks wild when you're ... well, ya know."

"I'm not on the prowl for a prostitute, D," I said, exasperated.

"C'mon, Cuz, let's both have a go at the same bird."

"Gross! I pass."

"Ah, don' get yer knickers in a twist. Although with Camilla,
that is on the menu ..."

"I got this, okay?"

"Fair enough, Mate."

A hint of lemon wafted into the pub as the door chime
announced someone entering, and I did a double take, for it was
not the scent of the perfume to which I had become accustomed.
Detective Constable Rya Shepard pulled up a bar stool next to me
and we sat in silence until Declan served her an ice-cold, vodka
martini with three olives. I raised what was left of my Guinness
and we toasted.

"Shaking up the fragrances, eh, Detective?" I asked.

"Oh, it's still Burberry. Just going with a new scent."

"Let me guess. Lemon Delight?"

"London Dream."

"Close enough," I said, before taking a big pull of my Guinness. With the pleasantries over, Rya got down to business, and Declan knew to keep his distance despite keeping an eye on us.

"I'm sorry about what went down the other day," she said bluntly.

"Thank you. But you were just doing your job."

"Jed, you're like my brother. I know you better than you know yourself. Of course the charge was bullshit and Cassian set you up. But when your fingerprints came in on the Dairy Queen cup, Cornish was all over my ass, and I didn't have a choice. I thought it would be better for everyone if I brought you in."

"Your *brother*?" I asked, unable to hide the disappointment in my voice.

Rya smirked. "Yeah, sort of. Why, what's wrong with that?"

I shrugged. "I guess I was hoping you thought of me more like a distant cousin where both parties might look the other way before taking a chance on one another."

Rya chuckled despite herself. "Let's go with that then," she said, patting my hand and giving it a loving squeeze. It was the happiest I had felt since Cassian nearly killed me.

"You know I love your big, dumb ass, right?" she asked.

I looked her in the eyes and tried not to give into the swell of emotions that were consuming me. "I do. And I love you too, Rya. Always have." I caught Declan's eye down the bar. He beamed while he wiped down the sticky countertop, before winking at me and pumping his fist in the air.

"And is Ms. Danielson okay with that?" she asked, cagily.

"Not sure. We broke up."

"I'm sorry," she said softly. After a few moments, Rya kissed me on a stubbly cheek, causing my heart to flutter. Like all good things, the hand-holding came to an end and she returned to her hard-nosed form, sipping her martini, determined to address whatever issue had brought her into the Shillelagh on a weeknight near closing time.

"Look, Jed. Unless something changes, things with the VPD are going to progress. I'm concerned this murder charge is going to stick."

"Bullshit."

"There's no other suspect or evidence. Just your fingerprints on the cup, which, I'm sorry, in your case may as well be the same as leaving your driver's licence at the scene. Factor in a witness willing to go on record that you returned to the scene of the crime while apparently trying to pass yourself off as a cop—it paints a pretty damning picture."

"McIntyre tried to stop Cullen before he kicked me off a building! Why would I want him dead?"

"I'm just telling you the optics aren't good on this one. And Cornish is on a mission to take revenge on you and your father, and he sees this as his golden ticket. Frank has some serious influence, but he can only buy you so much time, and the clock is ticking."

"So Cassian just gets to walk and keep rubbing out those who get in his way?"

Rya sighed. "You have to let this one go. Cullen's different from anyone you've gone up against before. You can't go toe-to-toe with him. I mean, look what's already happened. He's gotten the better of you every step of the way."

"Yeah," I muttered, finishing my Guinness. Declan appeared out of nowhere and swapped out my empty glass with a fresh pint without so much as a peep, which for him was quite an accomplishment.

"I know what you're like. If you keep going after Cullen, it's going to end ugly. I'm begging you, Jed. Walk away. Walk away and clear your name."

"How am I supposed to clear my name if I'm avoiding the guy who set me up?"

"I don't know. You'll think of something."

"Easier said than done, Rya."

We sat in silence nursing our drinks.

"Remember what I warned you about?" she finally asked.

"What?"

"That you can't be judge, jury, and executioner. It's a slippery slope that comes with a price you don't want to pay."

"And you have?"

Rya stook a big sip of her martini and bit an olive off the plastic spear in her cocktail. "Let's just say I've seen enough good cops fall victim to similar pressures. It's not worth it. And you're better than that."

"Am I, Rya?"

"How can you ask me such a question?"

"I never knew what my life was lacking until I met Johnny Mamba in a Dairy Queen a year ago and he asked me to find his kidnapped snake. Nothing—and I mean *nothing*—has ever given me more purpose than what I do for the people who come to me for help. Making my old man proud? Keeping up with Declan? Entertaining millions of people with my wrestling? It's all small potatoes compared to the feeling I get while working as a private investigator."

"You sound like you have a messiah complex."

I chuckled. "Perhaps I do. All I know is that I'm good at this, Rya. Really good. And I can make a difference," I said, thinking of my satisfied former clients and the promise I had made to my paralyzed former tag-team partner. "It makes it all worth it."

"Would you still say that if you wound up in prison?"

"Not sure. All I know is I finally found what I'm supposed to do with my life."

"Then don't screw it up. I know you're pissed about Lennox and his fishy *suicide*. But rather than hyperfocus on him and his mother, think of all the people you won't be able to help if you're sidelined. It's a numbers game, Jed. Your best work is still ahead of you."

"Yeah," I muttered weakly. "Maybe."

Rya downed the rest of her martini and reached for her purse.

"Don't," I cautioned, as Declan shook his head furiously from down the bar.

Rya stood and hugged me tightly from behind. "Please do the right thing, Jed."

I patted Rya's arm, and just like that, she was out the door and gone into the night. I sipped my Guinness, then Declan reappeared.

"I've been givin' things some serious thought, Laddie." He sighed deeply, like the weight of the world was on his shoulders. "This'll solve all yer problems."

He slid a folded piece of paper across the bar top toward me. I unfolded it and read what he had scribbled—a phone number underneath the name *"Mistress Tiffany."* I looked up at him confused.

"She's athletic as shite an' a bit o'a dom, so there'll be a wee bit o'spankin' before ya get into the sexy time. But Tiff will break you in proper until ya get enough experience under yer belt. I even went to the trouble o'settin' up a safe word for ya."

I rolled my eyes and rubbed my face, exhausted with my cousin.

"Rugger-Bugger," he said deviously.

"I don't know what that means and am not inclined to find out."

Our conversation was interrupted by the arrival of Melvin Van Lowe, dressed in his usual leather blazer, button-down shirt with skinny tie, and jeans. He approached carrying a small, black, hard-shell plastic box with a handle and pulled up a bar stool next to me.

Declan shot Melvin the stink-eye before glancing at me. I gave an approving nod. My cousin fixed him a glass of Jack and Coke and slung it down the bar top like a saloon bartender in a B-movie Western. Melvin caught the drink and downed half of it in a single gulp.

"Here," he said, placing the black box in front of me. "Do I even want to know what you need this for?"

I folded up *The Georgia Straight* newspaper and enjoyed a sip of my pint. "Probably not."

"Good," replied Melvin. "That way, if asked, I don't have to lie."

Declan couldn't take any more suspense while he stood drying Rya's martini glass with a dishtowel. "What's this poxy bollocks brought over here?" he asked, nodding toward the black box. Melvin scrunched his pointy nose at the barb but let it lie.

"I'll tell you later," I replied.

"Ah, piss off with that, already. I'm gettin' antsy, Jed. An' with yer arse in the VPD's crosshairs, well, I'd say it's high time you asked me for some real help with this case."

"I agree. And trust me, D. You're going to like this particular request."

Declan grinned from ear to ear. "Fuckin' deadly."

FORTY- EIGHT

Even from fifty feet away, I didn't need binoculars to see the pearly whites arcing through the air and showering down upon the rooftop like blood-stained ivory raindrops. The unfortunate fighter on the receiving end of the vicious right-handed hook spun around, his eyes rolling back in his head, before he face planted hard on the unforgiving terrain. The fighter left standing pumped his arms in the air victoriously. He was rewarded with whistles and cheers from his fellow fighters and a pack of drunken, disreputable spectators, as well as a supportive pat on his sweaty trapezius by none other than Cassian Cullen himself. The monstrous ex-soldier who had framed me for murder beamed with joy, positively thrilled by the violent scene that had just unfolded.

Mr. F, AKA Ferdinand, hobbled on his prosthetic leg to pay out those who had bet on the bout's winner. The remaining fighters congratulated the victor and dragged the loser to his feet. One of his fellow pugilists scooped up his front teeth before helping him off of the premises in a much gentler and kinder way than I had been shown. This fight was the last of the night, and

everyone on the rooftop began to make their way down the fire
escape leading to the alley below. InSite's twenty-four-hour safe
drug injection site on the ground floor of the five-storey building
meant this Downtown Eastside area was still witness to some
activity, despite the late hour.

I pulled out my phone and made the call. Cassian looked at
his mobile curiously, then answered.

"Cullen," he said.

"You know, you need a good nickname. After all, 'Hammerhead' has served me pretty well over the years. I'm thinking something like *Chrome Dome* or *Clumpy*. Alliterations are always good."

"Ounstead?"

"Yeah. Sorry, Pal, but I'm not rotting away in prison. Not
yet, anyway."

"How did you get this number?"

"The writing on the bathroom stall door said to call for a
good time."

Cassian cursed while I resisted a smirk, grateful Roland had
shared the number with me. It was also nice to have the bald
behemoth on the defensive for once.

"What do you want?" he snarled, turning around and pressing
his phone closer to his ear while the remaining fighters and fans
departed from the rooftop.

"To settle things between us. Once and for all."

"And why would I do that?"

"Because I have something you want."

Cassian laughed. "Bullshit."

"You sure about that? Look left, Asshole." Cassian, who was
now alone, except for Ferdinand, turned to face me. I was on the
rooftop directly across from him, a floor or two below, but had
the goods I knew he would want.

"Tell Ferdinand to take a hike," I said. I stood on the edge of
the building and waited until Cassian spotted me and dismissed
his partner. Once Ferdinand was gone and I was in Cassian's line

of sight, I took off the necklace I was wearing and held it up in the humid night air. Hanging from the chain were two custom made dog tags, which read "John Edward Ounstead."

"Had them made just for you," I said.

Cassian grinned despite himself. "Well played," he said, lovingly stroking his own necklace. "Those tags are mine."

"Try and take them," I replied, placing my tags back around my neck. I made my way down to the ground, walked over to the *InSite* building and climbed up the fire escape. Once on the rooftop, I approached Cassian and was within fifteen feet when he held up a giant hand.

"Stop right there," he commanded. "You wired?" I lifted my sweat-wicking T-shirt and turned around, offering proof I wasn't recording anything. Cassian nodded toward the extra inch that had recently appeared around my midsection. "I think all of those milkshakes might be catching up with you."

"Damn Italians," I muttered, pulling my shirt back down.

"What?"

"It's a long story. The gist is you shouldn't mess with a good thing. And that's what we both did. Me with giving into newly discovered calorie-bomb banana milkshakes, and you with punching people into comas, staging suicides, and committing murder."

Cassian glared at me. "I'm going to frisk you now."

"Have at it, Bub. But try not to get too worked up when you pat down my glutes. I did a killer set of squats today so they're probably tight as hell."

Cassian shook his head. "You got a fucking mouth on you, that's for sure."

"I was known to rock the mic back in my wrestling heyday."

Cassian followed through. He approached me cautiously before patting me down. After a good twenty seconds or so he seemed certain I wasn't wearing a recording device or carrying any weapons on my person. He took a step back. "You're clean."

"Told you so."

"I'm not stupid, Ounstead. You've done well for yourself in the past, but I warned you that I'm not some troglodyte, like one of the Steel Gods, or a moronic bloviating egomaniac like Spector who can be duped."

I nodded. "You're a formidable foe, Cassian. I'll give you that. But you do have one thing in common with them."

"Really?"

"Yep."

"And that would be?"

"You all made the mistake of underestimating me."

With that, and nary a moment's hesitation, I sprang forward, took a few running steps, leapt into the air, and delivered the most vicious Superman punch of my life. Cassian's head snapped back and he spat blood toward the full moon as he stumbled. Regardless of how things were about to play out, I mercilessly struck hard and struck first. The bastard deserved it.

Cassian dabbed the blood from the corner of his lip with his thumb, licked it, then smiled like Hannibal Lecter hosting a dinner party. "Impressive," he said.

"Let's go, Gigantor. I've been waiting for this."

"I'll bet you have," he replied, coming at me with more rage than that of a bull charging a matador's red cape.

Cassian caught me off guard with a succession of blows to my solar plexus that were so devastating I could barely breathe. I fell onto my back, clutching my midsection and gasping for air. Although he had gotten the upper hand, his punches had been focused on my core. Cassian hadn't realised that my ribs were still injured.

"Underestimated you, eh?" crowed Cassian, as he towered above me. "A well-timed sucker punch isn't a victory, you arrogant prick."

I started laughing.

"What's so funny?"

"You don't even know how hard you're going down tonight. That's what's funny."

"Get over yourself, Ounstead. I'm stronger than you. I'm tougher than you. And most importantly, I'm smarter than you. If you had anything at all on me, your VPD pals would be swarming this rooftop. But you don't. And you never will."

I leapt to my feet and stomped on the instep of Cassian's right foot, causing his ankle to wobble and the big man to stagger backwards. I tried to capitalize on the moment and put all my strength into an overhand right—which he managed to catch in the palm of one of his monstrous mitts. I was overcome with déjà-vu, a flashback to the parking lot of the Arms Pub in Port Coquitlam, where I defended Wally Fitzgibbons from his tormentor T-Money.

With the tables turned against me, Cassian tried to torque my fist downwards, but I fought back with every ounce of strength I had. As the stalemate continued, the Man-Beast stared down his nose at me, his facial expression an equal medley of fury and disbelief of my against-all-odds resilience.

I met Cassian's eyes as we both grunted, our arms trembling as we each tried to dominate the other and win this feat of strength. The standoff was cut short when Cassian threw a vicious left hook into my injured ribs, sending shockwaves of pain so intense throughout my body I collapsed to my knees.

"Weak spot," taunted Cassian, before delivering two additional left-handed hooks into my throbbing rib cage. If the already injured bones audibly cracked or broke some more, I couldn't hear it over the sound of my anguished screams. I let go of whatever supernatural strength I had been channelling into my fist and rolled belly up onto my back in the most pathetic and submissive way possible.

Cassian released my fist and snorted, pacing back and forth in front of me like a caged animal.

"You can't win," he said.

I struggled to breathe as I writhed in pain on the concrete, clutching my side and praying the searing agony would subside.

"But that doesn't mean this has to be the end, Ounstead."

I managed to sit up and muster a response. "What?"

Cassian kneeled in front of me. He lifted the custom dog tags hanging around my neck and jingled them in his hand.

"What if I told you I had a proposition for you?"

"I'd tell you …" I muttered, "to stick it where the sun don't shine."

"Of course you would," he replied, bemused.

"I … I've got a proposal for you, Cassian."

"Is that right?" he said smugly.

I cleared my throat and composed myself. "Would you like me to teach you about the Five Moves of Doom?"

"What?

A split second later I grabbed a handful of the crewneck collar of his black T-shirt, yanked it forward, and drove the top of my head as hard as I could into Cassian's face. I couldn't help but smile at the sound of the cartilage in his nose crunching. He bellowed in pain and tottered backwards, spewing out the blood from his nose across the rooftop, but he remained upright. Without missing a beat, I got back up and slipped into my old end-of-match, pro-wrestling routine. Except there was no pulling of punches this time around.

I followed up with two right-handed haymakers that clocked him twice on the jaw. Cassian teetered and swung his arms wildly in an effort to regain his balance. The space that opened up between us allowed me to shift into a three-point football stance. A moment later I charged forward like Usain Bolt with rockets strapped to my shoes. I took three powerful strides before launching myself horizontally into the air and used my right shoulder to spear Cassian's sternum with such force it knocked the giant man clean off his feet. He hit the concrete hard.

I heard Cassian moan in pain for the first time ever. With a hand clutching my ribs, I limped over toward him, until I was the one towering above.

"You … fucker," he wheezed at me.

"And then some," I replied.

I wrapped my right arm around Cassian's neck, pulled him upright, held on tightly, then dropped him to the concrete with my patented "Hammerlock DDT."

There was a stomach-churning crack as his head hit the ground. Cassian's forehead split open and started hemorrhaging even more blood than his nose. He groaned before crawling away until he was able to prop himself up against the rooftop's low protective wall. I approached him warily.

"Five Moves of Doom, eh?"

I looked down at the defeated man who had done the same to so many others. "I didn't want this, Cassian. But you left me no choice."

Cassian dug a hand into the pocket of his jeans, pulled out a lighter and a pack of cigarettes, slipped one in between his lips, and lit it.

"Okay, Ounstead. You win."

"What exactly did I win? You put Jerry Cripps into a coma. You destroyed his family to the point that Elijah Lennox was so racked with guilt he tried to con an insurance company out of a payout for a championship belt that was never stolen. All so he could give the settlement money to Cripps's wife and kids. Then you killed my client, faked his suicide, and murdered Reggie McIntyre to boot because he and Elijah were going to rat you out to the press."

"I don't know what on earth you're talking about," he said, with the corners of his lips slightly curled and a defiant glimmer in his eyes.

"I've run up against some evil bastards in my time, but you, Cassian, you take the prize."

Cassian lost whatever composure he had mustered. "They were pussies! Cripps was a little bitch. And I gave the other two a chance to reclaim what they once were. Fighters. Warriors. Champions. And they repaid me with betrayal! No, they all had it coming."

I shook my head, disturbed by the brutish bully's logic. "There's just one thing I don't understand. Why frame me for McIntyre's murder? Why not just take me out?"

Cassian smiled and took a long drag of his cigarette. "This is going to make you laugh. You want to know why?"

"I do."

"Because I like you, Ounstead."

"So what? You want to be friends?"

"Not necessarily. I just respect the fact you took a beating so bad—worse than pretty much any I've ever given or seen doled out—and yet you came right back at me. I don't see a lot of that."

"You're going to make me blush."

"Heh. So what now, Tough Guy?"

"Excuse me?"

"What is it your buddy says? *'To be the man, you need to beat the man?'*"

"Busting out the Ric Flair quotes. I'm impressed."

"Good. Then you can show your appreciation by telling me your plan."

"My plan?"

"That's right," he said, taking another drag from his cigarette which was now coloured with little red specks of blood. "You gonna call your daddy or your lady-cop friend? Try and drag the VPD into this? Whatever you attempt to spin won't stick."

My blood boiled at the mere thought that Cassian knew about my connection with Rya and that he would even indirectly threaten her safety.

"Face it. You got nothing on me," he said, chuckling.

I nodded. "You're right. But I can't let this stand."

"What are you going to do? Take me out? You don't have the balls."

"You know, someone once warned me about becoming judge, jury, and executioner. But at this point, I don't see an alternative."

"I do. Join me. Become part of this."

"What?"

"Think about it. Pooling our connections. Our mutual ability to put down anyone who gets in our way. My intelligence combined with your resourcefulness. We'd be unstoppable."

"If you wanted to partner up then why frame me for murder?"

Cassian smiled. "I guess I wanted to see what you'd do. And you didn't let me down," he said, as his Herculean body remained spread out across the rooftop. "You might not like me, Ounstead, but we could accomplish great things together. This city could be ours."

"I like the city the way it is."

"Then you're signing your death warrant."

"Right. Because if I don't do things your way, I'll be looking over my shoulder the rest of my life."

"You're not as dumb as you look."

"I'm sorry it's come to this."

"Think, Ounstead. You don't have it in you. Even when you took down the Steel Gods it was in self-defence and to save your father. You won't kill me."

"That's where you're wrong."

"Bullshit. If you were *really* planning to kill me, then why would you bother throwing down against me in the first place?"

I stood there on the rooftop while Cassian and I stared long and hard at each other. Eventually I answered.

"Because I had to know. You're right about one thing. I may not have the balls to pull the trigger myself. But I do to make this call." I touched Melvin's small, field ops communication unit in my ear. "*Take the shot.*" Cassian's eyes grew wide as saucers as a red laser dot appeared above his heart.

"*No!*" he pleaded. "*Wait!*"

I tapped the comm unit in my ear. "*Do it.*"

"*Thhhhwwwhack!*"

The hollow-point bullet ripped through Cassian's chest, leaving nothing behind but a whisper in the night and a red mist floating in the air. His hand went limp and hit the pavement, and I watched the glowing embers at the tip of his cigarette slowly go out. I gave a quick salute to Declan, who was on the adjacent rooftop across the street. He returned the gesture before packing up his sniper rifle and disappearing into the darkness. I stood over Cassian's body as it slowly exhaled a final breath. Once he was dead, I reached down, wrapped my hand around his chain of dog tags, and ripped it from his thick, tattooed neck.

"You don't deserve these," I muttered. I tucked his trophies into my pocket, then clambered down from the rooftop into the back alley, where Declan was waiting in a stolen sedan. How or where he procured it, I didn't ask. I jumped in, and with no one watching, we zoomed off into the night, leaving behind the corpse of a dangerous and deadly killer, one we knew would never be brought to justice by traditional means. Unfortunately, that justification did little to sugar-coat the fact that I had just knowingly—and willingly—crossed a line and become an assassin.

FORTY-NINE

Fading moonlight shimmered off the dark plumes of the great blue heron as the bird repeatedly stretched its S-shaped neck to use its sharp, yellow-orange beak to stab the belly of an over-turned crab on the shoreline. The small crustacean's legs flailed in all directions as the waterfowl strategically pierced the soft underside of the arthropod until it succumbed to its wounds and stopped moving. The heron went about snacking on its oceanside prey, a creature that was helpless and vulnerable once the largest wading bird in North America had conquered it by flipping it on its back and marking it for death.

I took a sip of my ice-cold Steam Whistle Pilsner and looked away. Ambleside Park was a beautiful, gateway destination to West Vancouver. During daytime hours, the park was a bustling public venue, with locals enjoying the skatepark, tennis courts, multiple trails, and pier. I had waited at the foot of 13th Street while Declan dumped the stolen sedan before returning in his Pontiac GTO. I hopped in and we drove into the park until my cousin found a spot for his car. He hoisted his mobile cooler and led the way toward a particular tribute bench that overlooked both the Pacific Ocean and the affluent waterfront community across the bay. West Vancouver's lights sparkled in the darkness, but I couldn't keep my gaze off of the equally illuminated Lions Gate Bridge on the horizon.

Declan placed an empty bottle in his cooler and replaced it with a fresh pilsner. He used his hand to pop the cap off of the beer and took a swig, despite the fact I was almost certain it wasn't a twist off. "'Tis a hell o'a site, Mate, I agree, but there's much more beauty to take in round here other than that sparkly glob o'concrete."

"It's not the lights, D. Although they are stunning."

"So what is it then?"

I took another sip of my beer. "That's where it all started."

"The Lions Gate?"

I nodded.

"Ya mean it's where—"

"I took a bunch of lives for the first time."

"Ah, shite on a shillelagh."

"Don't talk that way about the pub."

"I ain't. I said 'shite on a shillelagh' not 'the Shillelagh.'"

"Why?"

"Cuz I knew this wistful regret was comin' the moment ya pitched me yer grand plan for tonight."

I tore my gaze away from the bridge and looked at my cousin. "I get that you're cagey when it comes to your past and your time in the IRA, D. But I'm pretty confident you didn't do anything tonight that you haven't done before."

My cousin stifled a burp and sniffed. "Aye."

"Cassian was right, you know. Taking out those bikers on that bridge," I said, nodding toward the Lions Gate, "it was self-defence. And Pop's life hung in the balance."

"An' how many lives do ya think we saved tonight cuz we had the grit to do to Cullen what some bloke should o'already done a long time ago?"

"A handful at least. Maybe more."

"A lot more. Let me see that necklace o'his."

I retrieved Cassian's combat trophies from my pocket and handed them to Declan, who thumbed through the dog tags.

"Each one o'these tags was a life, Jed. A life that bastard took. An' he was bloody well proud of it. He'd developed a taste for it. I can only imagine the kind o'shite he saw over there in Afghanistan. But somewhere along the line he let a demon get a hold o'him. An' once ya let that kind o'darkness in—no matter how ya justify it—well, it becomes a part o'ya."

"So what makes us any different?"

"A lot, Boyo."

"Yeah. For now." We both finished our beers and swapped them out for more. This time we shared a bottle opener. "In all your time doing ... the things you've done. Did a demon ever get a hold of you?" I asked.

Declan stared at the tags in his hands for a long time before closing his fist around them. "Almost," he said solemnly.

"What stopped it?"

My cousin cleared his throat and took another sip of pilsner. "That's a tale for another time."

"So how do I know something sinister isn't working its way into me?"

"Did ya take pleasure in what we did tonight?"

I thought long and hard before answering. "Kicking his ass. Reclaiming my pride. Yes, I took pleasure in that. But having him killed? Not so much."

"Then there ya go."

"I did feel something though. The moment he died."

"What?"

"I don't know. A tinge of relief? Maybe even satisfaction?"

"Aye. As ya should. We did a good thing tonight, Jed."

"Did we? How many lives saved makes assassinating a defeated man like that okay? Where's the line between him and us?" I pounded half my beer and sighed. "Rya was right. It is a slippery slope."

Declan threw an arm around my shoulder and pulled me close. "Then it's a good thing I'm right by yer side, always ready to pull yer arse back if ya start to slide a wee bit too far."

I smiled. "Yes. I guess it is."

We clinked our bottles and sat there in silence until the moon was gone and the sky slowly began to lighten into gorgeous hues of purple, pink, and orange. The Lions Gate Bridge, the shores, and the ocean itself were all soon enveloped in vivid and golden rays of sunshine.

It was a new day.

EPILOGUE

The fallout from Cassian Cullen's death was swift, although his body wasn't found for a couple of days. His giant corpse had bloated under the sizzling, late-September sun and left the area around the InSite building stinking to high heaven—a place the bastard certainly wasn't headed, if he even believed in an afterlife.

I laid low at home, not even bothering to visit the Shillelagh or the upstairs office. I figured I had earned the break. I hadn't spoken with Declan either, and out of caution, we dared not mention what we had done by either phone or text. I suppose justice had been served in the names of Elijah Lennox, Jerry Cripps, and Reggie McIntyre, but their lives were still over. I placed an anonymous call using a burner phone to the Vancouver General Hospital to inquire about Cripps. He was still comatose, and the doctors were all but certain he would be permanently brain damaged. His wife Lynette and his children had still not been by, and I hoped wherever they were they had found a modicum of peace. It was a shame that Lennox's plan to give them an insurance payout for his missing belt had been ruined thanks to me, but then again, how could I hold myself at fault?

Confidentiality goes a long way in the PI game, and Lennox could have let me know what his plan was. I assume his efforts to expose Cassian and his rooftop fight club with *Vancouver Sun* reporter Kate Roland may have stopped him from confiding in me, not to mention his suspicion that he had been found out and was in Cassian's crosshairs.

Roland called me the day after Cassian's body was found.

"We're going to print the exposé," she said.

"But you still have no evidence."

"I have the testimony of Lennox and McIntyre, and after Cullen, uh, mysteriously turned up dead, my editor gave the story the green light. It also helps that the VPD have cracked down on Ferdinand Gonzales and that he's cutting a deal for being witness to Cripps's assault and conspiring to plan the murders of Lennox and McIntyre. That clears your name. Turns out a regular fight club spectator came forward and incriminated Gonzales once the news broke about Cassian's death."

"That's good."

"Funny thing though. You know how Cullen was well known for wearing his necklace of dog tags that he pilfered from the men he killed?"

"I may have heard something about that."

"They were gone when the body was found."

I bit my tongue as I sat at my dining-room table, holding the dozen pairs of dog tags that bore names of Cassian's many victims.

"That's odd."

"Uh-huh. Well, the cops think Cullen may have been mixed up with the Russian mob. Apparently one of the regular gambling enthusiasts at Cassian's fight club had mob contacts, and the execution-style killing was so precise, they think it was done by a professional."

"Looks that way. Say, Roland?"

"Yeah?"

"Can you do me a favour?"

"Name it."

"Can you contact Elijah's mother, Alma Lennox? Share the news that her boy didn't take his own life, and that Cassian killed him?"

"Okay, sure."

"Thank you. I just … I can't deal with that right now."

"I understand. Take care, Ounstead. And stay safe."

"You as well."

I clicked off the phone and knew without a doubt that Roland was no dummy. She had pieced it together, but apparently saw no reason to drag my name into it. Had Gonzales put me at the scene that night? It didn't look that way, but even if he could, he wasn't pointing the finger at me. It figures that the last thing he wants is to be on the radar of the man who had killed his boss. Regardless, Roland could now publish her story and do right by Lennox and McIntyre. Something also told me that she wanted to stay on good terms, and that I might hear from her again. I would certainly be open to quid pro quo exchanges down the line. The woman had saved my life after all, or at least prevented me from another brutal beating with her well-timed call to McIntyre's apartment.

About a week after Cassian's death, I finally dragged myself into the Emerald Shillelagh. It was midday and the place was nearly empty, except for two regulars, a couple of elderly ladies who came in on Wednesdays to split a soup and sandwich and talk over half-pints of beer. I pulled up a seat at the bar, and waited for Declan to appear. He was helping a mover load the karaoke machine onto a dolly, before the man wheeled the device out of the pub. After the front doors closed, my cousin came around the bar and went about pouring us pints of the black stuff. If what we had done that night was bothering him at all, it was hard to tell, as he whistled the theme music from *For a Few Dollars More*.

"You seem chipper."

"Sorry, Mate. Been kind o'goin' down a Western movie rabbit hole of late. Bloody hell do I love the Man with No Name."

"So, we're done with all of that, then?" I asked, nodding at the empty makeshift stage that no longer featured the karaoke machine.

Declan shrugged. "Kind o'ran its course, I think."

I left it at that, but nonetheless wondered if the gravitas of our expedient action had influenced the removal of the attraction that had proved so popular over the summer.

"Is Pop around?"

"He's golfin' with some o'his cop buddies. But he gave me a message for ya."

"And that is?"

Declan cleared his throat and so faithfully imitated my old man at his gruffest that it was hard not to laugh.

"Ya did good, Boy. It was him or us. Now get me a Peanut Buster Parfait for Christ's sake."

I smiled, remembering the same cautionary words of advice my father had shared with me when he executed Steel Gods leader Damian Kendricks that fateful night on the Lion's Gate Bridge. Declan served the pints. We clinked glasses and drank deeply. I licked the foam from my upper lip and left Declan to replace the old ladies' beers while I took my Guinness and headed upstairs to the Ounstead & Son office.

Tossing my keys on the desk, I dug Cassian's dog tags out of my pocket, retrieved a handful of envelopes from a desk drawer, and began separating them. I was determined to ensure they made their way anonymously to families of some of the men Cassian had killed.

I was about halfway through sealing the envelopes when I had to scratch the itch that had been bothering at me since the night Declan and I took out Cassian. I called Rya's number, and like the dozen times before, it went straight to voicemail. I listened to her smooth voice, but still didn't have the courage to leave a message. She must certainly have known what I had done. She was also aware that I had completely disregarded her warnings and advice. I wasn't worried about her coming after me or turning me in. She may have even found the Russian mob theory a convenient one to believe in herself. But I was distraught thinking that I had, perhaps forever, lost the woman I cared for most. I leaned back in my chair with a sigh. I had pushed Stormy away, made a mess of things with Rya, and, to top it off, crossed a serious line from which there was no returning. Was it even worth it?

I thought about my old friend Johnny Mamba and how it felt like almost yesterday that we had met at a Dairy Queen where he had begged me for help to find his kidnapped snake. My life was a lot simpler when I was nothing more than a washed-up professional wrestler who had nothing better to do than get drunk with his cousin and bounce punks from bars. I had convinced myself that the liberties I took as a private investigator were always for the greater good, but was that still the case? I just didn't know anymore.

I sat there thinking long enough that the lack of any motion to trigger the sensors caused the lights to go out. I didn't move or stop reflecting on the past year of my life and what it had cost me. Not until the phone rang and interrupted my melancholic memories. I leaned forward in the chair, a movement that both caused my tender ribs to ache and reactivated the lights. I squinted through the sudden brightness for a few moments before answering the call.

"Ounstead & Son Investigations."

"Is this 'Hammerhead' Jed?" asked a panicked man's voice. "The wrestler-detective?"

"It is."

"Oh, thank goodness. My name is Dr. Lee Mortimer. I'm a marine biologist at the Vancouver Aquarium."

"How can I be of help, Dr. Mortimer?"

"I've got a big problem."

"Which is?"

"Someone is poisoning my sea lions."

I hesitated before responding. "You think that someone is purposely making your sea lions sick?"

"I don't think it. I know it. And I have proof. But the cops didn't take me seriously when I went to the station to file a report. I don't know what else to do and, uh, I've heard that you sort of specialize in these kinds of things. Can you help me?"

I slowly spun around in the chair and looked at the framed copy of my private investigator's licence mounted side by side with my father's on the wall behind the desk. After a few moments, I responded.

"That sounds like a hell of a case."

ACKNOWLEDGEMENTS

With a pandemic hitting right before the launch of the pre-vious "Hammerhead" Jed novel *Rolling Thunder*, having to pivot last minute to a virtual book tour, and trying to complete this 'threequel' in time to secure a 2022 release date—all while home-schooling my kids in a sudden new world of uncertainty—it's safe to say writing this story was one of the most challenging things I've ever done.

While I have plenty of ideas for future "Hammerhead" Jed adventures and can't wait to get to them, there was something special and satisfying about finishing *Five Moves of Doom* and completing a trilogy.

I must begin by thanking my amazing publisher NeWest Press and everyone on their incredible team including Christine Kohler, Carolina Ortiz, and Meredith Thompson for their business and marketing savvy. I made my perspicacious editor Merrill Distad work his keister off on this one, but he gave me the feed-back and push I needed. NeWest's ubiquitous Production and Marketing Coordinator Claire Kelly maintains her status as the hardest working person in publishing as far as I'm concerned, and without her prowess and patience this book would not have come to be. Last but not least, NeWest's brilliant General Manager Matt Bowes offered endless support and faith in both me and "Hammerhead" Jed, just like he has during my entire journey as an author. It is an absolute honour to be able to call these publishing stalwarts friends in addition to collaborators and to be a proud member of NeWest Press. And I would also like to express my great respect and gratitude to the late Douglas Barbour, the former President of NeWest Press whose decades-long vision of giving a voice to Canadian authors resulted not only in "Hammerhead" Jed finding a home but also my wildest dreams coming true.

Speaking of Team NeWest, this time around I was able to get early feedback from my fellow authors and writer bros for life Niall Howell and J.T. Siemens. Both of these talented gents helped make this novel so much better, and if you are looking for crime writing of the highest caliber be sure to pick up copies of their critically-acclaimed and award-nominated books *Only Pretty Damned* and *To Those Who Killed Me*. And I have to give a long overdue nod to the brilliant Michel Vrana, who created a eye-catching and distinctive style for all of the covers of the books in the "Hammerhead" Jed mystery-comedy series.

My friend Joel Johnston, retired Vancouver Police Officer Badge 1314, served as a law enforcement technical advisor for Jed's hijinks yet again. With his wealth of experience, superior combat training, and success as a published author himself, it's impossible to think of someone more perfectly suited to give guidance to a fictional pro-wrestler PI who gets tangled up in the world of mixed martial arts while working a case than him.

I also have to thank my friend, writer, marketing mentor, and promoter Bob Harris for his generosity, as well as my pro-wrestling pal, entertainment ally, and original GLOW girl and squared circle legend Jeanne "Hollywood" Basone, as well as MMA legend Gerry Gionco, whose wealth of knowledge about combat sports is second-to-none. I would also like to express my appreciation to Elaine Guille and Sheilagh Simpson for their much-appreciated feedback.

Crime Writers of Canada continues to be an amazing organization to be a part of, and my sincere gratitude to my pals Erik D'Souza, Winona Kent, and Ludvica Boota, as well as all CWC staff and members who helped me navigate launching my last book virtually during unusual times while working so hard to keep the passion for Canadian crime fiction alive.

Thank you to my pals Andrey Schmidt and Andrew Huzar for their counsel, as well as my bud and fiction fanatic Andrew Hay, who upon hearing my pitch for *Five Moves of Doom*, strongly suggested that I focus on Jed embracing his identity as a "grappler" and "wrestler" first and foremost, which helped me to clarify my protagonist's emotional arc.

Thank you to my former professor and Academy Award nominated screenwriter Anna Thomas, as well as the entire American Film Institute Conservatory Alumni network for always being willing to offer support to an AFI grad.

I've been overwhelmed by the outpouring of interest in this trilogy and would be remiss if I didn't take a moment to mention how thankful I am to everyone who has ever taken the time to get to know my banana milkshake loving sleuth, with a special shout out to superfans Ariel Pastorek (a tattoo aficionado who actually has "Hammerhead" Jed themed ink!), Dan Copeland, Geoff Boyd, Kent and Erin Lockhart, law enforcement officer Derek Cheng, Twitter stars @fredthealien316 and @Magskall, and future "Ice Hawk" Jack Donohue.

My lifelong best friend, proof-reading savant, and surrogate brother Sean O'Brien had my back yet again during the ups and downs of the last couple of years and without him in my corner I would not have had the strength to pull through and get this trio of adventures out there.

My deepest thanks to my family and friends, especially my son Jack and daughter Scarlett for understanding that while Dad's work might be a bit atypical, their old man has a zeal for crafting mystery-comedies while they are busy with school, sports, and activities.

Finally, thank you to my wife Susie for her love and advice as well as my mother Dianne, who never gave up on the ambition of a kid who grew up adoring action movies, devouring crime fiction, and could never seem to get enough escapist entertainment.

Without being blessed with these two special women in my life there is simply no way I would have been able to create "Hammerhead" Jed Ounstead and his ongoing escapades.

—A.J.D.

A.J. Devlin grew up in Greater Vancouver before moving to Southern California where he earned a Bachelor of Fine Arts in Screenwriting from Chapman University and a Master of Fine Arts in Screenwriting from The American Film Institute. After working as a screenwriter in Hollywood, he moved back home to Port Moody, BC, where he now lives with his wife and two children.

Cobra Clutch, the first book in the "Hammerhead" Jed professional wrestling mystery-comedy series, was released in spring 2018 and nominated for a Lefty Award for Best Debut Mystery and won the 2019 Crime Writers of Canada Arthur Ellis Award for Best First Novel. The sequel, *Rolling Thunder*, was released in spring 2020 and was featured in the *Vancouver Sun, The Province, The Globe and Mail, Kirkus Reviews,* and *Library Journal,* and on *CBC The Next Chapter.*

For more information on A.J. and his books, please visit ajdevlin.com.